THESPECTACLEOFSPORT

THE SPECTACLE OF SPORT

from **SPORTS ILLUSTRATED**

compiled
and
edited
by
NORTON WOOD

PRENTICE-HALL INC.
Englewood Cliffs, N. J.
1957

The following articles are reprinted by permission of Harold
Ober Associates, Inc.: *When the Marlin Strikes*, by George
Weller; *I'd Rather Watch Fish*, by Philip Wylie; *Kentucky: May: Saturday*, by William Faulkner; and *The
Gentle Art of Swordplay*, by Paul Gallico. *My Life As a
Sports Widow*, by Cornelia Otis Skinner, is reprinted by
permission of Dodd, Mead & Co. from *Bottoms Up!* by
Cornelia Otis Skinner. *I Taught Bud Wilkinson to Play
Football*, by Patty Berg as told to Seth Kantor, is
reprinted by permission of Evelyn Singer. Other articles
are reprinted by permission of the respective authors.

82729

FOREWORD

The title of this book is derived from one of the most important departments in SPORTS ILLUSTRATED. SPECTACLE has been appearing in the magazine since the first issue in 1954. Happily, it was recognized from the outset as a journalistic innovation, and it is because of this that I think it would be of journalistic and historic value to reprint here the thinking about SPECTACLE that was put down on paper long before the advent of the magazine itself — when we at TIME INC. were indulging in the rare and beguiling exercise of trying to find words for our ultimate intentions for an unborn child.   A reading of this pre-publication aim will make abundantly clear the truism that good journalistic innovations are rarely accidents.

SPECTACLE

Sport, in all its endless variety, is always something to be seen. It is magic to the eye. It lingers in the life-long treasury of vision. And so, of course, in this great age of photography, the magazine of sports must be SPORTS ILLUSTRATED. *And not only must it have many, many moments of vision throughout its pages; there must be one place in the magazine where sport is saluted by a burst of the very greatest color photography. This spot in* SPORTS ILLUSTRATED *we call* SPECTACLE.

Spectacle and spectacular are words inherent in sport. The spectacular takes many forms. At opposite extremes there are:

1) The vast arena where countless thousands come together to share the sight of the completed pass or the knockout punch or the photo-finish.

2) The solitary individual, the man alone with his sail in the Gulf Stream, the man alone with his hunting dog in the piny wood.

For the man alone, all nature becomes his private vision, his unique communion. Of a sudden, in the piny wood, the quiet symphony of ordered peace flares into drama; 20 quail whirl up and about the lonely man and streak like brown lightning through the autumn twilight; his heart pounds and his eyes remember ever after that kaleidoscopic universe in the piny wood.

In 52 weeks SPECTACLE *will bring outstanding instances both of the tensely congregated scene and of the lonely vision. These extremes only illustrate the breadth of* SPECTACLE's *assignment.* SPECTACLE *has many tasks to do. It has a technical task: to show, for example, exactly how a pitcher pitches; to freeze a fish in the arc of its leap. These are sights which the human mind may sense but which the human eye itself cannot see.*

The pleasant scenery of sport, the congregations of sportsmen, the drama, the emotions, the history-making instants, the wonder and the beauty of sport — for all of this SPECTACLE *has a perpetual hunting license to become itself an outstanding weekly event in the calendar of sport.*

It seemed obvious to us at TIME INC., after our first anxious look at the subject, that the world of sport is one especially designed for photography. Certainly the spectator rarely sees sports as vividly as the camera, and never in the same richness of detail.

The skillful photographer is able to freeze the split second of furious action into patterns that escape the eye completely while the action is taking place. The fan has long been aware of this. Over and over again he has marveled at pictures that show the superhuman contortions of the player in mid-air at the start of a double play at second base; the odd bend of the pitcher's arm at delivery; the golfer's blast out of a sand trap; the plunging halfback half in, half out of the line.

But mostly the sports photographer was capturing these moments on black and white film. His resultant pictures, good as they sometimes were, still were incomplete, for, lacking color, they were lacking something that is the very essence of all sport. What is football, basketball or horse racing without the brilliance of the uniforms, the kaleidoscopic gaiety of crowd, turf, sky or drenching light?

The question answered itself when our photographers, experimentally at first, loaded their cameras with color film and let their creative instincts guide them through the world of sport. As the mood struck them, they went beyond the ball park and the stadium, which had been their familiar focal points. They went beyond to scenes that had been neglected before and they found compositions with new meaning, with new beauty, and in some cases they even added new dimensions to the art of employing the color camera.

Consider the Ghosts of Sindelfingen by David Douglas Duncan on page 69. When before had such an image been recorded in all the span of sports photography? Here is a truly new dimension. So, too, is the explicit pattern of the basketball play as shown from directly overhead by Hy Peskin on page 257. And the picture by Ed Fisher of the Pinder brothers, deep under the ocean, pursuing the enormous leopard ray on page 118. For sheer and moving beauty, stop at page 216 and see how the artist's eye of Jerry Cooke has caught the Lipizzans performing at the Spanish Court Riding School in Vienna. Then go on to page 250 and savor the stylish arrogance of the bullfighter before lingering over the shadowy pattern of the hockey players on page 299, which has a different kind of beauty all its own.

Now see how the magnetic force of the camera has often worked its magic in such a way as to draw the reader into the picture, making him forget for the moment that he is a mere observer of a recorded fact. This again is something new in sports photography which developed out of SPECTACLE. One of the first persons to comment on this force was not a journalist or an artist or a photographer. In the early days of our experimentation the great Jack Dempsey was shown some pictures that Mark Kauffman had taken of a championship fight. "It's the next thing to being in the ring yourself," he said in honest wonderment. What sailor (or landlubber, for that matter) would not exclaim in similar fashion when he looked at the picture of crew members aboard the yacht *Criollo* on page 94, and who would not similarly be drawn into the action which is pictured on page 290 and on page 318?

But there is much more than the initial impact of great color photographs in this volume and herein, perhaps, lies its true value. Look at the pictures and then savor them. Take a second look, for instance, at the picture of Tenley Albright on page 241. The initial impact is one of grace and beauty and wintry mood. But the photographer, Hy Peskin again, caught still more than that on his color film, and the perceptive reader will get much more out of the picture. He can, for instance, see that as the waning sun of late afternoon casts its long shadow, the skater, doggedly seeking perfection, has tirelessly cut a certain pattern again and again and again. How eloquent this is of the life of the young champion! On page 23 there is a picture of Ben Hogan, the master golfer, at the point of his follow-through after driving from the eighth tee in the Masters tournament. Consider how much more the picture has to tell, how much more Malcolm Wister, the photographer, through his discerning lens, has widened the understanding of the reader. The picture shows the nature of the hole, the kind of day it was, and through the size and tenseness of the watching crowd, the stature of the golfer himself.

I like to think that the new sports photographer has had his effect on the sports writer. In addition to the colorful examples of the work of SPORTS ILLUSTRATED's photographers, you will find in this volume a carefully selected anthology of writing from SPORTS ILLUSTRATED. Whether or not one has influenced the other is less important than the evidence that each has widened his scope and deepened his perception.

SIDNEY L. JAMES
Managing Editor
SPORTS ILLUSTRATED

THE CONTRIBUTORS

THE SPECTACLE OF SPORT is composed entirely of photographs and articles which appeared originally in SPORTS ILLUSTRATED. Credit therefore belongs to Managing Editor Sidney L. James and to the entire staff of SPORTS ILLUSTRATED who contributed in the initial research, writing, editing, layout and production of these word and picture stories for the magazine. To an equal degree they are contributors to THE SPECTACLE OF SPORT.

In the task of reshaping original material from SPORTS ILLUSTRATED to compose this book, the following staff members performed major functions:

Assistant Editor for Text	HAMILTON B. MAULE
Design and Layout	ALFRED ZINGARO

Since this book is primarily an adaptation from the SPECTACLE department of SPORTS ILLUSTRATED, Sid James occupies a special role of authorship. A fact which his Foreword on the preceding pages does not make clear is that he initiated the magazine's striking presentation of color photography and has personally shaped the character of SPECTACLE all along.

The concept of drawing together the best of SPECTACLE to form the heart of an enduring volume for the sports lover, while it grew slowly in the thoughts of many of us, took definite shape first in the mind of Assistant Publisher Richard L. Neale, without whose concrete efforts toward achieving publication THE SPECTACLE OF SPORT would never have appeared.

I should like to acknowledge a special debt to Assistant Managing Editor Richard W. Johnston, who is responsible for the original appearance of many of the major articles included here, and to Assistant Managing Editor John Tibby for the numerous short essays reprinted from the EVENTS AND DISCOVERIES section of the magazine. Acknowledgment is due also to SPORTS ILLUSTRATED's reporter-correspondents and to the members of TIME INC. news bureaus in cities around the world, whose reports to the editors provided the basis for many of the stories included. Finally, a word of thanks to Art Director Jerome Snyder for his final word on matters of styling the presentation of this book.

NORTON WOOD
Associate Editor
SPORTS ILLUSTRATED

CONTENTS

SPRING

Memory and invention
shape spring in the thrasher's throat,
guide the shortstop's suppliant hands
back of second.
But the yellow butterfly
moves by memory alone;
it is the procession of children
following into the wood
who invent.
Warm strokes of rain:
the thrasher silent
in the brown bottom of the bush;
the shortstop on the dugout bench
watching the infield tarpaulin
rise huge in the wind
like a whale.
Tomorrow, traveling player and bird
will set up at the old stands,
telling their easy rituals.
But the children running on
into the last ash-fall of light
have borne the butterfly back
across the fields,
a yellow fragment of today.

—GILBERT ROGIN

FIRST PITCH

Photographed by HY PESKIN

THE AMERICAN SPRING is very much like spring anywhere — lively green fingers of things poking their way up through the dull and barren ground, the sudden surprise of tulips, the great, quiet explosion of apple blossoms.

These are, in one form or another, universals. But the American Spring has something else, too — an element that is rich with the same awakening spirit of rebirth, life lived again. The boy, sensing the working of the earth, says to his friend: "It smells like baseball." The father picks up the son's baseball glove and tries it on, working his hand into it, punching it a couple of times.

The gardener rests, letting the sun warm his back, and thinks of the lush summer ahead. The boy and the man think of pitchers and batters, a sharp base hit, an outfielder running, the crowds, the cry of the vendor, the taste of the frankfurter.

The green grass grows, the tulip burns with color, the blossoms gently stroke the air. The ball, the bat, the glove and the hard (at first), then muddy (for awhile) diamond seem to grow, too, as dormant skills are slowly aroused in the small boy, the young man, the professional.

The sun crosses the equator on its journey north. At that moment, say the precisionists, it is spring. But in America (and perhaps wherever baseball is played) there is another moment. One day a major league pitcher such as Whitey Ford of the New York Yankees on the opposite page, standing in the center of the formal garden of the infield, working in union with his teammates but isolated from them, takes a deep breath, grasps the slick new baseball, winds up and throws to the opposing batsman. It is the first pitch of the new season.

Then, in America, it is spring.

—ROBERT CREAMER

16

While Old Glory ripples in a Lake Erie breeze, 70,000 spectators jam Cleveland's

nicipal Stadium, the largest in baseball, to cheer the Indians through a Sunday double-header

BASEBALL IS CARING

BASEBALL is caring. Player and fan alike must care, or there is no game. If there's no game, there's no pennant race and no World Series. And for all any of us know there might soon be no nation at all.

The caring is whole and constant, whether warranted or hopeless, tender or angry, ribald or reverent. From the first pitch to the last out the caring continues. With a score of 6-0, two outs, two strikes, nobody on, only an average batter at bat, it is still possible, and sometimes necessary to believe something can still happen—for the simple reason that it *has* happened before, and very probably will again. And when it does, won't that be the day? Isn't that alone almost enough to live for, assuming there might just be little else? To witness so pure a demonstration of the unaccountable way by which the human spirit achieves stunning, unbelievable grandeur?

If the caring isn't for a team (because a team won't come through, or can't), then for the game itself, the annual ritual, moving with time and the world, the carefully planned and slowly accelerated approach to the great reward—the outcome, the answer, the revelation of the best, the winner.

It is good to care—in any dimension. More Americans put their spare (and purest?) caring into baseball than into anything else I can think of—and most of them put at least a *little* of it there. Most of them know the game is going on all the time, like the tides, and suspect there's a reason, or at least wonder about it. What *is* all the fuss about the whole year, and all the excitement every October? *Is* this a nation of kids, or what? Why not existentialism instead of baseball, for instance? Well, for one thing, you've got to be tired to care for old existentialism, and Americans just aren't ready to be that tired yet. For another, baseball can be trusted, as great art can, and bad art can't, especially as it comes from Hollywood, where sharp dealing is an accepted principle of profit-making. And it doesn't matter that baseball is very, very big business—quite the contrary. That only makes its truth all the more touching and magnificent. It doesn't matter, either, that the great players don't think of baseball as I do, for instance. Why should they? It's enough for them to go after being great and then to *be* great—and then to be no longer able, as time goes by.

I'm devoted to the game, to all of the teams in both leagues and to the World Series, because I don't know of anything better of its kind to be devoted to—and it's always out there with that anonymous crowd of the hungry and faithful, watching and waiting, in the stadium—their eyes on the geometric design of the fresh diamond, all set for the unfolding of another episode in the great drama, which cannot be put anywhere else—not into movies, not onto the stage, not even onto the television screen (although that's pretty good when you're held captive somewhere 3,000 miles away from the great place and the grand moment), not into books, and not even into statistics, although the game has grown on them.

It's a game—the biggest and best and most decent yet. The idea is to win the most games in the American or the National League, and then to go on and win the World Series: to establish a statistic, and tie it forever to the ragtag experience of a whole people for a whole year.

It is a tradition that the President throw out the first ball of the season, but somewhere in the bleachers the poets are around, too.

I don't think you'd get Casey Stengel in any arena of human activity other than baseball, and not getting him would be a national disaster, unbeknownst as it might be. Alston, too—another kind entirely. Bragan. Tebbetts. All of them. Fighting it out with their players and their fans, their friends and enemies, umpires and newspapermen but, most of all, facts and figures—statistics. You don't get Sandy Amoros, either, running in from left field as fast as he can go after an inning in which he dropped one he *had* caught—knowing it might cost the team the pennant. Knowing and waiting, and then hitting and saving the damned pennant, and then fielding and saving it, and then hitting and saving it again—knowing, saying nothing, on the theory (some say) that he doesn't speak much English. That could be it, all right, but there could be another theory, too, and the kids know it, and the old men and the old women know it, and the cab drivers and the cops and people in hospitals and penitentiaries and other lonely places. They don't know Sandy—but what he did, they know *that*. And it's a good thing to know. You wouldn't get Robinson, either—from the beginning. Or Williams, twice back from the wars, or the heroic return of Sal Maglie, and all the others, each made great and more deeply human than ever by the game.

Well, *is* it a game? Is that all it is? So the Yanks win it again this year. So the Braves win. So what? What good does *that* do the nation? What good does that do the world?

A little good. *Quite* a little.

And there's always next year, too.

—WILLIAM SAROYAN

THE MASTERS

by HERBERT WARREN WIND

THE RISE to prominence of the Masters golf tournament is one of the relative miracles in modern American sport. In just about a score of years, the Masters, which started out in 1934 as just a notable competition, has grown so inexorably in prestige and honest glamour that today it has come to eclipse the National Open in the stir it arouses, and this stir is sufficient to place the event in just about the same category as the World Series (inaugurated in 1903) and the Kentucky Derby (first run in 1875) as a full-fledged national sports classic. During the first full week in April when the tournament annually takes place over the great green meadowland slopes of the Augusta National Golf Club in Augusta, Ga., millions of Americans who ordinarily can go right on living even if they confuse Hogan with Hagen and Little with Littler suddenly become interested in golf, golfers and Augusta, very much in the way they perennially become aware of horses, horsemen and Churchill Downs as the Derby approaches.

As for died-in the-cashmere golf fans, a consciousness of the Masters is in the air every day the year round. It is tacitly assumed by the men and women intimately connected with the game that all of their friends in golf, regardless of how many other major events they have to pass up due to private or business pressures, are jolly well going to see to it that they make the Masters. In any month of the year, when these far-flung inhabitants of golfdom bump into one another at banquets or tournaments or when they meet by chance on the street or in a parlor car, one phrase naturally and invariably accompanies the parting handshake: "Well, I'll see you at the Masters." They usually do.

text continued on page 27

The great Ben Hogan drives from the eighth tee betu

ranks of spectators lining the fairway at the Mas

In twilight, Dutch Harrison holes his final putt on the shadowy 18th green at Augusta before a sprinkling of onlookers; on final day, the 18th green is invariably banked by a huge horseshoe of spectators straining to see crucial shots

The fact that we live in an age of publicity and wildfire communication explains to a large degree the "overnight" progress of the infant tournament into a vital tradition, but it could never have happened even in this age unless the Masters were—as it is—just about all you could ask of a golf tournament and then some. (Perhaps it should be stated right here before proceeding any farther than it is still a higher honor for a golfer to win the National Open than the Masters, but the Open by its very nature changes its venue every year and consequently never acquires quite the especial patina that seems to affix itself to those events which have the advantage of taking place year after year in the same, ever-more-familiar locale.)

It takes four elements, really, to make a great tournament: a superb course; a strong field; competent and imaginative (if invisible) administrative organization; and, most important of all, the true and unmistakable spirit of golf at its best. The Masters has all of these requisites because it was born right and brought up beautifully under the twin talents of two men who could not be less alike and who have, almost because of their disparate abilities, dovetailed into an unbeatable combination. The better known of the two is Robert T. Jones, Jr., the one and only Bobby, the best-loved Southerner since Robert E. Lee and a man of such sensitive general intelligence that you wonder, when you look back, how he managed to harness it under the stress of competition when that kind of brains usually gets in an athlete's way. The other member of the team is Clifford Roberts, a 63-year-old, Chicago-born New York investment banker, a relentless perfectionist with one of the best minds for management and significant detail since Salmon P. Chase.

Jones's and Roberts' paths first crossed late in 1930 when Jones, a tired warrior of 28, had announced his retirement from tournament golf after completing his epochal Grand Slam. That autumn, at the invitation of Roberts and two other wintertime Augusta Regulars, Jones came to that city from Atlanta to inspect a plot of land they were recommending as a possible site for the "dream course" he had frequently remarked he would like to build when circumstances were hospitable. The plot was part of an ancient indigo plantation which had been purchased in 1857 by a Belgian nobleman, Baron Berckmans, who converted Fruitlands, as the estate was named, into one of the South's leading nurseries. Jones was driven down Magnolia Lane, a double row of magnolias leading to the antebellum manor house, today the heart of the Augusta National's rambling clubhouse.

"I stood at the top of the hill before that fine old house," Jones has since described that Balboa-like occasion, "and looked at that wide stretch of land rolling down the slope before me. It was cleared land, for the most part, and you could take in the vista all the way down to Rae's Creek. I knew instantly it was the kind of terrain I had always hoped to find. I had been told, of course, about the marvelous plants and trees, but I was still unprepared for the bonus of beauty Fruitlands offered. Frankly, I was overwhelmed by the exciting possibilities of the golf course that could be built in such a setting."

Each year the view from the hill, the view that instantly sold Jones, is breathed in by the thousands who journey to the Masters. There are few first-timers who, upon experiencing that view, do not exclaim either aloud or to themselves, "Yes, it's all it's cracked up to be and more." There are few "repeaters" who, after hurrying to the brow of the hill, do not affirm to themselves, "It's just as lovely as I remember it. I hope it always stays the same because of what it personally means to me."

The vista that Jones took in and the vista of later beholders is somewhat different if topographically the same. Since 1931, the cleared meadowland and its interrupting stands of giant pines and its banking clumps of southern flora have been articulated into 18 golf holes. The course that Jones designed in collaboration with Alister Mackenzie, the Scottish architect whose best-known other American course is Cypress Point, is very probably the most visually appealing inland course ever built anywhere and, architecturally, perhaps the only truly important course constructed since 1911 when the National golf links at Southampton, Long Island, was completed. These two courses, so dissimilar in appearance, are actually blood brothers. The Southampton links, featuring adaptations of classic British holes, first enunciated for Americans the beauty of *strategic* design. The Augusta National, coming after a period of wholesale infatuation with *penal* design, reaffirmed the superiority of the strategic and did it so well that a reversion to the penal has never since occurred. Instead of instantly penalizing the player whenever he strays from the straight and narrow and appointed, a golf hole of strategic design offers a player several lines of attack, permitting him, as he judges his capacities and how the hole is playing that day, to choose conservative, mildly aggressive or audacious tactics. A successful strategic hole rewards each shot fairly—that is, in proper proportion to the type of shot attempted and

Tournament golfers and caddies trudge beside pond on 16th hole while the crowd watches and the water gives back the image of tall pines

how well it was played. For example, the hole is prepared to bestow a worthwhile advantage on the golfer who attempts the shot that requires more skill and nerve than the safe shot and pulls it off. It is also prepared to make him pay in the same definite terms if he overassesses his shot-making ability.

At Augusta, the 13th and 15th holes probably offer the simplest illustrations of this strategic concept, although it is present in varying degrees of subtlety in all of the holes. Both the 13th and 15th are par fives, rather shortish ones, 475 and 520 yards respectively, in keeping with Jones's thesis that a par five should not be so lengthy that it cannot be reached with two absolutely first-class shots. At the same time, on each of these holes, a receptive water hazard lurks just before the green, a winding creek on the 13th, a small pond on the 15th. If a golfer has poled out a fine drive on either hole, then, if the wind is not against him, he has a decision to make: should he try to clear the water hazard and set himself up for a birdie or even an eagle, or should he play short of the hazard and accept the prudent probability of a par? Billy Joe Patton, who in the 1954 Masters was in no mood to accept the probability of a par when there was the remotest possibility of a birdie, elected on that pressureful last round to "go for" the green on both these holes. In both instances he was pressing the percentages; neither of his drives, the first pushed, the second pulled, afforded him a really good lie and a comfortable stance for that big second shot. On the 13th, though he lashed a terrific spoon shot from a side-hill lie, the ball drifted a shade and caught the upper creek, and before he was finished, Billy Joe had himself a seven. Quite similarly, trying to crack a spoon all the way from a close lie in the rough on the 15th, he was unable to get enough of the ball. The ducking shot eventually skidded into the pond before the green, and Billy Joe had a six that settled his fate once and for all. To be sure, the same all-out tactics were responsible for the slew of birdies Billy Joe picked up on his four adventurous rounds, but in most cases the odds were more in his favor than on the 13th and 15th in the final round, and this is the point of strategic architecture.

At the Masters, the course is the star of the show, and since it is, a few more observations on its manifold merits would seem to be in order. They are old stories to veteran Augusta hands.

1) While testing a pro for all he is worth, the course, as was the aim of its co-designers, is the friend of the average golfer. He has a minimum of lateral rough to worry about and no rough to clear in order to reach the start of the fairway. He has to contend with only 30 functional traps—Oakmont at its peak had well over 200. He generally scores three or four shots lower than on his far less lengthy and lordly home layout.

2) No golfer who is not an excellent putter can hope to win the Masters. The greens are immense, and their contours weave and roll like a young ocean. It is noteworthy that the one dark horse ever to win the tournament, Herman Keiser, is an extremely fine chipper and putter.

3) Power by itself cannot win at Augusta. As Jones has put it, "A long driver has a definite advantage over a short driver if he hits his long drive in the right direction."

4) The second nine at Augusta, while totalling about the same yardage as the first nine—3,495 yards—is considerably more perilous. There is water in front of or skirting the green on the 11th, 12th, 13th, 15th and 16th. This places a golfer under a sizeable strain, the penalty for a missed shot being so conclusive. At the same time, a hot golfer can score lower on this second nine than on the first. On his first round in the 1940 event, Jimmy Demaret galloped around it in 30.

5) Whenever a hole at the Augusta National has revealed that some key feature, perfect on the drawing board, doesn't "play," that feature has been corrected or remodeled. These modifications have been undertaken on the average of one or two features a year under the direction of Bob Jones. Bob now thinks that most of the really necessary adjustments have been made.

6) The Augusta National is in a class by itself when it comes to making provision for spectators. Just behind the second green, for instance, what was originally a mild slope has been bulldozed into a mound large enough to accommodate 2,000 people. From the crest of this mound it is possible to take in the approach and the putting on the 2nd, the drive on the 3rd, the approach on the 7th, and the drive and second shot on the 8th. There are any number of such choice vantage points, natural and man-made, for the spectator to use when he is not walking the holes with a favorite player or contender.

BECAUSE of the strategic come-hither of its holes, the Augusta National evokes the spectacular. Almost every Masters has either been won or roused to life by some dramatic shot or some burst of outrageous brilliance. This precedent was set back in 1935 in the second Masters when Gene Sarazen made his celebrated double eagle, a stroke less impressive financially and less final than Lew Worsham's wedge into the cup on the last hole in the 1953 Tam O'Shanter, but probably still the most sensational shot ever uncorked in a major event, double eagles being rarer birds than eagles. Playing his second on the par-five 15th (or 69th), aware that he needed a three-under-par finish on the last four holes to tie Craig Wood, Gene rode into a four-wood. The ball carried the pond, hit the green, ran headlong for the cup and dropped. Sarazen went on to tie Wood and eventually to defeat him in the play-off.

The Masters is never won until it is literally won, so suddenly can fortune shift for or against you at Augusta. In 1937, for instance, Ralph Guldahl, then the best medal player in the country, appeared to have the tournament all wrapped up when he entered the last nine with a lead of four strokes over the nearest man, Byron Nelson. Guldahl ran into trouble on the far bend, going two over par on the short 12th with a five and one over on the 13th with a six. Nelson came along and played the two holes in two and three and not only obliterated Guldahl's lead but went in front by two strokes, his eventual margin of victory. The shoe was on the other foot for Guldahl two years later. He needed a 34 home on the last day to catch Sam Snead and came in in 33, due chiefly to a wonderful eagle on the 13th where he gambled on clearing the creek with his second and stuck his spoon six feet from the cup. You can go on and on—Snead's final round in '49 when he picked up eight birdies; Nelson's six-under-par sprint over 11 holes in his play-off duel with Ben Hogan in '42; Hogan's four flawless rounds in '53; and so on and on. The great names have always dominated the Masters, and their doing so has brought new substance to the ivied adage that a great course will produce a great champion.

While it takes considerable yardage even to begin to describe the sheer and organic beauty of the course, to explain the atmosphere of golf at its best that has always pervaded the Masters requires only one word: Jones. When the first Masters was held in 1934, its principal attraction was that the tournament marked Bob's return to competition. Until 1948, when illness forced him into final retirement, Bob annually played in the Masters but in no other tournaments. He was never truly a factor, but as the host and the president of the club, he endowed (and endows) the Masters with its thorough-going distinction and its sporting flavor. Bob used to play the first round with whoever was the defending champion. This role is now filled by Byron Nelson, the perfect choice. At the presentation ceremonies held on the Brobdingnagian putting green, Jones acts as the master of ceremonies—though that is hardly the word for the charming way he reviews the tournament and introduces the winners in his soft and eloquent Georgia drawl.

Behind the scenes, metaphorically digging away to build a better sand trap so that the world will continue to beat a path to the Masters, is that one-man gang, Clifford Roberts, "the works" in the interior administration of the club and chairman of the tournament committee since the inception of the Masters. Along with Jones, Roberts devised the inspired system of determining which players receive invitations to the tournament, and to him belongs the credit for the planning and operation that distinguishes a big-time affair from merely a big one: having the course in perfect condition, handling the improvement of such facilities as the parking area, making certain the players are treated as welcome guests and, above all, trying to anticipate the every need of the spectators. In this last connection, for example, on arriving at the grounds, each spectator receives (gratis) the day's program. It is simply a sheet of typewriter-paper size, the names of the players and their starting times on one side, a map of the course on the reverse. This data is all a spectator needs to orient himself immediately, something he can never get from the high-priced, ad-filled programs put out by most tournament committees for commercial profit and which emerge so bulky that lugging them around is a burden, particularly since there is nothing to be gained by trying to read them. To enable the spectators to keep abreast of the scoring as it unfolds on so many corners of the course, Roberts has installed a permanent telephone-communications system which feeds the news to scoreboards set up at six junctions on the course. To mention only a few of the sundry "little touches" that spring from Roberts' passion for efficiency and order, the caddies, marshals and trash squads are decked out in standardized uniforms, a pamphlet on how to watch the tournament is available to spectators on request, the tall pines are protected by lightning rods, and the brown water in the hazards is touched up into a bright blue by adding a Calcozine dye.

When the weather is cooperative—and it usually is, though technically it is beyond Roberts' control—few pleasures in sport can compare with being at the Masters. Most of the drama, of course, is reserved for the last two days, when the tournament "shapes" and builds to a climax, but there are a lot of us who have at least an equal fondness for the first two days, before the big crowds and the heavy pressure set in. Then the air of a happy country fair hangs over the green, green grass, and as you follow at the elbow of your favorite players of this year and yesteryear, golf takes on the quality it used to have in the 20s—the quality of a game, an ageless game.

WHOOMPH!

Photographed by M. LUCY EDDINS

Head over heels goes his mount, and a gentleman jockey flies from his stirrups in the Maryland Hunt Cup race. Of all the many-sided contests of equestrian skill and courage there is none more exacting than steeplechasing, which springtime traditionally brings to the South. Spectators thrill to episodes like this monumental—but harmless—spill.

A TIME
FOR TROUT

WICKER CREELS hung beneath flaring apple trees on the banks of New York's fabled Esopus remind the restive angler with nostalgic eloquence that April is the month of the trout. From East to Far West, he will follow the compelling call, ignoring the sudden freshet which hopelessly roils his pet stream or the dying touch of winter which skims his lake with ice — for his is a passion bred of tradition.

By April's end the waters of 34 states are formally open to trout fishing, and laggards soon will follow as spring finds its way to snowbound high country. By June 1 the nation's 10 species are fair game for an awesome host of some 20 million fresh-water anglers, a host for which state and federal fisheries biologists have been quietly laboring for many months. In one year Wyoming stocks more than 5 million fish in its myriad of streams. Yet the angler there, as in many other western states, still creels three native trout to every hatchery-reared one. In the urban East the ratio of wild to tame is radically reversed, but even if eastern trout are largely stocked, that can scarcely dampen the pleasures of a blue sky, the raucous voice of water tumbling over rock and riffle, and all the other intangibles which lend trout fishing its very particular flavor. And, for the truly dedicated, there are the ancient and ponderous brown trout in the pools of such hallowed eastern streams as the Brodhead and Beaverkill.

They are lords of their pools, and when in the twilight they rise to a fluttering moth, anglers are stricken to reverent silence. These are the special quarry of the practiced and the patient, the disciples of Theodore Gordon, George LaBranche, Edward Hewitt and other high priests of the venerable art of fly fishing. To them a spinning rod is a sacrilege, a worm an abomination. But, for all trout anglers, the purists as well as that legion which simply likes to go fishing, April is the door to long-awaited days on stream and lake.

—THOMAS H. LINEAWEAVER

JAMES M. MEYER

Spring calls not only to the trout fisherman. Here in the tranquil setting of a wilderness bay in Wisconsin a pair of anglers seek out the small-mouth bass, an anything but tranquil fish which strikes the lure with ill-tempered abandon and submits to the rod only after a spectacular fight. The men wade into the shallows, casting among the green reeds, hoping, like every fisherman everywhere, that a record fish may lurk within range of the next cast.

WHITE GIANT
OF THE ICY NORTH

THE POLAR BEAR is one of the rarest and most prized of all big-game trophies. Living on the almost inaccessible ice floes of the Arctic Ocean, huge, wily, and without any instinctive fear of man, it represents to the hunter the ultimate in dangerous prey. Here is how one of these formidable animals died, on a bright afternoon with the sun casting blue shadows behind the piled ice and the heavy slug from a 375 Magnum deep in his vitals.

The hunt started from an airplane wheeling low over the moonlike wastes of the Arctic, the pilot and hunter watching for bear sign and setting down quickly on landing skis when they saw this 1200-pounder waddling heavily over the spongy ice between floes. A brief stalk — the men ducking behind hillocks of ice, the bear moving steadily, head swinging and big paws shuttling, on whatever business led him to his appointment with the deadly bit of lead from the hunter's rifle. It was not a hard stalk because the polar bear kept moving toward the hunter and was only 20 yards away, aware for the first time of a stranger in his kingdom, when the impact of the bullet knocked him from an ice ridge and sent him sliding down into the frigid waters of the Arctic.

It took five men to haul the heavy carcass out of the water, a long time to peel off the thick hide. The hide alone weighed 250 pounds and squared at a little over 11 feet. It was worth the cold and the wet and the long trip for Dr. William Fisher, a Bellingham, Wash., dentist who hunted and killed the bear.

Photographed by **ROBERT HALMI**

Firing from 60 feet, Fisher watches blood spurt from bear as 300-grain slug from custom-made 375 Magnum thuds into its shoulder. (Right) Out of the water into which he tumbled, pilot, guides and Fisher snake huge bear to firm ice

Heading upward to a pressure ridge, the ponderous bear is almost lost in the glittering ice field. To keep his prize in sight, Bill Fisher scrabbled up the heap of ice slabs only to find the bear there first, in close range

Happy hunter squats by his half-ton kill. Bear skin alone weighed over 250 pounds, squared at 11 feet 2 inches. A 10-foot hide is considered exceptional

CALLING ALL CROWS

"IF MEN had wings and bore black feathers," Henry David Thoreau once said, "few of them would be wise enough to be crows." Despite the likely truth of this observation, men keep trying to become as smart as the big, black, swashbuckling con men of the avian world, and down in Baltimore a team of six men has made the project almost a life work.

The Baltimore six include a team of four brothers—Ray, Lou, Jerry and Eddie Foehrkolb—and a father-and-son team, Charlie and Buddy Weaver. The team started to hunt crows back in 1947, but for four full years they hit nothing but fresh air while the crows cawed themselves sick.

The reason for their failure was simple enough. The crows were just too smart. They could spot the boys coming a mile away and hear a car door slam farther away than that. And the crows never relaxed their vigilance or sat around cutting up a few caws without leaving a sentinel on the nearest fence post. This sentinel crow would call out interesting bulletins which, freely translated, might mean: "Station wagon pulling off the highway!" or "Break it up, fellows, these guys got guns!" or perhaps "Hey! A great horned owl just flew in! Let's go get the — —!" Crows hate horned owls as much as other birds hate *them*.

Well, sir, the Baltimore boys decided, after four years of failure, to start at the very beginning. They set out to learn to talk and think like crows. They read every book on crows in the library. They bought every kind of crow call manufactured and practiced around the house until their wives were frantic. They hid in the woods and just listened to crows. Soon they were able to dig the talk real good and a little later they were able to duplicate the one about the great horned owl so well that crows blackened the sky as they rushed pell mell toward the enemy.

But the Baltimore hunters played it cozy. Having mastered the talk, they designed a blind out of mesh wire covered with dark chicken feathers. They got some of those jungle suits the Marines used to wear and made masks out of the same material. (A crow can spot a white-faced hunter through the thickest foliage.) Next, the hunters worked on decoys until they developed specimens of owls that would fool another owl, to say nothing of a crow.

It paid off. Sitting in their blind, the decoys out front, the now skillful imitators began to talk like crows. They told of Marilyn Monroe-type crows preening themselves in the underbrush. They broadcast alarms of crow riots (crows dearly love a free-for-all), and they cawed of crows in distress in a way that would melt the heart of even a heartless crow. They kept talking without a break, for that is a crow's way. If there is even a split-second interruption, the oncoming crows will whirl and flee.

Now they had the hang of it, the Baltimore boys got crows by the thousands. For three years straight now, one of them has won the contest put on by the National Sporting Goods Co. of Baltimore. Recently Charlie Weaver brought in 1,229 crows' feet (as evidence of number of crows caught) to take the title. No one knows how a one-footed or three-footed crow got in there.

Who cares about this slaughter of crows? Farmers and conservationists care very much. So do crows.

—GERALD HOLLAND

THOROUGHBRED COUNTRY

Photographed by RICHARD MEEK

Lexington is a land of fences—solid, strong and high fences. At Calumet they are clean and white, glistening in the sun as they twist gracefully around the tulip poplars.

In all of America there are few localities that can match the Bluegrass country of Kentucky for springtime beauty and splendor. Across the rolling sweep of the hills of this rich and magnificent acreage the gentle breezes of spring ripple the length and breadth of carefully nurtured pastures surrounded by romantic dogwood and stately locust and sugar maple trees. This is the land of tobacco and whisky, of the last of the authentic Kentucky colonels. It is also the home of the Thoroughbred-race-horse-breeding industry, a business so enormous today that a horse can sell for more than a million dollars.

In early April visitors begin pouring into the land of the Bluegrass — many as house guests of the owners of such breeding establishments as Calumet Farm, Normandy Farm and Circle M Farm (pictured on the following pages), some moving cheerfully into Lexington hotels to spend a pleasant week or more on a round of leisurely farm inspections by morning and immersion in the intimate atmosphere of racing at the Keeneland Race Course during afternoons. Of one thing visitors can be sure: wherever they go in Lexington until the Kentucky Derby post-mortems are over in May, the conversation will center around race horses. Experts will discourse on bloodlines, breeding theories and the merits of a new crop of wobbly-legged foals. What looks like a prize group of yearlings to one breeder is often nothing more than ordinary to his critical neighbor. But at the Keeneland track, many a Kentucky-bred — including some choice Kentucky Derby candidates — will have a chance to show his wares.

—WHITNEY TOWER

ring in the shadowy yearling paddocks and on the soft pastures

is an exciting and inspiring time of every year, bringing out the frisky yearlings

to nip and romp, the breeders to watch and hope for future champions

Grazing peacefully in a pasture beside an enormous Calumet brood mare barn, a conten

...re remains close by her resting newborn foal, who soon enough will leave her side forever

Lexington has its memories of the pas
as well as occasions for happy rejoicing. Pin.
and white dogwood surround the quiet Thoroughbre
graveyard on the C. V. Whitney farn
where rest the remains of such as Whisk Broom II
Regret and Equipoise. Nearby
before a blue-tiled reminder of France (left
at E. Barry Ryan's Normandy Farm, a groom walk
leisurely with a young foal. And at Leslie Combs II'
Spendthrift Farm (opposite) a post-Derby part
meets under the shade of a black locus
against the gentle backdrop of a rolling pastu

More sturdy fences create symbolic partitions among the stallion paddocks

at Mrs. Edward S. Moore's Circle M. Farm, once part of Idle Hour, a home of champions

KENTUCKY: MAY: SATURDAY

THREE DAYS TO THE AFTERNOON

by WILLIAM FAULKNER

Three Days Before

This saw Boone: the bluegrass, the virgin land rolling westward wave by dense wave from the Allegheny gaps, unmarked then, teeming with deer and buffalo about the salt licks and the limestone springs whose water in time would make the fine bourbon whiskey; and the wild men too—the red men and the white ones too who had to be a little wild also to endure and survive and so mark the wilderness with the proofs of their tough survival—Boonesborough, Owenstown, Harrod's and Harbuck's Stations; Kentucky: the dark and bloody ground.

And knew Lincoln too, where the old weathered durable rail fences enclose the green and sacrosanct pace of rounded hills long healed now from the plow, and big old trees to shade the site of the ancient one-room cabin in which the babe first saw light; no sound there now but such wind and birds as when the child first faced the road which would lead to fame and martyrdom—unless perhaps you like to think that the man's voice is somewhere there too, speaking into the scene of his own nativity the simple and matchless prose with which he reminded us of our duties and responsibilities if we wished to continue as a nation.

And knew Stephen Foster and the brick mansion of his song; no longer the dark and bloody ground of memory now, but already my old Kentucky home.

Two Days Before

Even from just passing the stables, you carry with you the smell of liniment and ammonia and straw—the strong quiet aroma of horses. And even before we reach the track we can hear horses—the light hard rapid thud of hoofs mounting into crescendo and already fading rapidly on. And now in the gray early light we can see them, in couples and groups at canter or hand-gallop under the exercise boys. Then one

alone, at once furious and solitary, going full out, breezed, the rider hunched forward, excrescent and precarious, not of the horse but simply (for the instant) with it, in the conventional posture of speed —and who knows, perhaps the two of them, man and horse both: the animal dreaming, hoping that for that moment at least it looked like Whirlaway or Citation, the boy for that moment at least that he was indistinguishable from Arcaro or Earl Sande, perhaps feeling already across his knees the scented sweep of the victorious garland.

And we ourselves are on the track now, but carefully and discreetly back against the rail out of the way: now we are no longer a handful clotting in a murmur of furlongs and poles and tenths of a second, but there are a hundred of us now and more still coming, all craning to look in one direction into the mouth of the chute. Then it is as if the gray, overcast, slightly moist post-dawn air itself had spoken above our heads. This time the exercise boy is a Negro, moving his mount at no schooled or calculated gait at all, just moving it rapidly, getting it off the track and out of the way, speaking not to us but to all circumambience: man and beast either within hearing: "Y'awl can git out of the way too now; here's the big horse coming."

And now we can all see him as he enters the chute on a lead in the hand of a groom. The groom unsnaps the lead and now the two horses come on down the now empty chute toward the now empty track, out of which the final end of the waiting and the expectation has risen almost like an audible sound, a suspiration, a sigh.

Now he passes us (there are two of them, two horses and two riders, but we see only one), not just the Big Horse of professional race argot because he does look big, bigger than we know him to be, so that most of the other horses we have watched this morning appear dwarfed by him, with the small, almost gentle, head

51

and the neat small feet and the trim and delicate pasterns which the ancient Arab blood has brought to him, the man who will ride him Saturday (it is Arcaro himself) hunched like a fly or a cricket on the big withers. He is not even walking. He is strolling. Because he is looking around. Not at us. He has seen people; the sycophant adulant human roar has faded behind his drumming feet too many times for us to hold his attention. And not at track either because he has seen track before and it usually looks like this one does from this point (just entering the backstretch): empty. He is simply looking at this track, which is new to him, as the steeplechase rider walks on foot the new course which he will later ride.

He—they—go on, still walking, vanishing at last behind the bulk of the tote board on the other side of the infield; now the glasses are trained and the stopwatches appear, but nothing more until a voice says: "They took him in to let him look at the paddock." So we breathe again for a moment.

Because we have outposts now: a scattering of people in the stands themselves who can see the gate, to warn us in time. And do, though when we see him, because of the bulk of the tote board, he is already in full stride, appearing to skim along just above the top rail like a tremendous brown hawk in the flattened bottom of his stoop, into the clubhouse turn still driving; then something seems to happen; not a falter nor check though it is only afterward that we realize that he has seen the gate back into the chute and for an instant thought, not "Does Arcaro want us to go back in there?" but "Do I want to turn off here?" deciding in the next second (one of them: horse or man) no, and now driving again, down to us and past us as if of his own intention he would make up the second or two or three which his own indecision had cost him, a flow, rush, the motion at once long and deliberate and a little ungainly; a drive and power; something a little rawboned, not graceless so much as too busy to bother with grace, like the motion of a big working hunter, once again appearing to skim along just above the top rail like the big diminishing hawk, inflexible and undeviable, voracious not for meat but for speed and distance.

One Day Before

Old Abe's weathered and paintless rails are now the white panels of millionaires running in ruler-straight lines across the green and gentle swell of the Kentucky hills; among the ordered and parklike grove the mares with recorded lineages longer than most humans know or bother with stand with foals more valuable head for economic head than slum children. It rained last night; the gray air is still moist and filled with a kind of luminousness, lambence, as if each droplet held in airy suspension still its molecule

of light, so that the statue which dominated the scene at all times anyway now seems to hold dominion over the air itself like a dim sun, until, looming and gigantic over us, it looks like gold—the golden effigy of the golden horse, "Big Red" to the Negro groom who loved him and did not outlive him very long, Big Red's effigy of course, looking out with the calm pride of the old manly warrior kings, over the land where his get still gambol as infants, until the Saturday afternoon moment when they too will wear the mat of roses in the flash and glare of magnesium; not just his own effigy, but symbol too of all the long recorded line from Aristides through the Whirlaways and Count Fleets and Gallant Foxes and Citations: epiphany and apotheosis of the horse.

The Day

Since daylight now we have moved, converged, toward, through the Georgian-Colonial sprawl of the entrance, the throne's anteroom, to bear our own acolytes' office in that ceremonial.

Once the horse moved man's physical body and his household goods and his articles of commerce from one place to another. Nowadays all it moves is a part or the whole of his bank account, either through betting on it or trying to keep owning and feeding it.

So, in a way, unlike the other animals which he has domesticated—cows and sheep and hogs and chickens and dogs (I don't include cats; man has never tamed cats)—the horse is economically obsolete. Yet it still endures and probably will continue to as long as man himself does, long after the cows and sheep and hogs and chickens, and the dogs which control and protect them, are extinct. Because the other beasts and their guardians merely supply man with food, and someday science will feed him by means of synthetic gases and so eliminate the economic need which they fill. While what the horse supplies to man is something deep and profound in his emotional nature and need.

It will endure and survive until man's own nature changes. Because you can almost count on your thumbs the types and classes of human beings in whose lives and memories and experience and glandular discharge the horse has no place. These will be the ones who don't like to bet on anything which involves the element of chance or skill or the unforeseen. They will be the ones who don't like to watch something in motion, either big or going fast, no matter what it is. They will be the ones who don't like to watch something alive and bigger and stronger than man, under the control of puny man's will, doing something which man himself is too weak or too inferior in sight or hearing or speed to do.

These will have to exclude even the ones who don't like horses—the ones who would not touch a horse or go near it, who have never mounted one nor ever intend to; who can and do and will risk and lose their shirts on a horse they have never seen.

So some people can bet on a horse without ever seeing one outside a Central Park fiacre or a peddler's van. And perhaps nobody can watch horses running forever, with a mutuel window convenient, without making a bet. But it is possible that some people can and do do this.

So it is not just betting, the chance to prove with money your luck or what you call your judgment, that draws people to horse races. It is much deeper than that. It is a sublimation, a transference: man, with his admiration for speed and strength, physical power far beyond what he himself is capable of, projects his own desire for physical supremacy, victory, onto the agent—the baseball or football team, the prize fighter. Only the horse race is more universal because the brutality of the prize fight is absent, as well as the attenuation of football or baseball—the long time needed for the orgasm of victory to occur, where in the horse race it is a matter of minutes, never over two or three, repeated six or eight or 10 times in one afternoon.

4:29 P.M.

And this too: the song, the brick mansion, matched to the apotheosis: Stephen Foster as handmaiden to the Horse as the band announces that it is now about to be the one 30 minutes past 4 o'clock out of all possible 4 o'clocks on one Saturday afternoon out of all possible Saturday afternoons. The brazen chords swell and hover and fade above the packed infield and the stands as the 10 horses parade to post—the 10 animals which for the next two minutes will not just symbolize but bear the burden and be the justification, not just of their individual own three years of life, but of the generations of selection and breeding and training and care which brought them to this one triumphant two minutes where one will be supreme and nine will be supreme failures—brought to this moment which will be supreme for him, the apex of his life which, even counted in lustra, is only 21 years old, the beginning of manhood. Such is the price he will pay for the supremacy; such is the gamble he will take. But what human being would refuse that much loss, for that much gain, at 21?

Only a little over two minutes: one simultaneous metallic clash as the gates spring. Though you do not really know what it was you heard: whether it was that metallic crash, or the simultaneous thunder of the hoofs in that first leap or the massed voices, the gasp, the exhalation—whatever it was, the clump of horses indistinguishable yet, like a brown wave dotted with the bright silks of the riders like chips flowing toward us along the rail until, approaching, we can begin to distinguish individuals, streaming past us now as individual horses—horses which (including the rider) once stood about eight feet tall and 10 feet long, now look like arrows twice that length and less than half that thickness, shooting past and bunching again as perspective diminishes, then becoming individual horses once more around the turn into the backstretch, streaming on, to bunch for the last time into the homestretch itself, then again individuals, individual horses, the individual horse, the Horse: 2:01:4/5 minutes.

And now he stands beneath the rose escarpment above the flash and glare of the magnesium and the whirring film of celluloid immortality. This is the moment, the peak, the pinnacle; after this, all is ebb. We who watched have seen too much; expectation, the glandular pressure, has been too high to long endure; it is evening, not only of the day but the emotional capacity too; Boots and Saddles will sound twice more and condensations of light and movement will go through the motions of horses and jockeys again. But they will run as though in dream, toward anticlimax; we must turn away now for a little time, even if only to assimilate, get used to living with, what we have seen and experienced. Though we have not yet escaped that moment. Indeed, this may be the way we will assimilate and endure it: the voices, the talk, at the airports and stations from which we scatter back to where our old lives wait for us, in the aircraft and trains and buses carrying us back toward the old comfortable familiar routine like the old comfortable hat or coat: porter, bus driver, pretty stenographer who has saved for a year, scanted Christmas probably, to be able to say "I saw the Derby," the sports editor who, having spent a week talking and eating and drinking horse and who now wants only to get home and have a double nightcap and go to bed, all talking, all with opinions valid and enduring:

"That was an accident. Wait until next time."

"What next time? What horse will they use?"

"If I had been riding him, I would have rode him different."

"No, no, he was ridden just right. It was that little shower of rain made the track fast like California."

"Or maybe the rain scared him, since it don't rain in L.A.? Maybe when he felt wet on his feet he thought he was going to sink and he was just jumping for dry land, huh?"

And so on. So it is not the Day after all. It is only the 81st one.

GRACE IN A DIVE

THE PERFECT FORM shown by California diver Paula Jean Myers on the opposite page as she heads for the water to complete a half gainer helps explain why exhibition diving is to its devotees the most beautiful of all sports. The combination of agility and grace which characterizes diving produces a symphony of coordinated motion, magnificently demonstrated in John Zimmerman's picture sequence on the following pages of Olympic gold medal winner and former Ohio State springboard star Bob Clotworthy.

Because of the exact precision required in competitive diving, it takes at least five years of exhausting daily workouts to develop championship form. And diving can be cruelly punishing. Besides the tension and mental anguish that goes with competition — the lonely walk out on the high board in a meet where one slip can cost a title — there is always the risk of injury. Hitting the board, striking the water improperly at a speed of close to a mile a minute, and failing to recover under water in time to avoid bumping the bottom of the pool all take their toll. At a recent physical examination a flabbergasted doctor found that many of the best U. S. divers are scarred like prizefighters.

Strangely, many divers are acrophobic. Pat McCormick, two-time Olympic champion, is one of these and readily admits it. But if high places scare her, it has never shown on the judges' sheets.

—LEE GRIGGS

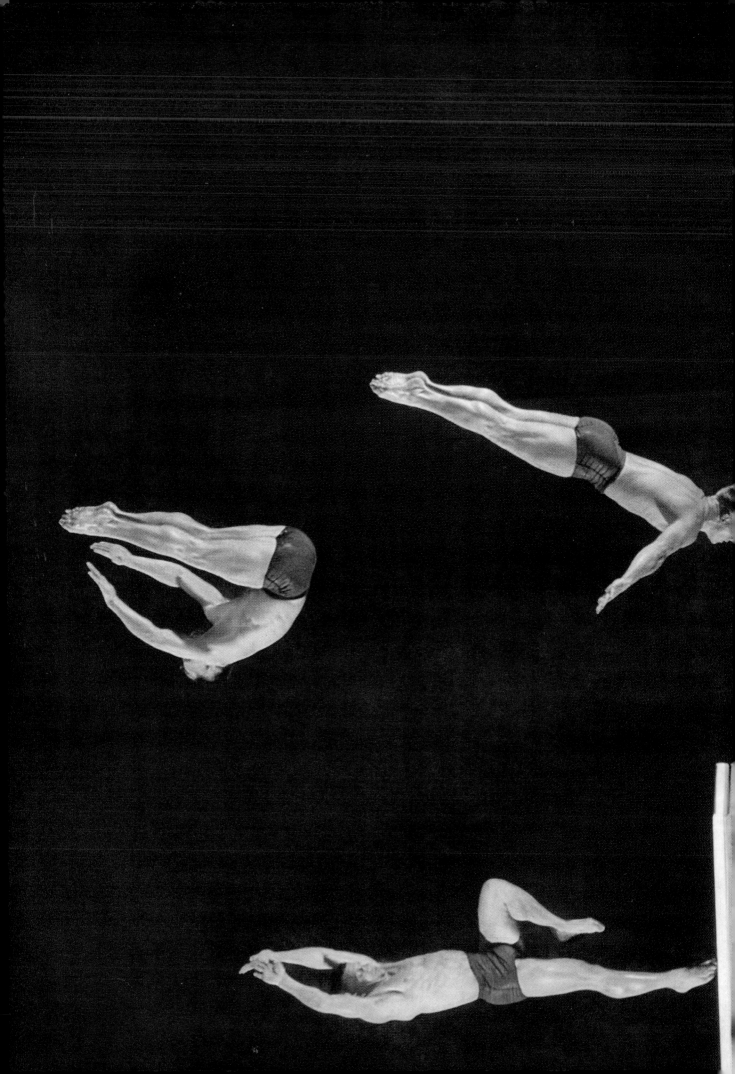

Sequence picture shows Olympic champion Bob Clotworthy as he moves through the four critical phases of a perfect reverse pike dive

As seen from below. Clotworthy's knife-like entry into pool cuts a sheer hole in water surface

DIVING MASTER

MANY YEARS AGO, when footballs were almost round and shortstops wore mustaches, men argued as fiercely as they do today about what college was best in what sport. In that day the arguments seldom included swimming: before World War I there were simply no swimming teams or kings worth defending or knocking. Then along came Yale, followed by Michigan and Ohio State. Today a swimming debate among real believers can be lively, as long as it skirts the special art of diving, for at this point defenders of Yale and Michigan will fall silent and may, in fact, become morose. The divers of Ohio State are better than anybody.

To take the facts coldly from the record book, in the past 20 years the springboard divers of Ohio State have won 81 national titles. Everybody else has won 21.

A championship record of 81 wins and 21 losses is the sort of percentage many colleges have sought in other sports by swinging the ax at a succession of coaches. Ohio State's diving supremacy has been achieved by leaving the coach's head alone. The University started competitive swimming in 1931 with a 32-year-old coach named Michael Peppe, an eager, compactly built all-round athlete who stood 5 feet 4 inches with his head on. Mike Peppe is still coach, he still has his head but not much hair, he is still fairly compact, but shaped now at age 59 a bit more like a barrel. Because his present duties entail more than coaching, he now ranks as professor and rates the proper fancy title Director of Swimming. The title is academic at this point. He has long ranked high as a swimming coach and in a class by himself as diving master of the world.

A master of a sport as precise as diving might be expected to have some qualities of an Old World fencing maestro—a flinty eye, the taut nerves of a cat, a cavalier flair and a temper that can blow higher than a Roman candle. Mike Peppe has quick moments, but his eyes are a soft mahogany, and his mien and pace are usually that of a Newfoundland dog. In a tough season he behaves like a man who will live through the next 20 years if his divers lose everything except their trunks.

Beyond his years of experience, other coaches pick two things that perhaps serve Peppe best: firstly, a seldom obvious but deep love of perfection, which he never achieved himself as an uncoached diver 40 years ago; secondly, a remarkably quick eye to spot the hidden, split-second error that is marring a near-perfect dive. Joe Hewlett, the Ohio coach of gymnastics, a sport with some affinity to diving, has a point to add. "Peppe doesn't overcoach," Hewlett remarked recently. "The fault of most of us today is overcoaching. When a coach keeps saying 'Do this,' where does a boy get insight into his ability? You'll see Peppe going over fundamentals with his best divers one day, then you'll see him leaving the kids to coach each other, so they beat their brains out and get some insight into diving."

Rival coaches think well of Peppe but wish him less success—starting as soon as possible. In the National Outdoor championship at Cuyahoga Falls, Ohio, which preceded the Olympic trials in 1956, the top six places were won by undergrads or grads of Ohio State. For a publicity picture the local junior chamber of commerce brought on two bathing-suit cuties to pose with the winning divers. While the girls kissed the boys, and cameras snapped, someone realized Ohio State had made a six-man sweep. The cry went up, "Get Mike Peppe for a picture." Peppe was close at hand, merely hidden by taller men. While the photographers fired away at him, Peppe stood submissively, face somewhat red from sun and possibly embarrassment, shifting uneasily from foot to foot, looking out of the top of his eyes so he seemed shorter than he is. The total effect of the diving master at this grand moment was that of Walt Disney's bashful dwarf meeting Snow White for the first time.

Olympic Coach Karl Michael, who was on hand, waved at the posed array of diving talent. "Right now," Michael said. "I'd take any three of Peppe's boys for the Olympic team." As it turned out, Coach Michael got three of them. Bob Clotworthy won the gold medal at Melbourne; Don Harper took second; and Glen Whitten, going for broke with two tough dives, mushed both slightly and finished fourth.

In the football city of Columbus, Ohio, surrounding the Ohio State campus, a fancy diver doing three somersaults out of a downtown window into High Street would get some notice, but a good quarterback would probably rate as much if he got a foot stuck in the water pail. The fact that the best divers in the world compete in Columbus and rarely attract 500 off-campus customers does not bother Peppe. He is fairly famous around town. On the street, friends and strangers often stop him to ask how the football team is shaping up.

—COLES PHINIZY

59

THE NEEDLES OF CHAMONIX

Photographed by HOWARD FRIEDMAN

MOUNTAINS — nature's most impressive creations — have since time immemorial been objects of fear. And for the climber, one of the greatest tests of skill or nerve is the Needles of Chamonix — a classic forest of granite spires clustered around the east and northern sides of Mont Blanc where Alpine France and Switzerland meet.

Looking at the Needles, or Aiguilles, with their jagged pillars and weathered flying buttresses, is like observing the ruined temples of the Titans. Symbols of impregnability — Grand Charmoz, Grépon, Aiguille Verte, Aiguille de Blatiére — the very names of these fragile sentinels suggest high adventure.

Though Mont Blanc was climbed as long ago as 1786 by a chamois hunter and local doctor, the highest of the steely Needles — Aiguille Verte (13,520 ft.) — was not conquered until 1865. Since then they have had an irresistible attraction for rock-climbers the world over.

Rock-climbing, which to some is the training phase of mountaineering, is a western notion, an idea that never came to the ancients in the east. As a sport, it was the invention of imaginative Englishmen who were born in the secure environment of the 19th century. Though the basic rope techniques have not changed, mechanical innovations like the climbers' pitons, karabiners and stirrups have made the most awesome wall of the Chamonix Needles possible.

—FRED BECKEY

Balanced atop a needle rock high up in the Chamonix area,

a daring English climber adjusts his rope for the descent

Rappeling a foot at a time, climber works his way down the sheer side of the rock pinnacle toward river of cloud below

SIX NIGHTS ON A NEEDLE

THE GREAT PEAK of Mont Blanc looms in its cold white grandeur above uncounted bristling granite spires, among them the *aiguilles* (needles) of Chamonix. There are scores of routes to the summit of Mont Blanc, just as there is an "easy" way to the peak of Aiguille du Dru (sharp needle), but the wall face of the Dru is the sheerest in the Alps. Until the summer of 1955 it never had been climbed.

Walter Bonatti, a blue-eyed Alpine guide who the year before was the youngest member (24) of the Italian expedition that conquered K-2 in the Western Himalayas, set out to climb it alone. He made it, at the cost of skinless hands and nights of enshrouding fear.

"On Dru," he said, "I knew fear as I have never known it before. There were many moments in which the whole of the thoughts which filled my brain cried to me, 'Go back, go down, go back!' It was fear of the mountains' solitude as much as of physical difficulties. But at night sleep mercifully came."

Sleep meant sitting for most of the six nights in a loop of rope to which he lashed himself to hang in a sleeping bag over black void. One night he was lucky. He found a ledge he could sit on, legs dangling over a precipice.

"The first night," he went on, "I bivouacked at the foot of the *direttissima* (the most direct route).

"Next morning at dawn, I threw up a loop to a projection and it caught hold. Without resting I was then able to lift myself 150 meters up the wall's face. Then night came. I regretted my earlier decision to leave my small transmitting radio behind so as to lighten my load. Silence and solitude suddenly loomed immense. They were broken only by the deep voice of the glacier beneath me and the whistling wind. Some stones every now and then dropped from the wall face

down into the pit below. They frightened me, too. But then dawn came.

"But day also brought me trouble: a sort of chimney covered with ice into which I couldn't get the point of a nail. Therefore I could make no use of the rope. I embraced that chimney with all my strength—it projected outward over a precipice—and I pressed against it with all I had, including my nose, and gradually edged up. When I reached the top of the chimney, I realized with terror that I would never be able to climb down it. Once I started sliding down, I would inevitably slither into the abyss. I was beyond the point of no return, and though the actual amount of the face I had climbed was short, night was upon me. But then, after another night, I saw the sun.

"And so it was on the following days. On the last day, the whole of the skin on my hands had gone, left on the wall face or on the rope. I grew terribly thirsty. Below I had quenched my thirst with snow; but there was no snow on the wall's smooth face now.

"Then, suddenly looking up, I saw the sun on Dru's peak. It was only 100 meters higher than me. I said to myself, 'I have won;' and I loved Dru and I loved all mountains in that moment."

At the top he met friends who had traveled the "easy" way: "I hardly saw them. I threw myself on a water flask they had brought. Then I ate two chickens."

Why did Bonatti invite the terrible risks of his ordeal? "They call me a conqueror of mountains," he says. "I am no conqueror . . I must confess that the sentiment which mountains inspire in me might well be called fear. It is a sentiment of preoccupation, of uncertainty, or—let us be honest and use the right word—of fear of the unknown.

"I am not happy till I have conquered this fear. I manage to overcome it but it is still there."

—MARTIN KANE

WHITE WATER'S WRATH

Photographed by

MARGARET DURRANCE

THE ELEMENTAL FURY of a white-water river can be a vicious threat to a racer like the one shown at right battling the rapids of the Arkansas in a thin-skinned kayak. As the canoe slides onto the glassy tongue of the rapid that sucks it into the boil, even the most seasoned riverman feels a bolt of fear. Spray stings his face and cuts his vision. He hunches forward, thighs and feet braced against the fragile birch frames, his hips swiveling with each sudden wrench of the canoe. A wave smashes against his face and for a moment he is completely under. But he bobs up and finally breaks through to safe water. Once out, he may risk a look back at the rapids and experience a great lift of exultation. He has challenged nature and won, and there is no other feeling quite like it.

Each June some score or more canoeists challenge the Arkansas River in the annual white-water race at Salida, Col. Not all of them can count on a triumphant look back after the 25.7 miles of tortured water which makes up the course. After a winter of heavy snow, the Arkansas sometimes runs two feet higher than normal, and veterans know that just a few inches can make a tremendous difference in a river so powerful that even in the knee-deep shallows a kayak that spins broadside to a rock may be snapped in half by the force of the 10-mile current. But the river gives signs to the people who know it. By its green or blue color it tells the bottom; by its high or deep sounds it points out the rocks. The Arkansas is an honest river, and the brave men who fight its white water know from the beginning what they have to fight. Which is all that any brave man can ask.

—ROBERT AJEMIAN

Roaring white water in the rugged Cottonwood Rapids of the Arkansas River flings ka

ward bank as racer paddles hard to stay in the channel and keep his light, fragile craft afloat

THE GHOSTS
OF SINDELFINGEN

Photographed by DAVID DOUGLAS DUNCAN

IN GERMANY, the land which gave birth to the brothers Grimm and other spinners of fairy tales, almost every city, town or village of medieval age has its private store of ghosts and legends. They may concern the robber baron who lived in the castle now quietly crumbling on a hillside nearby; or the dungeon keep beneath the ivy-covered city walls; or the lovely daughter of the wealthy merchant who many generations ago pined away for love of the gooseherd's son. But no other place can boast the ghosts which Sindelfingen, an ancient Swabian town near Stuttgart, has today. They appear in full daylight, in bright colors and with a roaring sound, filling the old cobbled streets briefly with a vision far more familiar in different settings in many distant lands. Photographer David Douglas Duncan took their pictures in Sindelfingen recently. To find out what they are, turn the pages.

—PERCY KNAUTH

The speeding ghosts of Sindelfingen here take on their concrete form: Mercedes sports cars, which are test-driven by factory mechanics through the village streets. The 300SL shown below and the 190SL at left are among the very finest of the breed: proud, fast and beautiful. The true miracle of their existence lies in the fact that a decade before these pictures were taken, Mercedes lay in ruins; Sindelfingen, site of the final assembly plant, was in very fact a ghost town. Thus, Phoenix-like, these cars stand as symbols of Germany's extraordinary industry: the magic, to those who admire and those who own them, of a dream come true.

BLACK MARLIN

Photographed by CORNELL CAPA

To hook the great Pacific black marlin, to watch it break skyward time and time again in the fury of battle, tearing the ocean to shreds of foam, is that once-in-a-lifetime experience that big game fishermen dream about. Largest of the marlin species, the black marlin often exceeds 1,000 pounds, and to boat one of these fighting monsters is a wrenching test of angling skill and stamina. To meet that test, man journeys to the far, lonely place where the chill Humboldt Current hurries northward past a barren Peruvian headland known as Cabo Blanco. Here the senior marlin fins in abundance, and this is the site of the famed Cabo Blanco Club, one of the world's most exclusive fishing fraternities. Its members pay $10,000 to join, but the club welcomes non-members as well, if the lure of the great fish draws a sportsman as far as Peru.

From a Cabo Blanco Club cruiser in 1953 member Alfred C. Glassell, Jr., of Houston, Texas, caught a black marlin which tipped the scales at 1,560 pounds, world record for the species and the largest billfish ever taken on rod and reel. The fish shown here exploding from the sea, a modest-sized 500-pounder, is being wrestled in by the same Mr. Glassell. It fought for 30 minutes and jumped 14 times before it was finally subdued and boated (*next page*).

74

WHEN THE MARLIN STRIKES

Raymundo d. castro maya is a small Brazilian who has probably caught more black marlin in proportion to his weight than any other man in the world. On the dock at Cabo Blanco one evening he told how it is done.

"We always find the marlin going north," he explained. "The first thing to make sure is that it is not a swordfish. A swordfish shows two fins, dorsal and caudal, a marlin only one. After you see it, the next thing is to show the marlin the bait."

Baiting for marlin is really the art of serving a highly fastidious guest. The marlin may want mackerel at 11, but fancy only bonito at 12. When finning out on the surface, it is rarely hungry. It has usually eaten heavily downstairs and risen to the sun only for a snooze. The hunter is offering it not dinner, but a second dessert. Full already, it can be finicky.

Sometimes the marlin is lazying along in a school of helpless giant squids. "If it is already eating squid," said Castro Maya, "you offer it something else. Marlin are like humans. They like surprises."

The marlin likes to overtake its prey smartly, rear back its bill like a club and deal it a hearty swipe on the snout. With its three-inch deep-blue eyes, which have the scrutinizing powers of binoculars, the marlin scans the behavior of the meal after its blow. If the creature looks stunned, loses speed, goes into a flurry and faces suicidally into its jaws, the marlin opens wide and swallows it.

Generally, to catch marlin, two fist-size hooks are sewed inside a mackerel, the tips customarily facing toward the head of the fish. Once it has taken the hooks, the marlin may jump 40 times with one hook inside its gills, the other in its jaw.

Castro Maya now explained how to play the fish. "When it takes the bait, you let go, give it a good chance to swallow. You throw the reel off gear, into free spool. The marlin swims away, very quietly and fast at first. I count 10. Zzzz-zz—it runs out the line— zzzzzz—it runs. When I am sure it has the bait, I strike it. I lift the rod. Now the fight begins. Fix your belt. Check your gloves. You will be very busy, and nobody, under the rules, can help you.

"For the next hour, at least, you will be pumping. Let it go. Pump it back. Let go. Pump. The marlin jumps in the air. That is well. You count the jumps. The jumps tell you about the courage of your marlin."

Unlike other great fish, the black marlin does not cheat its aggressor by hiding itself or its agony in the depths. It dies as openly as the bull in the ring. It stands upright on the waves, momentarily superior to its element, like a naked man flying. It rolls its great dark-blue eyes over the boat in hate and permits the fisherman to see its contempt. Again and again it climbs up, enormously blue against the sky, water spewing from its glistening back. Every fin is spread in anger. It courses over the water in great flat leaps, a hurdler clearing invisible barriers 25 feet apart. It stands up and whirls like a Spanish dancer, bending down its angry head with its reddened mouth open, whirling its white waistcoat.

What the marlin wants is to chop away the snaffle tearing at its mouth. It starts hacking the wire with its four-foot spearlike bill, an all-purpose tool. Whether it wins freedom or loses depends on where it strikes. If it strikes close to its own mouth, as is natural, the blow falls somewhere along a 30-foot length of stainless-steel cable, the leader hanging from its mouth. Sometimes the wire breaks. Usually, however, it holds.

If the marlin has a good hunch, or is lucky, it may strike farther up, beyond the wire leader, where there is about 25 feet of No. 39 thread, doubled. If it strikes here with the line tense, the line breaks and the marlin wins. Rarely does its guesswork carry it so far back toward man, the ultimate cause of its agony. And it almost never attacks the halfway cause, the boat.

"When it tires of jumping and goes down," said Castro Maya, "you must fight it in a different way. You must not let it hang dead on the line, like a manta ray. You must plane it." "Plane" means to gun the boat's engine and move gently ahead. This forces the marlin to rise and fight.

For fisherman and for marlin the 30 feet of wire leader is the last measure of death or freedom. Not until all the line has been gathered into the boat can the struggling fish be clubbed or gaffed. At the moment that the marlin feels the first human tug on the leader, it has clear warning that death is near. It starts the fight all over again. It darts away in a white flurry. Or, it dives to the bottom and sticks its bill in the sand, thrashing for leverage.

A fight can last almost any time, from 10 minutes— a freak, when the marlin has two hooks deep in its stomach—up to six hours. There is, of course, a way of simply murdering the marlin, rather than catching it: to creep up on it in the pulpit of a cruiser and plunge a harpoon in its back. Marlin up to 2,200 pounds have been stabbed in this way. But to the sportsman this is only one step above feeding it bait with dynamite filling, as is done to sharks on the Great Barrier Reef of Australia.

—George Weller

RACE TO GLORY

Photographed by JOHN G. ZIMMERMAN

The strain of maximum effort shows on the faces of gold medal winners Tom Courtney (left) and Charley Jenkins as they race headlong into Olympic history to bring the U. S. another victory in the 1,600-meter relay before the vast crowd in Melbourne's Olympic Stadium.

THE STORY

OF

JOHN LANDY

by PAUL O'NEIL

THE TOWNSPEOPLE of Fresno, California, Raisin Capital of the World and Pearl of the San Joaquin Valley, share one obsession: they are track and field fans. Kids in Fresno can recite the latest clockings in the 100- and 220-yard dash the way kids in Brooklyn recite baseball averages, and their elders—waitresses, ranchers, truck drivers and bankers—recall the feats of the great men of running with a pride and awe which is probably unique in the U.S. On a Saturday evening in May, 1956, 16,000 of them—as many as could possibly jam past the gates of Fresno State College's little Ratcliffe Stadium and into its seats, its infield and the grassy areas around the ends of its famed, sand-colored clay track—were present there and garrulous with anticipation.

At 7:14 o'clock, give or take a few seconds, every man, woman and child of them were on their feet and emitting a pleading roar which must have been heard on the distant Sierras, for around the far turn at Fresno came Australia's John Landy, one of the loveliest runners ever born, floating like blown tumbleweed toward a new world record in the mile run. The air was chilly, although the declining sunlight still slanted brightly on the green grass and the motley of 1,400 athletes—now spectators almost to a man—who had gathered for the 30th running of the West Coast Relays. A plaguing wind was blowing down the backstretch in gusts up to seven miles an hour. But Landy, whose warm smile and shock of curly brown hair had become familiar to millions of newspaper readers and televiewers during the two weeks of his U.S. tour, had built the foundations of a historic race.

He had been boxed momentarily on the first turn between ex-Occidental College Miler Jim Terrill and former Yaleman Mike Stanley. But he had slid clear at 200 yards, with Villanova's young Dublin Irishman, Ron Delany, at his heels, and from then on, running like some tanned Inca courier, he had steadily left the field behind. He had hit the quarter miles with almost absolute precision—59.9, 2:00.1, 3:00.8. Then, fiercely bent on penance for his one-yard defeat at the hands of his fellow Australian, Jim Bailey, seven days before, he fled into the final lap with 57 seconds to go to break his own world record.

How was he doing? It was impossible to say. But the crowd, remembering that he had run 57.2 in the final quarter against Bailey in the Los Angeles Coliseum, urged him on with a steady, deafening torrent of sound. He was 35 yards ahead of Delany in the backstretch, 40 yards ahead as he lengthened his stride in the turn, and 50 yards ahead and running all alone as he came rolling down the stretch. He went through the tape with his style unflawed by weariness, and turned back, strolling casually, to find out the news. The time was 3:59.1—his sixth sub-four-minute mile, and his second in one week. He had missed.

He walked immediately toward an Australian radio

80

man, waiting near the turn with a microphone. As he did so, his chest rose and fell laboriously beneath the green jersey of the Geelong Guild Athletic Club. But he took one last deep breath and then spoke almost as normally as if he had simply hiked the mile. He was bitterly disappointed. "It just wasn't there to give," he cried. "I had no sparkle in me at all. It was ridiculous not to have run 3:56. A near-record-breaker —perhaps that's my fate. I'm disappointed. I know in my heart I can run better than that. It was just another run—a time trial—just another performance."

A little later, back in the red brick dressing room, surrounded by reporters, he went on: "It may be that I've had too many hard races this year. In both cases here I doubt that I was running as well as in Australia, although I felt better tonight than last week. I was not exhausted at the end. I had the energy but I was just not getting it out. I was very strong." Had competition aided him in the race against Bailey in Los Angeles? "The competition," he said with a wry grin, "didn't present itself until it was too late to be of any use." He continued: "This may have been my last mile. I'll be running 1,500 meters before the Olympics, and I had hoped to give you a new record."

Thus ended one of the most astonishing and admirable adventures in the history of athletics in the U.S. And one, in the minds of those who listened to him in Fresno, which was only dramatized by John Landy's unfeigned disappointment. In a single fortnight he had flown 9,000 miles from Australia to the U.S., had not only accepted a burden of press conferences, newsreel performances, radio shows and television spots which would have staggered a candidate for the U.S. Senate, but had won his auditors to a man with his poise, his patience and an articulate honesty.

In accepting, without reserve, the responsibility of serving as an "ambassador" for Australia and a sort of salesman for the Melbourne Olympics, he had virtually promised to run two four-minute miles in eight days. And, for all the nervous strain of his incessant extracurricular activities, he had done so—a feat without precedent in the annals of track. If he had been beaten by a jump in the surprising race with Jim Bailey he had also made the pace and thus opened the door of fame to his fellow countryman.

Landy is a complex human—an intellectual with a compulsion for the arena and a stoic disregard for pain and exhaustion; a reserved and sensitive man whose mind is repelled, but whose spirits are kindled, by the roar of applause and the incandescent glare of publicity. The mile is much more than a race to Landy; it is, one gathers, almost a problem in esthetics. "I'd rather lose a 3:58 mile," he says, "than win one in 4:10." He has never betrayed by the slightest word or gesture anything but the utmost admiration for those who have beaten him. But he burns to win. "I'm vicious underneath," he said last week in

a burst of almost apologetic candor. Then, lapsing back to understatement: "I'm terribly irritated when I lose."

Landy's career can be roughly divided into two sections—before and after his historic loss to Roger Bannister in the Mile of the Century in August, 1954. He was bruised by defeat at Vancouver. He had been running, literally, almost every day for four long years, and he suffered a massive emotional letdown. "Everybody beat me when I got home," he says. "A schoolboy beat me in a quarter mile. I could see no reason for going on. Running is not a big sport in Australia, and I had run against the best in the world on the best tracks in the world. At home I faced the prospect of running badly on mediocre tracks against mediocre competition in little meets attended by three people. It was too much. Running is not a life; I had to quit sometime. I decided that the time had come to scrub it."

HE BECAME a schoolmaster. Landy, a graduate in agricultural science from Melbourne University, is probably the most famous alumnus of Australia's exclusive Geelong Grammar School. Geelong itself—an institution patterned rigidly after the English public school—is housed in a series of stately Georgian buildings not far from Melbourne. But four years before, influenced by progressive educational theories evolved in Scotland by German-born Educator Kurt Hahn, it had also established a remote branch called Timbertop, a cluster of rustic wooden buildings scattered through a great forest of peppermint gum trees in the Australian Alps. No formal sports are permitted at Timbertop and the patterns of scholastic existence are broken as much as possible; Geelong boys all go there for one year and are encouraged to be on their own in the surrounding wilderness. When Geelong's English headmaster, Dr. J. R. Darling, invited him to teach biology at this mountain retreat, Landy gratefully accepted.

He could hardly have found a better place to rest, to lick his wounds, to contemplate his fate and assess his own nature. He found the life of a schoolmaster rewarding in many ways. But his first seven months were, in many other ways, "the low point of my life." He had forced himself, for years, to live a life of iron self-discipline and self-denial, but it was a life which involved gladiatorial excitement, enormous emotional strain and release, globe-trotting and waves of publicity and acclaim such as seldom wash over any but movie stars or heads of state. Now he found himself immersed in a quasi-monastic life without competition or excitement.

Landy has been fascinated, since boyhood, with Australian Lepidoptera and has spent many a day walking through open country looking for rare manifestations of moths and butterflies. He turned back to it, but his amateur entomology was, after all, only a hobby. And teaching demanded a degree of self-effacement which, he was surprised to discover, came hard to him. He missed the violent individual self-expression, the feel of combat, which, almost without his realizing it, the mile had been giving him.

Landy had become a miler almost by accident. As a teen-ager he tried sprinting, and, at one point was clocked in a 10.6 hundred on wet grass, but he soon decided that the God-given talent needed for 9.4 was not his. Later, he seriously took up rough 18-man Australian football, as audacious a venture for a youth of 145 pounds as if he had set out to play American football against 200-pounders. But he concluded that he would never be among the top 16 men in the country ("I would have needed an extraordinary degree of agility against big men") and finally, while attending Melbourne University, attacked the mile. At first, feeling he had little talent, he was interested in it simply because he considered it an event at which he might become proficient through sheer doggedness.

But gradually it became a tremendous, a fascinating challenge to him. It was, he came to feel, "the human struggle" artificially contrived. "In any running event," he says, "you are absolutely alone. Nobody can help you. But short races are run without thought. In very long races you must go a great distance simply to be present in the laps that really count. But almost every part of the mile is tactically important—you can never let down, never stop thinking, and you can be beaten at almost any point. I suppose you could say it is like life. I had wanted to master it." But in the early months at Timbertop—although he had retired as the world record holder—he could not shake the feeling that he had failed: "I could not forget the shock I got when I saw Roger Bannister whipping past me on the final bend."

FOR SEVEN MONTHS Landy did no training at all, although he counteracted his restlessness with hundreds of miles of hiking through the mountainous country. But gradually he found himself attempting, sometimes on paper, to analyze the mile, to reduce the art of running to an essence and thus find where he had erred. He finally decided that the key lay in one simple fact: the race was run in a circle—or at any rate on an oval. "If you ran it on a straight it would be completely different. The circular track means it must be run in Indian file and the circular track divides the runners into the hunters and the hunted, the sitters who lie back and wait and the man who makes the pace. Every psychological aspect of the mile depends on that, and the man who sets the pace accepts a tremendous psychological disadvantage.

"All the responsibility for making the race rests on the pacer—the hunted. It is an exhausting thing, and you can only attempt to guess what is happening be-hind you and what is in the minds of the hunters. Of course, you can get a half-miler to make the pace for two laps and then drop out, but that is artificial. It is not running the mile. Or you can simply sit on your man—stay behind no matter how slow the race goes and wait. It is very comforting to do it—you can draw a bead on him and relax and sooner or later you will find a moment to attack him and if you do it at the right time you will inevitably beat him. But I don't like slow miles. I wanted to run record times and win. And after I set the pace against Bannister it seemed that the two things would not be reconciled."

But couldn't they? What, he began wondering, was to prevent the hunted from exercising discouraging pressures on the men behind him? An even pace had always been the ideal. Why not make an uneven pace? Thinking back on his 50 competitive miles, he decided that there was a "dead spot" a thousand yards from the start—on the first turn of the third lap—a place where men tired, but did not yet have recourse to the exhilaration of the final battle for the tape. If the hunted pulled away at that point, the hunters might never get within striking distance again. Making one bold move there, the pacer might inflict "a blow to the stomach," might turn the confidence of his pursuers to hopelessness.

The very difficulty and dangerousness of the idea was stimulating. With sufficient flexibility, sufficient virtuosity, he thought it might be possible to run anywhere, even in a good field, to lie back if the pace was fast enough, to move up and lead if necessary, and still be dominant.

That would be true mastery. According to Franz Stampfl, the Austrian coach who gained fame at Oxford, runners are divided by nature into pacers and sitters, into runners and racers, and are incapable of filling more than one role. Landy decided that was "sheer nonsense." "A lot of people," he says, "believed I had no kick at the finish. I disagreed. I've sat on men and kicked them to death. The sprint at the end is only relative. It is a matter of acceleration rather than real speed. After all, Chataway is famous for his kick, and he can't run 220 yards under 25 seconds. I felt that, if I could run the last 120 yards of a four-minute mile in 15.4 seconds, I could win. I decided that I could run the first half mile more slowly, as slowly as 2:02, or perhaps even 2:03, save more for the finish and still run under four."

Landy began training again, and for the first time in his life discovered that he could enjoy running. There is no level ground at Timbertop; he simply put on old clothes and sand shoes (tennis shoes) and ran, uphill and down, around a wandering course through the trees for two hours every afternoon. As he ran he came to new conclusions about training and its objectives. A man who sets out to become an artist at the mile is something like a man who sets out to discover the most graceful method of being hanged. No matter how logical his plans, he cannot carry them out without physical suffering. In his early years Landy performed chilling feats of toil simply to convert his body into the instrument he needed to satisfy his ambitions. In four short months in 1951 he cut 30 seconds off his time, brought it from 4:45 to 4:15 by literally running himself into a state of absolute exhaustion daily. "But that was as far as I could go until I saw Zatopek in the Olympics and learned that I had to have form as well. After that I got down to 4:02—and finally the record."

LANDY still believes in massive doses of work. By the time he began anew at Timbertop he had already converted himself into a fantastically efficient running machine (the average man's lungs hold 4½ quarts of air and can take in 120 quarts a minute; Landy's, it was discovered in recent tests, hold seven quarts and can utilize 300 a minute. He has a "huge" heart and a pulse rate of 42 as opposed to the average of 60 or 70). With this background he felt that further "formal" training was unnecessary, that he should strive instead to strip away the impediments and artifices of civilization, to become a "running animal." The level of fitness in animals—in, say, a race horse—he thought, was higher than in humans even before the horse was trained. "Animals move constantly. There is no such thing as convalescence in the animal kingdom—a dog with a broken leg will not rest."

Landy felt that he would have been a better runner if he had been raised on a farm or had run through the woods as a child like Paavo Nurmi. Unfortunately his family had "not lacked for a shilling" (the Landys are well-to-do people, and the runner's father has the distinction of serving on the board of the Melbourne Cricket Club), and he led a conventional middle-class boyhood. He reflected with admiration upon the colored tribesmen—"those fellows from Kenya who ran at the Empire Games. They were not used to tracks or running shoes, and after they ran they must have been in agony. A trainer told me that if you touched their legs, spasms would run through their muscles. But they gave no sign of pain at all. They didn't even grunt."

For 10 months Landy ran, uphill and down, estimating his speed simply by sensing the energy he had used for certain periods. He did exercises constantly "to bring up my speed." He refused to decide whether he would try for the Olympics or not. But when he came within inches of beating California's 880 World Record Holder Lon Spurrier in his first formal race, a half mile at Melbourne's Olympic Park, the die was cast, Australia rejoiced and the limelight and pressures of active competition engulfed him again.

Landy himself felt jubilant. Turning a half mile at the pace he had run meant that he had new speed to use in laying siege to the world's milers. When he ran the first mile of his comeback a little later he was doubly reassured. The time was 3:58.6. He felt strong at the finish. He ran an identical mile again. His 17 months in the hills had given him a maturity, a positiveness he had lacked before and, he was certain, a "basic performance" under four minutes—a professional ability to approach the record whenever he chose. He felt almost sheepish about it and still does. "I've been fooling the public," he says. "The four-minute mile is vastly overrated. It is just four times around the track. If I were doing this for a living, I could run it twice a week. But that would just be a performance. It's winning in real competition that counts, and there's not much purpose in running if you can't keep running faster, is there?" For all this, he was full of hope that he could reach new heights. The reason: the Melbourne Mile, in which he had stopped stock-still in the third lap to see if a fallen runner named Ron Clarke was hurt.

"I stopped involuntarily. Then I thought, 'I've been disqualified.' Then I thought, 'No, no—I'm still in the race.' It looked impossible. Mervyn Lincoln (Australia's young 4:00.6 miler) and the field were 30 yards ahead. I was in a blind panic. I didn't think about time. I didn't plan. I just ran after them. How I caught them and won I don't know, but I ran the last 120 yards in 14.4 seconds. I was dead at the end. The time was only 4:04.2, but I reckoned the energy expended was equal to a 3:56."

At this point he was asked to make the U.S. tour. He was extremely reluctant to do so, if only because he would be "pressurized," would be forced, as a sort of theatrical performer, to run for time no matter what the competition, and do so in strange surroundings, but Melbourne City Councilor Maurice Nathan, a wealthy merchant and a leader in promotion of the Olympics, all but insisted. Nathan, back from an American junket, realized Landy's popularity in the U.S. and also felt that Australia could never attract interest in the Games abroad simply by dispatching press releases. Landy finally agreed.

The pressure began in Honolulu. Reporters besieged him for a half hour after he got off the plane there; he gulped a quick lunch, held a press conference from 2 to 4 in the afternoon, made an appearance at a high school track meet, was interviewed on the radio and swamped by autograph hunters. He escaped with difficulty, went to the University of Hawaii campus, ran eight miles, drank some pineapple juice and hustled to the airport. He could not sleep on the plane. The schedule was more hectic in San Francisco the next day. He ran eight more miles after nightfall. In Los Angeles he went through the same routine. "If you don't get used to it," he said, "you just aren't good enough, that's all." But as the week wore on, he confessed to a leaden sense of "apprehension." He was appalled by the stone-hard surface of the Coliseum track, and at one point in midweek was fearful that he might not be able to finish a race on it. His weight sank from 146 to 143 pounds and he slept badly. He was more nervous, before the start, than he could remember.

Afterward he doubted that either the track—which he finally conquered by filing his spikes short—or his schedule, which had provided "a compensating excitement," had affected his running. He refused to attach any significance to the fact that his feet were cut and blistered by his heavy training. "There is no gray —just black and white—in this injury business. If you're hurt badly enough to limp, you can't run at all. If you aren't, it makes no difference." But he was hard hit by Bailey's stretch victory. "Jim had a big day," he said. "He's improved tremendously; his style used to be prohibitive. I don't want to take anything away from him, but I doubt that he could do it alone, or that he could do it again right off [Bailey ran 4:06.4 the following Saturday]. The point is—he has the equipment to do it. So have a lot of others. I'm mortally afraid, now, that nobody, including myself, has the margin of superiority to be able to make the pace and win."

Yet if he was discouraged he kept it to himself after that moment. When Pete Rozelle, former public relations man for the Los Angeles Rams, who shepherded him through the tour, announced that Landy hoped to "relax a little" after the meet, a reporter cracked: "What does he do for relaxation—take a Miltown?" It was an unfair estimate of Landy's nature. He did just what any sensible man would have done after so difficult a week: he sat up rehashing his adventures, drank a few Scotches and went to bed with a mild glow.

Afterwards, with the heat subsiding, he proved himself a humorous and extremely sociable fellow, albeit one with a sardonic eye. When Shepherd Rozelle announced, amid a long-distance call to Melbourne, that Australian newspapers were reporting the tour on Page One daily, Landy muttered: "Sickening." As Rozelle recounted his ambassadorial triumphs, Landy marched up and down the room, grinning accusingly and lifting an imaginary pitchfork. He was fascinated by Los Angeles' speeding automobiles ("I keep expecting to see everybody in town arrested en masse") and by Los Angeles' radio advertising ("Henry Ford himself wouldn't have enough money to buy what I've been asked to buy in the last 10 minutes"). At Fresno when an Australian newsman reported, in some excitement, that he had just seen a real cowboy, Landy asked: "What's he look like?" Said the informant: "Tight blue jeans, cowboy boots, black shirt and a big hat." Landy broke in: "Oh, I know him—Wes Santee." He was outspoken in his disappointment after the Fresno race, but once the post-finish questioning was through, Landy spoke no more about it.

"I had hoped to be able to pull out a big one," he said. "But right now, I'm going to have two hamburgers with French fries on the side. Perhaps I'll have a good go at racing in the Games."

SUMMER

*Thickened with light, the spaces of summer
hold sound like the sea.
A playing-field shout outlives the play;
an outboard motor is put up, its drone preserved,
as it were, in summer's amber.
Only at night are the sounds quick and falling:
the water breaking each time the jumping fish falls;
in the white barns, horses stamping
in their dreams' dark furlongs;
grooms sitting out under the elms
in canvas chairs, on tack boxes,
telling lies*

—Gilbert Rogin

SEA, SUN AND SAIL

AMERICAN SAILORS, by and large, are the best in the world, and the reason for their superiority is simple: they have more good places to sail, and more boats to sail in, than the yachtsmen of any other country. For example, the New England coast from the northern tip of Maine to the Sandy Hook light is one long succession of deep, protected harbors where classboats can race in safety, and big, graceful ocean cruisers can lay over between adventures on the open sea. At the southern end of the classic New England sailing ground lies the long arm of Long Island Sound, perhaps the best-known sailing area in the entire U.S. And it is here that the beautiful sloops and yawls, like those shown at right in the annual New York Yacht Club cruise, carry on a summer-long rivalry that many yachtsmen consider the absolute pinnacle of all sailing competition.

Eastern skippers, however, are a long way from holding a monopoly on U.S. yachting. All across the country the quick little Comets and Snipes, graceful Internationals, flat-faced Inland Scows, and innumerable other categories of sailing craft skitter across the lakes and bays of America as half a million day sailors join the summer festival of wind and water.

No one who has fiddled nervously with a stop watch through the five minutes after a warning gun, then known the bursting excitement of the charge to the starting line, will ever be completely free of the urge to race small boats. Nor will the man who has taken the night wheel on a Pacific cruise ever forget the lazy roll of the long swells as the masthead waggles and tips across the dark sky. Nor will the 12-year-old who has been brought up bailing a sneakbox in a Jersey salt marsh ever doubt the truth of the words spoken by the water rat in Kenneth Grahame's *Wind in the Willows.* "There is nothing," said the rat, "absolutely nothing half so much worth doing as simply messing about in boats."

—EZRA BOWEN

Nimble girl crew hikes out onto leeboard of Class C scow as skipper mans the tiller during regatta at Lake Arrowhead, high in the Sierra Mountains of California

The Arrowhead regatta gives these scrambling California youngsters a chance to show off their skill in full-scale race

...pping out of regatta with broken mast, crew of 18-foot ...tie makes emergency repairs while waiting for towboat

Against a massive backdrop of brick and concrete along the Detroit water-front, racing sloops maneuver between Great Lakes passenger steamer and cargo vessel laden with new cars, before start of Detroit's annual Riverama

DAVID KITZ

Fog from the Pacific rolls under North tower of Golden Gate Bridge as procession of Rhodes 3.

...ops, their sails graceful as gull wings, slides over the blue surface of San Francisco Bay

In a fresh breeze, crew members brace to keep balance on the canted, wet deck of 67-foot ya

ollo as ocean racer drives toward the mark across blue Bahamian waters in Nassau Cup race

Rushing downwind with spinnaker set, mainsail hard against starboard spreaders, Seattle yawl Ad

...ges past Race Rocks light during rugged Swiftsure race in the stormy Straights of Juan de Fuca

KENNETH G. OLLAR

BOOM IN BIG BATS

THE BASEBALL SPOTLIGHT, which plays fitfully over the wide stage of the diamond, stays longest at home plate. There the young men with the big bats — such as Mickey Mantle on the page opposite — wage their throw-by-throw warfare with the pitchers. Always present is the possibility which makes this duel the most dramatic part of baseball — the threat of a long, lifting drive into the far seats. No one in the stands or watching a game on television can stifle a thrill of expectation when a Ted Williams or a Stan Musial or a Duke Snider moves into the white-lined oblong of the batter's place and whips a bat easily and gracefully back and forth, the heavy ash light and threatening in thick hands driven by heavy-muscled forearms and directed by the quick, keen eye of a hitter. So baseball reserves its fattest paychecks for the men with the big bats and the thunder in their swing and the drama they carry when they step quietly to the plate.

There is menace implicit in the tight-wound strength of Mantle as he crouches to await the pitch, his bat — soon to arc in a shimmering, white circle — now poised and heavy with danger. Here in the heart beat of time before the ball reaches the plate and the big bat connects or misses, is the starting point of all the excitement that is baseball.

—TEX MAULE

Stan Musial of the St. Louis Cardinals coils before he strikes. As ball approac

hifts weight, whips bat around, and follows through as the ball heads for seats

WILLIAMS' CORNER

AT FENWAY PARK in Boston, a corner of the left-field grandstand juts sharply to the left-field foul line, and there was a time when Red Sox fans vied for seats in it, the better to ride Ted Williams. There is a legend that one day Ted filled his hip pocket with hamburger and, at a proper moment, flung it to the corner critics with the implication that, being wolves, they might relish some raw meat.

Today Ted Williams enjoys a sort of peaceful co-existence with his corner. Indeed, the corner cannot be said to exist as it did in the old days. All of Fenway Park is Williams' corner now and to sit in any part of it is to become part of the endless Williams debate.

"He's mellowed, there's no doubt of that at all," said a fan the other afternoon, speaking with a rich South Boston brogue. "You take the way he treats the kids. Here the other day didn't he pose with his arm around the boy who got into a fight over him and give him a baseball, too? Do you remember when he'd tell a kid to scram?"

"I mind the time," said another fellow, taking a pipe out of his mouth, "when there'd be one big boo as he came out on the field. Today I'd venture to say its 85% cheers to 15% boos. Do you agree?"

"No, I don't," said a third man, South Boston like the others. "I mean to say I don't go along with the idea that Mr. Ted Williams has mellowed and that everything is sweetness and light between him and the fans. The man has contempt for the fans."

A man wearing a sports shirt you could see through leaned over from the row behind. "Excuse me," he said, "no offense intended, I'm sure. But you gentlemen miss the point entirely."

The man with the pipe glanced at the others meaningly. "Well," he said, winking, "if you'll put us straight on the matter, we'll be most humbly grateful, I'm sure."

"The point about Williams is," the man in the sports shirt went on, "the point is he doesn't *have* to give a tinker's damn. He's just so good at his job that he can say, 'Take it or leave it.'"

The man with the pipe broke in: "Did you ever hear of a certain Mr. Babe Ruth? Wasn't he good at his job and at the same time on good terms with everybody?"

"Will you let me complete my thought?" said the man in the sports shirt irritably.

"Oh, go ahead," said the man with the pipe.

"I'll be brief," said the sports shirt. "I was here Memorial Day. Well, sir, Ted comes up for the first time and takes a count of two and nothing. Now an ordinary hitter would be required to let the next one go by but, as we all know, the take sign is never on Ted. So, lo and behold, if the next one isn't down the middle and the next thing you heard was that crack of the homerun ball and the whole stand was on its feet applauding—not yelling, mind you—but applauding as if it was a performance of the grand opera. And then there was Ted racing around the bases, not trotting like your Babe Ruth, but sprinting as fast as he could. As usual, he didn't tip his cap, but just streaked into the dugout as much as to say, 'There's your home run now, take it or leave it.'"

"What's the point of the story?" said the man with the pipe.

"The point is," exclaimed the man in the sports shirt, "wouldn't all of us like to be the same, so good at our jobs that we could tell the boss to take it or leave it or go to blazes? Isn't Mr. Ted Williams the living symbol of the same independence that makes the Irish character the wonder of the world?"

The others exchanged glances. "May I ask your name?" said the man with the pipe.

"Moriarity," said the man in the sports shirt, "from Framingham."

"Well, hell," said the man with the pipe, "bring your beer and come and join us. There's plenty of room in this row."

—GERALD HOLLAND

k Aaron, the Milwaukee Braves' great young hitter, sets
eyes on the flight of the ball, the bat still in his hand

UP A LAZY RIVER

Photographed by W. EUGENE SMITH

MAN WOULD not be man if, somewhere in his heart, he was not a bum—if he did not nurse a recurring dream of indolence and irresponsibility, and did not yearn to stretch out on a tropic beach or under a western watering tank and let his whiskers grow and occasionally have a shot of something rousing from a bottle. It is a dream which has a way of growing stronger in summer, but in most strata of society a fellow just can't hustle off to hunt for Tom Sawyer's island, or for pearl oysters—he can't, indeed, even doze off on the courthouse steps at noon —without causing a raise of eyebrows and a wag of tongues. Fish, however, are a bum's best friend. Not the lusty salmon, nor the leaping trout, nor any fish which must be pursued, but the flounder and the catfish—fish which inhabit the tide flats and the back eddies of slow rivers, fish which may be lured to the bait from a recumbent position. Millions of men annually escape that constricting maze erected over the centuries by their women with no more equipment than is reflected in the still life at left. They escape in every country under the sun—the photograph was made by W. Eugene Smith in a Portuguese tidal inlet off the Gulf of Cadiz— and, though the red wine in the jug might be white mule, or cider, or muscatel or rye in other parts of the world, it is a picture which reflects a universal aspect of the masculine soul. A man need not row a weather-beaten boat such as this Portuguese fisherman's craft more than a dozen strokes to achieve Purpose and, hence, a suspect but unassailable license for bumhood. After that languid series of motions he is free to drop an anchor (a tin can full of cement), bait his hook, float his bobber upon the softly gurgling flood, pull out the cork, tilt his jug, lower his hat over his eyes and sink back into that comatose and reflective state in which man reaches true nobility of character. In the process, although the odds are against it, there is a chance that he might even catch a fish.

—PAUL O'NEIL

BOATERS
AND OARS
AT HENLEY

Photographed by WALKER EVANS

THE HENLEY ROYAL REGATTA, England's grand old rowing classic, goes on as steadily and as unchanged as the flowing waters of the Thames on which it is held. Since it was established in 1839, the regatta has managed (except during World Wars I and II) to bring together the pick of blueblood English crews and attract outside competitors from all over the world without ever losing its agreeably old-fashioned air. In 1955, when a red-vested, bare-shouldered, shaven-headed team showed up from Moscow and carried off a chestful of trophies, including the coveted Grand Challenge Cup, there was an uneasy rustling in the enclosures. But there is no sign that Henley suffered a permanent trauma.

"Sturdy oarsmen," murmured an Old Blue in the tight-lipped way that distinguishes a Henley regular. "After a few years, I'm sure they could get the hang of it."

Nobody thinks of Henley as all rowing. For four midsummer days the sloping meadows and shaded lawns on either side of the mile-and-550-yard course blossom with white and candy-striped marquees which glisten in the sunshine (or, just as probable, sag in a summer rain). Punts and houseboats are moored with nudging intimacy behind the booms which protect the course. The ladies wear their prettiest, summeriest frocks. The males top their white flannels with blazers and boaters and caps of startling hues which almost any competent ornithologist would recognize as mating plumage (*see right*). Behind the enclosures there is a funfair with dodgems and shooting galleries to attract the young gentlemen from Eton and Radley. At night there are fireworks.

Despite its Victorian birth, there is something decidedly raffish about Henley. Nowhere else would a proper Englishman be seen dead wearing a shrimp-pink bow tie.

—JOE DAVID BROWN

106

*Bending forward for the final pull to the finish, the London Rowing Club
crew surges past the grandstand pavilion during the semifinals
of the Grand Challenge Cup race in Henley's Royal Regatta*

HORSE UP;
RIDER DOWN

Photographed by HY PESKIN

HIGH SPOT of the Canadian summer for rodeo followers is the six-day Calgary Stampede, which draws tens of thousands to Alberta to cheer the toughest and best of rodeo cowboys. The spectators are rewarded with the thrill of sights like the wildly leaping bronco on the opposite page, photographed at the peak of his man-high lunge as he menaces the fallen rider with pawing hoofs.

No one knows what makes a bronc explode when he feels the weight of a rider, but the good ones react with a spectacular fury over and over again. Before the days of the ASPCA, a horse sometimes bucked because of a bit of tabasco under the tail, a burr under the saddle or an electric buzzer. But today the use of such artful stimulants has been almost entirely eliminated by rodeo officials.

The bucking horse, usually unprepossessing in appearance and of heterogeneous ancestry, may have been born mean. Or he may have started life as a dependable ranch animal and suddenly, one day, been seized with a violent contempt for man. In any case, the more evil-tempered he is, the better the rodeo cowboys like it; they get small credit in the eyes of judges for sitting a bronco that just crowhops half-heartedly around the arena.

Calgary's rodeo is not only one of the most famous and spectacular of the year's big meetings, but is one which rewards winners with some of the richest purses on the year-round rodeo wheel. The top hands among the roughly 1,000 professional cowboys who compete in 600 rodeos in the U.S. and Canada each year split up some $3 million in prizes. The broncs will split up several of the top hands.

In a steer-decorating contest, cowhand leaps from his horse to slip a tiny flag over rushing steer's horn. This is a gentler version of American rodeo's bulldogging, in which steer is thrown. Below, in wild-cow milking contest, cowboys rush to milk animals roped by partners

A lurching steer fails to dislodge rider clinging desperately to comple the 10-second ride which will qualify him for the winner's ca

Slashing hoofs send cowhands scrambling during wild horse race in which the contestants try to sade

...cking, kicking horses and ride them across finish line. It is one of the most dangerous rodeo feats

BROTHERS UNDER THE SEA

Photographed by ED FISHER

NO ONE can say who was the first hunter to spear fish under water, or where or how the sport began. For as long as any man can guess, slippery young Fiji Islanders, armed with wooden spears, have perched like cormorants on the fringing reefs of their volcanic islands, dived into the crashing surf, and come back alive with fish. Today Fijians are still plunging through the boiling water into the quiet below, but they have put aside their wooden spears. Times have changed. The Fijians now carry spearguns as fancy as any used by vacationers in the swank Caribbean.

Spearfishing has become in recent years a sport of the world. Japanese are at it; so are Russians, South Americans, South Africans and Alaskans (though it probably takes another Alaskan to understand why). Spearfishermen go under ice and in the dismal murk of tidal guts and estuaries, but of it all nothing cheers the sporting soul so much as prospect of a hunt in the glass-clear wonderworld of the tropics. There, where the refracted sunlight skips across the sea fans and coral prongs of a reeftop, a spangled array of parrotfish, tangs and doctorfish scurry in the shimmer, hanging in the water one moment, then all of them suddenly wildly riding the breadth of the reef in a surge of sea. Down the reefside, where the warm light flickers weakly and is lost in twilight, the big game moves about.

It is in the wonderworld of the Caribbean that three Florida brothers —Art, Fred and Don Pinder — hunted for 20 years and came to be the world's best spearfishermen, developing the ability to dive on their own lung power 80 feet down after 200-pound fish and learning the special ways of each breed. "This sport is not fishing, but more like hunting," the masterful diver, Art Pinder concluded, thinking back on 20 years of it. "It is, in fact, more like hunting than hunting itself."

—COLES PHINIZY

116

In a Bahamian inlet, using the simple, pliable sling spear with which he and his brothers hunt all game up to 800 pounds, Diver Art Pinder boats a hogfish

After a 20-minute chase across grassy flats, brothers Art and Fred Pinder slowly close

tance on a 300-pound leopard ray, clutching for the bent spear protruding from its back

In green shoal water Fred Pinder snatches a lobster from a coral crevice. He uses a gaff as protection against the lobster spines and as a safeguard in case the lobster shares its niche with a moray eel. From the same crevice where Fred got his lobster, Art Pinder comes up with a five-foot moray (right). Even though he has speared the eel solidly, Art applies pressure with a second spear to keep the eel's strong jaws away from his hands

I'D RATHER WATCH FISH

by PHILIP WYLIE

IN A LIFELONG QUEST for fish, many a sportsman will gradually change from an angler to what I call a fish watcher. Of course, most fishermen die in harness —no figure of speech where deep-sea angling is concerned; but some become more interested in fish themselves than in catching fish. Just the other day, for example, I learned of a research expedition that will spend five years off the South and Central American coasts under the aegis of an eastern oil executive who, until lately, was a big-game angler, pure and simple. Now he is a fish watcher.

Fresh-water anglers, especially those who seek trout, have long had a concern for the life cycle and habitat of their favorite fish. But an interest in fish that is motivated by the hope of a loaded creel does not describe the true "fish watcher"; he is likely to find his reels stored away in grease from one year to the next. It is more exhilarating to him to find out about the submarine world than to catch samples with a hook.

What's the spell?

I know the day it began for me. We were trolling over the big reef outside the middle Florida Keys— in the open sea, some miles offshore. The morning was fair and the fishing fine—until the breeze died away entirely. We trolled after that in a sea as slick as blue enamel, so smooth you could see the wake of the outrigger baits, let alone of the boat, for a thousand yards astern. Then the engine conked out and we drifted. We were impatient until somebody happened to look over the side—and down.

There, 50 feet below, was the bottom, the reef— vivid in the clean Gulf Stream water—and there were the fish that had stopped biting in the calm: amber-jacks, grouper, 'cudas, big snappers and the rest. There, too, were smaller fish by the thousands, the tens of thousands, fish as brightly colored as Christmas tree ornaments. All around them was the unearthly landscape of living coral, the many colored miniature cordilleras, with sand "deserts" between. On the sand, rays dozed, half buried; sharks swam above. Under a natural bridge of coral a huge jewfish lay. All that afternoon, until an onshore breeze riffled the surface and spoiled our fun, we leaned over the gunwales and just looked. Nobody even thought of lowering a bait to see if the fish would bite down there: nobody wanted to ruin the view by bringing a splashing fish to boat.

What bemused me afterward, as I meditated a spectacle I knew I could never forget, was my ignorance. I'd just seen corals (I supposed they were) of a hundred forms and as many colors: the reef looked as if a boatload of dye had foundered upon it, and I had seen 50 varieties of fish and other animal life to which I could give no name. Yet—for years and years —I'd been trolling over just such spots as that!

It was easy to find books which helped with fish identification; it was much harder to learn the names of the madrepores and millepores, the corals, anemones and sponges which gave the reef its lunar aspect. At about that time, however, I built a house on Biscayne Bay and discovered my sea wall supported a miniature cross section of reef life. After that, on almost any calm day I might be seen lying on my lawn on my belly, my head projecting over the wall, watching; and on any calm night I might also be found in the same place—with a powerful flashlight.

In my case, the next step came with the glass-bottomed bucket. I'd taken my family to Bimini in the Bahamas with a view to marlin fishing. But I developed a secondary sport which I herewith commend to any fish-interested swimmer. The beach at Bimini is sandy, but a few yards offshore lie patches of coral only a yard or two under mean tide. Simply by hooking my chin over the rim of the bucket (which I padded soon, when my chin wore out), by grasping the opposite rim with both hands, and by kicking my feet, I turned myself into a glass-bottomed boat.

The little inshore reefs are the habitat of many of the young of deep-water species. They are also a dwelling place of great numbers of the most gorgeous fishes that live: beaugregories and other demoiselles, butterflyfish, wrasses and so on.

Skin-diving equipment, of course, has enabled bold swimmers to do their watching at the fish's level; but "bucket fishing," as we called my sport, is highly recommended for all who can swim and care to see sights that are beautiful, astonishing—and sometimes startling, like wrasses persistently trying to nibble your legs, or finding yourself face to face with a barracuda five feet long!

In casual and innocent ways the angler can become a fish watcher. It doesn't have to happen to him in the sea or in the tropics. He may be a man with a rowboat dock in a fresh-water pond in Wisconsin who happens, on some pellucid afternoon, to look down into the green weeds and minnow schools and starts to wonder. He may be a man with a house on a brook or one with a salt-water marsh in his backyard; anglers are usually the ones who become fish watchers merely because angling takes them where fish are.

As the enterprise took an increasing hold on me I gave decreasing attention to fishing, per se. What boots it to catch the hundred-and-umpteenth sailfish if instead, by patience, one can actually watch sailfish swimming about at peace in the depths, or behold them schooling up—apparently to mate; or study a sailfish that chooses—for no comprehensible reason, to lie at the surface, his vast "sail" spread until wind and sun dry it out completely?

Catching a common shark, as a rule, is a dull sport; watching a shark feed naturally in its own cerulean world is something else! And feeding fish simply to attract them in numbers becomes an extraordinary diversion. Indeed, on the island of Bimini there is now a glass-bottomed boat that is probably the most popular sea-going sports vessel in the Bahamas. A trip in this vessel to the reef outside is regarded by many first-time viewers as the most breath-taking experience in their lives.

The watcher of fishes sees so much that is mysterious and unexplained that he often turns to books first for an answer and finally to the authors of such books, the scientists. He thus finds himself allied with the researchers. That is what happened to Mr. Lou Marron, who financed the South American expedition mentioned earlier. It happened to Michael Lerner, president of the International Game Fish Association, who established a laboratory in Bimini for the American Museum of Natural History. Other marine research stations, laboratories, institutes and the like have been founded in California, Texas and elsewhere by anglers who took to watching fish.

MARINELAND, the gigantic "aquaria" south of St. Augustine, is simply ocean "fish watching" brought ashore and made available to the general public. Its immense success is evidence of the latent urge for this sport. Silver Springs, in Florida, is a fish watcher's paradise; and at Homosassa Springs, in the same state, a glass-walled tunnel takes tourists underwater for a fish-eye view of fish. The voyage of the raft *Kon-Tiki* across the Pacific was, above all else, a constant adventure in observing the life of the sea.

Where does all this fish watching lead? It doesn't provide the excitement of a screaming reel and hissing line; it doesn't put fresh mackerel or pompano on the dinner table.

The sport of observation leads, however, to as exciting adventures—and to adventures far more *diverse*. That goes without saying, of course, if the angler puts on a face mask and flippers and dives overboard to do his watching among the fish. The less enterprising fish watcher, however, has his moments, too.

I know one, for example, who had his skiff upset by a huge tiger shark which, fortunately, left its teeth marks in the bow of the boat rather than the stern of the man thrown overboard. And if the fish watcher doesn't bring home any bacon, he may still help the world to eat better. Fish watchers—scientists and laymen together—have located many new sea-food treasuries, including some vast and as yet untapped resources. We've also learned, for instance, a great deal about fish which has been of inestimable value to the scientists. We have found, by experiment, that if a food fish is tossed into a captive community of larger fish, and if it escapes their first appalling rush, it is left alone to become an accepted resident of the community—which is the way people act, too, quite often. And, through glass-bottomed buckets and boats, we have found that some such "citizenship"—though perilous—seems to be available to all fishes, everywhere, most of the time. For the depths of seas and lakes and ponds are *not* disordered submarine stage sets, the constant background for massacre, mayhem, cannibalism and bloodletting—as almost everybody rather shudderingly supposes.

Sure, fish are predatory and, sure, they eat each other. But, most of the time, they are peaceable creatures that live in an environment as beautiful as a temple with stained-glass windows—or an orchid-hung glade in a rainy forest. The sea around is cobalt, or it is green as jade; the reef is lavishly decorated with "flowers" planted by paint-crazy Nature; the fish themselves and the rest of the living things are exquisite as butterflies, even when they weigh a half ton.

I well remember my last blue marlin. Not big: 330 pounds. We cut up the carcass to feed fish that some scientists were keeping alive—and threw the head off the dock into the bay. The next day, while hunting sea shells on the beach, I came upon that head—the eyes still limpid and inquiring, the incredible blue hues of the gill covers still luminous. I sat down on the stratified beach sand rock, remembering what I'd seen of the reef and the other places where marlin swim, and I wondered why I'd dragged him out of his elegant domain and done him in.

Since then, I haven't fished for blue marlin. It isn't a moral matter: I might, if the mood hit me, set a bonefish dancing behind a charter boat any afternoon. And I enjoy watching others catch a first marlin as much as I enjoyed my own first one. But it struck me then, and the feeling has not yet changed, that I would rather learn fish than fish, rather watch than catch. That's why I'm more apt nowadays to be seen peering into the water in the company of an ichthyologist, or swimming around with my head in a glass-bottomed pail, than to be found with a six-nine outfit in my hands and a bait dancing astern. I'm a fish watcher. A terrific sport!

THE AUGUST

DELIGHTS

OF SARATOGA

Photographed by RICHARD MEEK

THE NAMES of the horses that have danced victoriously over the turf at Saratoga, oldest functioning race track in the U.S., read like a memory book of American Thoroughbred racing: Man o' War, Gallant Fox, Equipoise, Exterminator stir up the echoes of the past.

For ninety-three summers Saratoga has stood quietly, graciously, untouched by change. No bands play, no monuments clutter the elm-shaded paddock, no rattling trains interrupt the stillness of its twenty-four-day meeting. Saratoga is more than a period in the calendar year of racing; it is a special world in itself.

The founding fathers of the little, sleepy community, nestled in the foothills of New York's Adirondacks, long ago deemed it only humane that the Saratoga racegoer not be required to reach the track for the first race until 2:30 P.M., and the rule has never been altered. Across from the archaic red grandstand (right) swans glide gracefully in an infield pond and an empty blue canoe drifts on the fancy of the wind. The canoe becomes an immovable point of consternation to the young visitor, but the older ones know that the canoe is there for no reason at all, except that it was there during the first meeting and out of respect for tradition it must remain.

Not many years ago a Saratoga regular, who had not missed a race in thirty years, declared in his will that when death took him he would like his ashes to be spread across the stretch at Saratoga. And his wish was fulfilled, without clamor or sensation.

Attendance at Saratoga is poor, betting paltry compared to the rest of the American tracks. For the past twenty years experts in the economics of racing have said that each season at Saratoga would be its last. And for twenty years the old track has proven how consistently wrong experts can be.

—WILLIAM LEGGETT

As much a part of the Saratoga scene as the morning workouts for the race horses is

...tional breakfast on the clubhouse terrace enjoyed by relaxed horsemen and their guests

WAIKIKI'S WILD WHITE HORSES

THE SPORT of wave riding, like the good waves on which it depends, comes from the open ocean. The first known wave riders were the primitive Polynesians who were at ease both on and in the water long before civilized Europeans were smart enough to take a bath. In old Hawaii, wave riding was the sport of kings and commoners.

As the solitary Hawaiian pictured on the opposite page throws his weight forward to keep his board on the rising wave, it seems the waves at Waikiki still belong exclusively to the islanders. But this is true only in the big surf out far. In Waikiki's 12 square miles of water, waves of varied types and heights roll in from a half dozen surf lines. Any tourist with the poise of Humpty Dumpty can get in an outrigger canoe with a veteran Hawaiian and ride fringing crests four to eight feet high in the Canoe Surf line.

The average beginner learns to ride a board in four-foot waves of the Malihini Surf in a few hours (ski buffs often catch on in half an hour). Then after several months' practice a novice may have the knack of angling down a wave to gain speed and to keep clear of the plunging boil he will encounter in the fast, curling 10-foot waves of the Queen's Surf. On the best days, a quarter mile beyond Queen's Surf, 20-foot waves spill over in the Castle Surf and the First Break line. Out in the First Break, a Humpty Dumpty may take very many great falls and never learn to ride these big, wild white horses.

—COLES PHINIZY

A half mile at sea, a skillful Hawaiian board rider throws a smoking trail of spray beh

as he rockets 30 miles an hour along the unbroken shoulder of a 12-foot fringing wave

Through a torrent of spray thrown up by the bow of their outrigger canoe, tourist

waiian beach boys slide down a wave at start of quarter-mile ride into Waikiki Beach

DIAMOND IN THE NIGHT

THE ODD JEWEL shining against the velvet of the night on the opposite page is venerable old Yankee Stadium. The occasion is a night baseball game, and, down on the field, everything looks a little larger than life under the brilliant synthetic sunshine of the batteries of lights. The bright green of the outfield picks up some of the shine from the lights, the ball is a white streak through the night air, and the customers, veterans now of two decades of nighttime games, bask as happily beneath the stars as ever they did in the bright sun of midafternoon.

When Larry MacPhail brought night baseball to the major leagues in the 1930's, he pumped new life into a flagging spectacle and, incidentally, saved the lives of no telling how many office boys' grandmothers in the next 20 years. The ballplayers, most of them, did not like it. Joe DiMaggio, at the end of his great career, said it took five years off his baseball life. But a new generation has grown up since then, and the modern player, nurtured on the bright lights during his minor league life, blinks in the sunlight of the infrequent day game and finds nothing strange in his nocturnal business.

Photographer Hy Peskin leaned out of a helicopter circling above New York to get this contemporary view of U. S. baseball.

—TEX MAULE

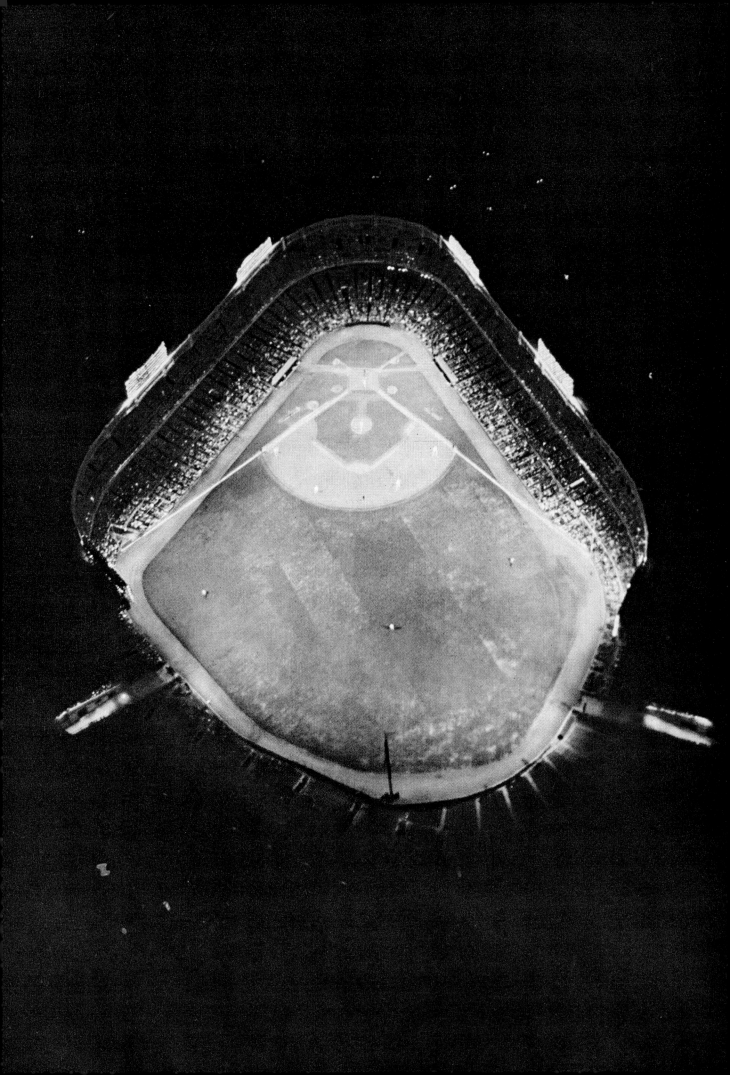

Pigeon's-eye view of Yankee Stadium, brilliantly lighted against the fading glow of the ea

ing sky above New York, shows the warm, wide-ranging spectrum of baseball at night   Marvin Newman

MR. RICKEY AND THE GAME

by GERALD HOLLAND

"I AM ASKED to speak of the game," said Branch Rickey, restating a question that had been put to him, "I am asked to reflect upon my own part in it. At the age of 73, on the eve of a new baseball season, I am importuned to muse aloud, to touch upon those things that come first to mind."

Seated in his office at Forbes Field, the home of the Pittsburgh Pirates, Branch Rickey nibbled at an unlighted cigarette and sniffed the proposition like a man suddenly come upon a beef stew simmering on a kitchen stove.

Abruptly he threw himself back in his chair and clasped his hands over his head and stared up at the ceiling. He looked 10 years younger than his actual age. Thanks to a high-protein, hamburger-for-breakfast diet, he was 30 pounds lighter than he had been three months before. His complexion was ruddy and his thick brown hair showed only a little gray at the temples. Now his great bushy eyebrows shot up and he prayed aloud:

"Lord make me humble, make me grateful . . . make me *tolerant!*"

Slowly he came down from the ceiling and put his elbows on the desk. Unconsciously, perhaps, a hand strayed across the desk to a copy of *Bartlett's Familiar Quotations*. The hand was that of an old-time catcher, big, strong and gnarled. He turned slowly in his chair and swept his eyes over the little gallery of framed photographs on the wall. Among them were George Sisler, Rickey's first great discovery, one of the greatest of the left-handed hitters, now at work down the hall as chief of Pittsburgh scouts; Rogers Hornsby, the game's greatest right-handed hitter, a betting man for whom Rickey once dared the wrath of baseball's high commissioner, Kenesaw Mountain Landis; Jackie Robinson, chosen by Rickey as the man to break down baseball's color line; Honus Wagner, the immortal

Pittsburgh shortstop, now past 80, at this moment growing weaker by the day at his sister's house across town; Charley Barrett, the old Cardinal scout, Rickey's right arm in the days when St. Louis was too poor to make a Southern training trip.

Turning back to his desk, Rickey grimaced and then spoke rapidly, almost harshly:

"Of my career in baseball, let us say first of all that there have been the appearances of hypocrisy. Here we have the Sunday school mollycoddle, apparently professing a sort of public virtue in refraining from playing or watching a game of baseball on Sunday. And yet at the same time he is not above accepting money from a till replenished by Sunday baseball."

He paused and bit the unlighted cigarette in two. He dropped his voice:

"A deeply personal thing. Something not to be exploited, not to be put forward protestingly at every whisper of criticism. No, a deeply personal thing. A man's promise, a promise to his mother. Not involving a condemnation of baseball on Sunday, nor of others who might desire to play it or watch it on Sunday. Simply one man's promise—and it might as well have been a promise not to attend the theater or band concerts in the park."

His eyes went around the room and were held for a moment by the blackboard that listed the players on the 15 ball clubs in the Pittsburgh farm system. His lips moved and the words sounded like, "But is the boy *ready* for New Orleans?" Then, with a quick movement, he leaned across the desk and waggled an accusing finger.

"Hell's fire!" he exploded. "The Sunday school mollycoddle, the bluenose, the prohibitionist has been a *liberal!* No, no, no—this has nothing to do with Jackie Robinson. I contend that there was no element

138

of liberalism there. I will say something about that perhaps, but now the plain everyday things—the gambling, the drinking, the . . . other things. I submit that I have been a liberal about *them!*"

He was silent. He did not mention or even hint at the names of managers who won major league pennants after everyone but Branch Rickey had quit on them; nor the men who gladly acknowledge that they are still in baseball because of the confidence Rickey placed in them.

The telephone with the private number rang. Branch Rickey picked it up and traded Southpaw Paul La Palme to the St. Louis Cardinals for Ben Wade, a relief pitcher. "You announce it," he said into the phone, "and just say La Palme for Wade and an unannounced amount of cash. We'll talk about a Class A ballplayer later. Anybody but a catcher. I don't need a catcher at that level." He put down the phone and his eyes twinkled. "Later in the day I may make a deal with Brooklyn," he said, "if I can get up the nerve." As things turned out, either he did not get up the nerve or he was unable to interest the Flatbush authorities.

He whirled around in his chair and stared out the window. He could see, if he was noticing, the end of a little street that runs down from Hotel Schenley to the ball park. It is called Pennant Place, a reminder of happier days for the Pittsburgh fans, now so ashamed of their eighth-place Pirates that only a few of them would show up at the ball park—even for doubleheaders.

Rickey ran both hands furiously through his thick hair.

"A man trained for the law," he said, "devotes his entire life and all his energies to something so cosmically unimportant as a game."

He examined minutely what was left of his cigarette. Carefully, he extracted a single strand of tobacco and looked at it closely before letting it fall to the floor. Usually he chews unlighted cigars, but this day it was a cigarette.

He began to laugh.

"The law," he chuckled, "I might have stayed in the law. I do not laugh at the great profession itself. I am laughing at a case I had one time—the only case I ever had as a full-time practicing attorney. I had gone to Boise, Idaho, from Saranac to try to gain back my strength after recovering from tuberculosis. I got an office and hung out a shingle and waited for the clients. None came. Finally, I was in court one day and the judge appointed me attorney for a man who was being held on a charge the newspapers used to describe as white slavery.

"I was apprehensive, but at last I summoned enough courage to go over to the jail and see my client. Oh, he was a horrible creature. I can see him now, walking slowly up to the bars and looking me up and down with contempt. He terrified me. I began to shake like a leaf. After a minute he said, 'Who the hell are you?'

"I tried to draw myself up a little and then I said, 'Sir, my name is Branch Rickey. The court has appointed me your attorney and I would like to talk to you.' He looked me up and down again and then spat at my feet. Then he delivered what turned out to be the final words of our association. He said, 'Get the hell out of here!'"

Rickey threw back his head.

"I not only got out of there," he said, "I got out of the state of Idaho and went to St. Louis and took a job with the St. Louis Browns. I intended to stay in baseball for just one year. But when the year was up, Mr. Robert Lee Hedges, the owner, offered me a raise. There was a new baby at our house. And not much money, new or old. So I was a moral coward. I chose to stay with the game."

Rickey thought a moment.

"I might have gone into politics," he said. "As recently as 14 years ago, there was the offer of a nomination for a political office. A governorship. The governorship, in fact, of Missouri. I was tempted, flattered. But, then as I ventured a little into the political arena, I was appalled by my own ignorance of politics. But the party leaders were persuasive. They pledged me the full support of the regular party organization. They said they could not prevent any Billy Jumpup from filing, but no Billy Jumpup would have the organization's backing. It is an overwhelming thing to be offered such prospects of reaching high office. I thought it over carefully and then tentatively agreed to run, on condition that another man—a seasoned campaigner—run on the ticket with me. He said that was utterly impossible. He invited me to go with him to New York and talk to Mr. Herbert Hoover about the situation in Missouri. But afterward I still was unable to persuade my friend to run. He was Arthur Hyde, Secretary of Agriculture under Mr. Hoover. Later I learned to my sorrow the reason for Mr. Hyde's decision. He was even then mortally ill. So, regretfully, I asked that my name be withdrawn. The man who ran in my place was elected and then went on to the United States Senate.

"So, conceivably, I might have been a governor. Instead, I chose to stay with the game."

RICKEY made elaborate gestures of straightening the papers on his desk.

"A life of public service," he said, peering over his glasses, "versus a life devoted to a game that boys play with a ball and bat."

He turned and picked up a baseball from a bookcase shelf.

"This ball," he said, holding it up. "This symbol. Is it worth a man's whole life?"

There was just time for another mussing of the hair

before the phone rang again.

"Pooh," said Rickey into the phone after a moment. "Three poohs. Pooh-bah." He hung up.

"I was listening last night to one of the television interview programs," he said. "Senator Knowland was being interrogated. It was a discussion on a high level and the questions involved matters affecting all of us and all the world. I was listening intently and then I heard the senator say, 'Well, I think the Administration has a pretty good batting average.' "

Rickey blew out his cheeks and plucked a shred of tobacco from his lips.

"It must have been a full minute later," he went on, "and the questions had gone on to other things when I sat straight up. Suddenly I realized that to answer a somewhat difficult question this United States senator had turned naturally to the language of the game. And this language, this phrase 'a pretty good batting average,' had said exactly what he wanted to say. He had not intended to be frivolous. The reporters did not smile as though he had made a joke. They accepted the answer in the language of the game as perfectly proper. It was instantly recognizable to them. I dare say it was recognizable even in London."

He frowned, thinking hard. Then his face lit up again.

"The game invades our language!" he exclaimed. "Now, the editorial page of the New York *Times* is a serious forum, not ordinarily given to levity. Yet at the height of the controversy between the Army and Senator McCarthy, there was the line on this dignified editorial page, 'Senator McCarthy—a good fast ball, but no control.' "

Rickey slapped his thigh and leaned over the desk.

"Now, didn't that tell the whole story in a sentence?"

He waved an arm, granting himself the point.

He cherished his remnant of a cigarette.

"A man was telling me the other day," he went on, "he said he was walking through Times Square in New York one blistering day last summer. The temperature stood at 100° and the humidity made it almost unbearable. This man happened to fall in behind three postmen walking together. Their shirts were wringing wet and their mailbags were heavily laden. It struck this man that these postmen might well be irritable on such a day, and, since he saw that they were talking animatedly, he drew closer so that he might hear what they were saying. He expected, of course, that they would be complaining bitterly of their dull drab jobs on this abominable day. But when he had come close enough to hear them, what were they talking about with such spirit and relish?"

He paused for effect, then with a toss of his head, he exploded:

"Leo Durocher and the New York Giants!"

Carefully, he put down his cigarette butt. Then he leaned back and rubbed his eyes with the back of his fists. He tore furiously at his hair and half swallowed a yawn.

"Mrs. Rickey and I," he said, "sat up until 2 o'clock this morning playing hearts."

He straightened the papers on his desk and said as an aside: "I contend it is the most scientific card game in the world."

He searched the ceiling for the point he was developing, found it and came down again.

"The three postmen, heavily laden on a hot, miserable day, yet able to find a happy, common ground in their discussion of this game of baseball. And in their free time, in their hours of leisure, if they had no other interest to turn to, still there was the game to bring color and excitement and good wholesome interest into their lives."

He took up the fragment of paper and tobacco that was left of the cigarette as though it were a precious jewel.

"Leisure," he said, sending his eyebrows aloft, "is a hazardous thing. Here in America we do not yet have a leisure class that knows what to do with it. Leisure can produce something fine. It may also produce something evil. Hell's fire! Leisure can produce a great symphony, a great painting, a great book."

He whirled around to the window and peered out at Pennant Place. Then, turning back like a pitcher who has just cased the situation at second base, he let go hard.

"Gee!" he cried. "Leisure can also produce a great dissipation! Leisure can be idleness and idleness can drive a man to his lowest!"

He recoiled, as from a low man standing at the side of his desk.

"Idleness is the worst thing in this world. Idleness is doing nothing and thinking of wrong things to do. Idleness is the evil that lies behind the juvenile delinquency that alarms us all. It's the most damnable thing that can happen to a kid—to have nothing to do."

He put the tattered cigarette butt in his mouth and spoke around it.

"The game that gives challenge to our youth points the way to our salvation. The competitive spirit, that's the all-important thing. The stultifying thing in this country is the down-pressure on competition, the something-for-nothing philosophy, the do-as-little-as-you-can creed—these are the most devastating influences today. This thinking is the kind that undermines a man's character and can undermine the national character as well."

He studied his shreds of cigarette with the deliberation of a diamond cutter.

"Labor and toil," he intoned, "by the sweat of thy brow shalt thou earn thy bread. Labor and toil—and something else. A joy in work, a zest. Zest, that is the word. Who are the great ballplayers of all time? The ones with zest. Ty Cobb. Willie Mays. The man down the hall, one of the very greatest, George Sisler. Dizzy Dean. Pepper Martin. We have one coming back to us this year here at Pittsburgh. Dick Groat. He has it. Highly intelligent, another Lou Boudreau, the same kind of hitter. He has it. Zest."

Rickey smiled. "Dick Groat will be one of the great ones. There will be others this year. We have 110 boys coming out of service, 475 players under contract on all our clubs. A total of $496,000 invested in player bonuses. There will be other good prospects for the Pirates among these boys. This ball club of ours will come in time. No promises for this year, but in '56, I think, yes."

He turned to look down the street to Pennant Place, then added: "A *contending* team in '56—at least that."

(At the barbershop in Hotel Schenley it is related that Rickey's defense of his eighth-place ball club is considerably less detailed. "Patience!" he cries, anticipating the hecklers as he enters the shop.)

T HE DOOR opened and Harold Roettger, Rickey's assistant, entered the room. A round-faced, studious-looking man, Roettger has been with Rickey since the old St. Louis Cardinal days. He was in the grip of a heavy cold.

"Do you remember a boy named Febbraro?" he asked, sniffling, "in the Provincial League?"

"Febbraro, Febbraro," said Rickey, frowning. "A pitcher. I saw him work in a night game."

"That's the boy," said Roettger, wiping his eyes. "He's been released."

"Aha," said Rickey, "yes, I remember the boy well. Shall we sign him?"

"We ought to talk about it," said Roettger, fighting a sneeze.

"Harold," said Rickey, "Richardson [Tommy Richardson, president of the Eastern League] is coming down for a meeting tomorrow. I wish you could be there. I devoutly wish you were not ill."

"I, too, devoutly wish I were not ill," said Roettger. "I'll go home now and maybe I'll be ready for the meeting."

"Please try not to be ill tomorrow," said Rickey. "I desperately need you at the meeting."

"I will try very hard," said Roettger, "and will you think about Febbraro?"

"I will," said Rickey. "Go home now, Harold, and take care of yourself."

(Later, Roettger recovered from his cold and signed Febbraro for Williamsport in the Eastern League.)

As Roettger left, Rickey searched for the thread of his soliloquy.

"Hornsby," he said suddenly, "Rogers Hornsby, a man with zest for the game. And Leo, of course.

"Leo Durocher has come a long way, off the field as well as on. A quick mind, a brilliant mind, an indomi-table spirit. A rugged ballplayer—and I like rugged ballplayers. But when he came to St. Louis, Leo was in trouble. No fewer than 32 creditors were breathing down his neck, suing or threatening to sue. An impossible situation. I proposed that I go to his creditors and arrange for weekly payments on his debts. This meant a modest allowance of spending money for Leo himself. But he agreed.

"There were other matters to be straightened out. Leo's associates at the time were hardly desirable ones. But he was not the kind of man to take kindly to any criticism of his friends. I thought a lot about Leo's associations, but I didn't see what I could do about them.

"Then one day during the winter I received a call from the United States Naval Academy at Annapolis. The Academy needed a baseball coach and they asked if I could recommend a man. I said I thought I could and would let them know.

"I knew my man. But I didn't dare tell him right away. Instead, I called his wife [Durocher was then married to Grace Dozier, a St. Louis fashion designer] and asked her to drop in at the office. When she arrived, I told her that I intended to recommend Leo as baseball coach at the Naval Academy.

"She looked at me a moment. Then she said, 'Would they take Leo?' I said they would if I recommended him. Then I told her I proposed to get a copy of the Naval Academy manual. I said I knew that if I handed it to Leo myself, he was quite likely to throw it back in my face. But if she were to put it in his hands, he might agree to look it over. Mrs. Durocher thought again. Then she said, 'Get the manual.'"

(Rickey has a habit of presenting ballplayers with what he considers to be worthwhile reading. When Pee Wee Reese was made captain of the Dodgers, Rickey sent him Eisenhower's *Crusade in Europe*.)

"When I told Leo," Rickey continued, "he was stunned and unbelieving, then enormously but quietly pleased. I told him that I would arrange for him to report late for spring training. I made it clear that he was to decline any payment for his services. Treading softly, I mentioned that the boys he would be coaching were the finest our country had to offer. I suggested gently that any leader of such boys would, of course, have to be letter perfect in his conduct. Leo didn't blow up. He just nodded his head.

"When he reported to spring training camp, he was bursting with pride. He showed me a wrist watch the midshipmen had given him. He said, 'Mr. Rickey, I did it, I did it!'

"I said, 'You did half of it, Leo.'

"'What do you mean, half!' he demanded.

"'To be a complete success in this undertaking, Leo,' I said, 'you must be invited back. If they ask you back for next season, then you may be sure you have done the job well.'"

Rickey smiled.

"They did invite him back," he said. "And this time the midshipmen gave him a silver service. He had done the job—the whole job—and I rather think that this experience was a big turning point for Leo. It lifted him into associations he had never known before and he came away with increased confidence and self-assurance and, I am quite sure, a greater measure of self-respect."

(Years later, just before Leo Durocher was suspended from baseball for a year by Commissioner A. B. Chandler, Rickey called his staff together in the Brooklyn Dodgers' offices to say of his manager: "Leo is down. But we are going to stick by Leo. We are going to stick by Leo until hell freezes over!" At this writing, in a manner of speaking, it is Rickey who is down—in eighth place—and Leo who is up, riding high as manager of the world champions.)

Rickey straightened his tie. He was wearing a four-in-hand. Ordinarily, he wears a bow tie, but once a month he puts on a four-in-hand as a gesture of neckwear independence.

"More than a half-century spent in the game," Rickey mused, "and now it is suggested that I give thought to some of the ideas and innovations with which I have been associated. The question arises, 'Which of these can be said to have contributed most to making baseball truly our national game?'

"First, I should say, there was the mass production of ball players. The Cardinals were three years ahead of all the other clubs in establishing try-out camps. We looked at 4,000 boys a year. Then, of course, we had to have teams on which to place boys with varying degrees of ability and experience. That brought into being the farm system.

"There were other ideas not ordinarily remembered. With the St. Louis Browns, under Mr. Hedges, we originated the idea of Ladies Day, a very important step forward. Probably no other innovation did so much to give baseball respectability, as well as thousands of new fans.

"With the Cardinals, we developed the idea of the Knot Hole Gang. We were the first major league team to admit boys free to the ball park and again the idea was soon copied."

(In the beginning, boys joining the Cardinal Knot Hole Gang were required to sign a pledge to refrain from smoking and profanity — clearly the hand of Rickey.)

"These were ideas," Rickey went on, "and baseball was a vehicle in which such ideas might comfortably ride."

Rickey's eyes strayed to a framed motto hanging on the wall. It read: "He that will not reason is a bigot; he that cannot reason is a fool and he that dares not reason is a slave."

Rickey bent down and went rummaging through the lower drawers of his desk. In a moment he came up holding a slender book. The jacket read: "Slave and Citizen: the Negro in the Americas. By Frank Tannenbaum."

"This book," said Rickey, "is by a Columbia University professor. Let me read now just the concluding paragraph. It says, 'Physical proximity, slow cultural intertwining, the growth of a middle group that stands in experience and equipment between the lower and upper class; and the slow process of moral identification work their way against all seemingly absolute systems of values and prejudices. Society is essentially dynamic, and while the mills of God grind slow, they grind exceeding sure. Time will draw a veil over the white and black in this hemisphere, and future generations will look back upon the record of strife as it stands revealed in the history of the people of this New World of ours with wonder and incredulity. For they will not understand the issues that the quarrel was about.'"

Rickey reached for a pencil, wrote on the flyleaf of the book and pushed it across the desk. He leaned back in his chair and thought a moment. Then he sat straight up.

"Some honors have been tendered," he said, "some honorary degrees offered because of my part in bringing Jackie Robinson into the major leagues."

He frowned and shook his head vigorously.

"No, no, no. I have declined them all. To accept honors, public applause for signing a superlative ballplayer to a contract? I would be ashamed!"

He turned to look out the window and turned back.

"Suppose," he demanded, "I hear that Billy Jones down the street has attained the age of 21. Suppose I go to Billy and say, 'You come with me to the polling place.' And then at the polling place I take Billy by the arm and march up to the clerks and say, 'This is Billy Jones, native American, 21 years of age.' and I demand that he be given the right to cast a ballot!"

Rickey leaned over the desk, his eyes flashing.

"Would anyone but a lunatic expect to be applauded for that?"

IT IMMEDIATELY became clear that although Rickey deprecated his right to applause, he had never minimized the difficulties of bringing the first Negro into organized baseball.

"I talked to sociologists," he said, "and to Negro leaders. With their counsel, I worked out what I considered to be the six essential points to be considered."

He started to count on his fingers.

"Number one," he said, "the man we finally chose had to be right off the field. Off the field.

"Number two, he had to be right on the field. If he turned out to be a lemon, our efforts would fail for that reason alone.

"Number three, the reaction of his own race had to

be right.

"Number four, the reaction of press and public had to be right.

"Number five, we had to have a place to put him.

"Number six, the reaction of his fellow players had to be right.

"In Jackie Robinson, we found the man to take care of points one and two. He was eminently right off and on the field. We did not settle on Robinson until after we had invested $25,000 in scouting for a man whose name we did not then know.

"Having found Robinson, we proceeded to point five. We had to have a place to put him. Luckily, in the Brooklyn organization, we had exactly the spot at Montreal where the racial issue would not be given undue emphasis.

"To take care of point three, the reaction of Robinson's own race, I went again to the Negro leaders. I explained that in order to give this boy his chance, there must be no demonstrations on his behalf, no excursions from one city to another, no presentations or testimonials. He was to be left alone to do this thing without any more hazards than were already present. For two years the men I talked to respected the reasoning behind my requests. My admiration for these men is limitless. In the best possible way, they saw to it that Jackie Robinson had his chance to make it on his own.

"Point four, the reaction of press and public, resolved itself in the course of things, and point six, the reaction of his fellow players, finally—if painfully—worked itself out."

Rickey reached across the desk and tapped the Tannenbaum book.

"Time," he said, "time."

He despaired of his cigarette now and tossed it into the wastebasket. His eyes moved around the room and he murmured half to himself: "We are not going to let anything spoil sports in this country. Some of the things I read about boxing worry me, but things that are wrong will be made right . . . in time."

He laughed.

"I don't think anyone is worried about wrestling. Isn't it a rather good-natured sort of entertainment?"

He chuckled a little more, then frowned again.

"I am asked about the minor leagues The cry is heard, 'The minors are dying!' I don't think so. The minors are in trouble but new ways will be found to meet new situations and new problems. Up to now, I confess, the major leagues have been unable to implement any effort to protect the minor leagues from the encroachment of major league broadcasts."

(A baseball man once said that Branch Rickey is constitutionally unable to tell a falsehood. "However," this man said, "sometimes he pours over the facts of a given case such a torrent of eloquence that the truth is all but drowned.")

The door opened and Rickey jumped to his feet. His eyes lit up as he cried: "Mother!"

In the doorway stood Mrs. Rickey, carrying a box of paints the size of a brief case.

"Well, Mother!" cried Rickey, coming around from behind the desk. "How did it go? Did you get good marks?"

Mrs. Rickey, a small, smiling woman, stood looking at her husband. Childhood sweethearts in Ohio, they have been married for 49 years.

Rickey pointed dramatically to the paintbox.

"Mother has joined a painting class!" he exclaimed. "At 73 years of age, Mother has gone back to school! Well, Mother? Did you recite or what? Do they give marks? What is the teacher like?"

Mrs. Rickey walked to a chair and sat down. It was plain that she was accustomed to pursuing a policy of containment toward her husband.

"They don't give marks," she said quietly. "The teacher is very nice. He was telling us that painting opens up a whole new world. You see things and colors you never saw before."

Rickey was aghast.

"Wonderful!" he cried. "Isn't that just wonderful! Mother, we must celebrate. I'll take you to lunch!"

"All right," said Mrs. Rickey. "Where will we go?"

"The Duquesne Club," said Rickey.

"That'll be fine," said Mrs. Rickey.

(In sharply stratified Pittsburgh society, there are two standards by which to measure a man who stands at the very top: one is membership in the Duquesne Club, the other is a residence at Fox Chapel, the ultra-exclusive Pittsburgh suburb. Rickey has both; the residence is an 18-room house set down on 100 acres.)

Rickey was the first to reach the sidewalk. He paced up and down waiting for Mrs. Rickey, flapping his arms against the cold, for he had forgotten to wear an overcoat that morning. Guido Roman, a tall, handsome Cuban who is Rickey's chauffeur, opened the car door.

"You want to get inside, Mr. Rickey?" he asked.

"No Guido," said Rickey, blowing on his fingers, "I'm not cold."

A car drew up and stopped across the street. A tall, muscular young man got out.

Rickey peered sharply and ducked his head. "A thousand dollars this lad is a ballplayer," he muttered out of the side of his mouth. "But who is he, who is he?"

The young man came directly to Rickey.

"Mr. Rickey, you don't remember me," he said. "My name is George—!"

"Sure, I remember you, George!" Rickey exploded, thrusting out his hand. "You're a first baseman, right?"

"Yes, sir," said George, blushing with pleasure.

"Go right in the office and make yourself at home,

143

George," Rickey said, beaming. "There's another first baseman in there named George—George Sisler. Say hello to him!"

"Say, thanks, Mr. Rickey," George said, hurrying to the office door.

In a moment Mrs. Rickey came out and the ride downtown in Rickey's Lincoln began. As the car pulled away from the curb, Rickey, a notorious back-seat driver, began a series of barked directions: "Right here, Guido! Left at the next corner, Guido! Red light, Guido!"

Guido, smiling and unperturbed, drove smoothly along. As the car reached the downtown business district, Rickey, peering this way and that, shouted, "Slow down, Guido!"

Guido slowed down and then Rickey whispered hoarsely: "There it is, Mother! Look!"

"What?" smiled Mrs. Rickey.

"The largest lamp store in the world! Right there! I inquired about the best place to buy a lamp and I was told that this place is the largest in the whole wide world! Right there!"

"We only want a two-way bed lamp," said Mrs. Rickey.

"I know," said Rickey. "But there's the place to get it. You could go all over the world and not find a bigger lamp store. Right turn here, Guido!"

"One way, Mr. Rickey," said Guido, cheerfully.

That was the signal for a whole comedy of errors, with Rickey directing and traffic cops vetoing a series of attempts to penetrate one-way streets and to execute left turns. Rickey grew more excited, Mrs. Rickey more calm, Guido more desperate as the Duquesne Club loomed and faded as a seemingly unattainable goal.

"Judas Priest!" Rickey finally exclaimed. "It's a perfectly simple problem! We want to go to the Duquesne Club!"

"I know how!" Guido protested, "I know the way!"

"Then turn, man, turn!"

"Get out of here!" yelled a traffic cop.

"For crying out loud!" roared Rickey. "Let's get out and walk."

"I'm not going to walk," said Mrs. Rickey, mildly. "We have a car. Let Guido go his way."

"Oh, all right," Rickey pouted. "But you'd think I'd never been downtown before!"

In a moment the car pulled up at the Duquesne Club and Rickey, serene again, jumped out and helped Mrs. Rickey from the car.

"Take the car home, Guido," he said pleasantly. "We'll call you later."

"Yes, Mr. Rickey," said Guido, mopping his brow.

A group of women came out of the Duquesne Club as the Rickeys entered. The women nodded and smiled at Mrs. Rickey. Raising his hat, Rickey bowed low, then crouched to whisper hoarsely behind his hand:

"Classmates of yours, Mother?"

He stamped his foot and slapped his thigh, choking with laughter.

"One of them is in the painting class," said Mrs. Rickey placidly. "The others are in the garden club."

At the luncheon table on the second floor, Rickey ordered whitefish for Mrs. Rickey and roast beef for himself. There were no cocktails, of course; Rickey is a teetotaler.

("I shudder to think what might have happened if Branch had taken up drinking," a former associate has said. "He does nothing in moderation and I can see him facing a bottle of whiskey and shouting: 'Men, we're going to hit that bottle and hit it *hard!*'")

THE LUNCHEON ORDER given, Rickey excused himself and made a brief telephone call at the headwaiter's desk. Returning to the table, he sat down and began to speak of pitchers.

"The greatest pitchers I have ever seen," he said, "were Christy Mathewson and Jerome Dean."

(Rickey likes to address a man by his proper given name. He is especially fond of referring to Dizzy Dean as "Jerome.")

"Mathewson," Rickey continued, "could throw every pitch in the book. But he was economical. If he saw that he could win a game with three kinds of pitches, he would use only three. Jerome, on the other hand, had a tendency to run in the direction of experimentation. Murry Dickson (formerly of the Pirates, at the time with the Phillies) has a fine assortment of pitches, but he feels an obligation to run through his entire repertory in every game."

The food had arrived and Rickey picked up knife and fork and, eyeing Mrs. Rickey closely, began to speak more rapidly.

"Yes," he said loudly, "Murry is the sort of pitcher who will go along splendidly until the eighth inning and then apparently say to himself: 'Oh, dear me, I have forgotten to throw my half-speed ball!' And then and there he will throw it."

Abruptly, Rickey made a lightning thrust with his fork in the direction of a pan-browned potato on the platter. Mrs. Rickey, alert for just such a stratagem, met the thrust with her own fork and they fenced for a few seconds in mid-air.

"*Jane!*" pleaded Rickey, abandoning the duel.

Mrs. Rickey deposited the potato on her own plate and passed over a small dish of broccoli.

"This will be better for you," she said quietly. "You know you're not to have potatoes."

Rickey grumbled: "I am weary of this diet. It is a cruel and inhuman thing."

"Eat the broccoli," Mrs. Rickey said.

"Jane," said Rickey, "there are times in a man's life when he wants above everything else in the world to have a potato."

"You get plenty to eat." said Mrs. Rickey. "Didn't you enjoy the meat patty at breakfast?"

Rickey shrugged his shoulders, conceding the point, and attacked his roast beef and broccoli with gusto.

"The subject of my retirement comes up from time to time," he said. "And to the direct question, 'When will you retire from baseball?' my answer is, 'Never!' But I qualify that. Now, I do foresee the day, likely next year, when I shall spend less time at my desk, at my office. I shall spend more time in the field, scouting, looking at prospects, and leave the arduous responsibilities of the general manager's position to other hands."

He looked admiringly at the baked apple before him. He put his hand on the pitcher of rich cream beside it and glanced inquiringly across the table. This time the veto was not invoked and, happily, Rickey drained the pitcher over his dessert.

After he had dropped a saccharin tablet in his coffee, he leaned back and smiled at Mrs. Rickey. Then he leaned forward again and rubbed his chin, seeming to debate something with himself. He grasped the sides of the table and spoke with the air of a conspirator.

"Here is something I intend to do," he said. "My *next* thing. A completely new idea in spring training."

He arranged the silverware to illustrate the story.

"A permanent training camp, designed and built for that purpose. Twin motels—not hotels, *motels*—with four playing fields in between as a sort of quadrangle. A public address system. Especially designed press accommodations. *Now:* One motel would be occupied by the Pittsburgh club, the other by an *American League* club. They would play a series of exhibition games and would draw better than two teams from the same league.

"Everything that went into the camp would be the result of our experience with training camps all through the years. It would be foolproof. And it would pay for itself because it would be operated for tourists after spring training. I *have* the land. At Fort Myers, Florida, the finest training site in the country for my money. I *have* an American League club ready to go along with me. I *have* two thirds of the financial backing necessary."

Rickey leaned back in triumph, then came forward quickly again.

"Everybody concerned is ready to put up the cash now," he whispered, "*except me!*"

He paused for effect, then suddenly realized he had not said exactly what he intended. He burst into laughter.

"Sh-h-h," said Mrs. Rickey.

"What I mean," he said, sobering, "is that I can't go along with the plan until we have a contending ball club. But we'll get there. We'll put over this thing. It will revolutionize spring training."

It was time to get back to the office. Rickey was for sprinting down the stairs to the first floor, but Mrs. Rickey reminded him of his trick knee.

"Ah, yes, Mother," he said. "We will take the elevator."

On the street outside, Rickey remembered he had sent his car home.

"We'll get a cab down at the corner," he said. "I've got a meeting at the office. Where can I drop you, Mother?"

"Well," said Mrs. Rickey, "I thought I'd go look at some lamps."

"Oh, yes," Rickey exclaimed. "Go to that store I showed you, Mother. I understand they have the largest selection of lamps in town."

Mrs. Rickey looked at him and shook her head and smiled.

Rickey, already thinking of something else, studied the sidewalk. He raised his head and spoke firmly over the traffic.

"The game of baseball," he said, "has given me a life of joy. I would not have exchanged it for any other."

He took Mrs. Rickey by the arm. They turned and walked down the street together and vanished into the crowd.

EDGE OF THE SUMMER SEA

IN THE CAREFREE DAYS of August before the Weather Bureau's farthest outpost has looked into the malicious eye of the season's first hurricane and sent out a warning cry, it is a time to escape from the withering heat. At the edge of the timeless, tumbling sea, armies of vacationers and weekenders raise their gaudy umbrellas in a salute to the sun. It matters not where they are — whether at crowded Coney Island, the New Yorker's refuge from the sweltering city, or among the hosts who flock to Long Beach outside of Los Angeles, or on any other strip of sand along America's variegated coastlines; each seeks and finds his own little place and plants himself and family in a patch of territory which henceforth will be called their own. At no other time, in no other place will they so cheerfully endure the close-crowded neighbor, the painful sunburns, the sand that seeps in seam and sandwich. Such is the summer ritual at the edge of the sea. The special enchantment that it holds for one and all is captured in the photographs on the following pages.

—WILLIAM CHAPMAN

Photographed by JERRY COOKE

146

Here on the ocean's shaggy mane is room for all. Poet and peasant,
 banker and candlestick maker, join the joyous ceremony of being buffeted
in the glorious razzle-dazzle of the billowing surf.

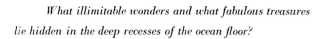

What illimitable wonders and what fabulous treasures
lie hidden in the deep recesses of the ocean floor?

All the summer day long,
in the whirling spume and
the hurtling wave,
a bit of the sea's endless drama
and its way is unfolded.

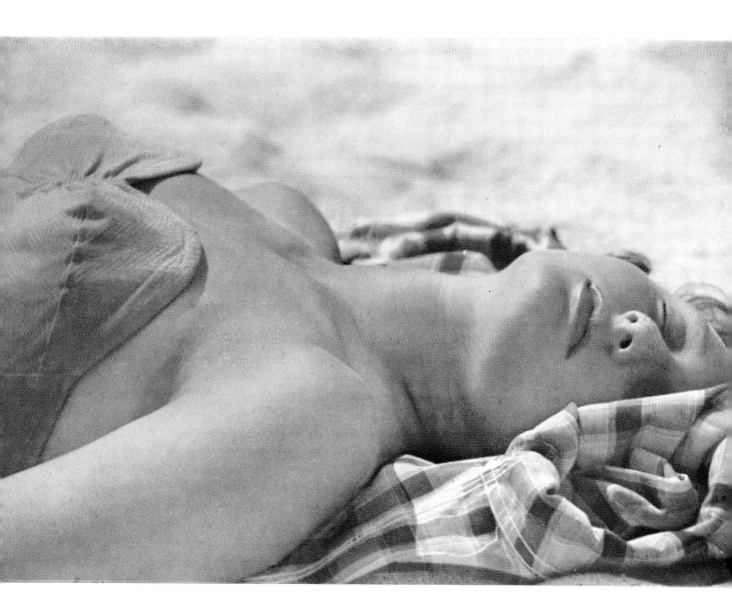

On the shining strand, with the tumbling laughter of the wild sea water
playing through her dreams, a sand-flecked young girl drowses
in the long sleepy August afternoon.

Near that magical line of the beach where the white shells tinkle
in the last whisper of the spent wave,
children build their moated castles, already doomed by the rising tide,
to be rebuilt tomorrow.

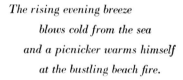

The rising evening breeze
blows cold from the sea
and a picnicker warms himself
at the bustling beach fire.

AND A ZING ZING ZING

Policeman, policeman, do your duty,
Here comes Diana, the American beauty.

THE EERIE POETRY that small girls chant (or compose) as they skip rope and the strange rhythmical games involving hand-clapping or bouncing balls that children improvise on city streets have been recorded by an imaginative sound engineer named Tony Schwartz, in what *The New York Times* has called the most original piece of work ever put on records. It probably is. Schwartz describes himself as a "sound hunter"; for the past 10 years he has been carrying his tape recorder around Manhattan, capturing the assorted groans, rumbles and shrieks of the city, and in the midst of its ceaseless clamor the quaint humor and liveliness of the children playing games of their own invention provide a counterpoint that is often astonishingly beautiful.

Most of the sounds of New York that Schwartz has collected suggest a sound track for some ancient Greek myth: the awful bellow of the West Side subway as it emerges above ground at 123rd Street or the mournful complaint of the *Queen Mary* leaving Pier 90. Once Schwartz was passing a yard between two tenements when he heard a strange, repeated call: "One, two, three and a zing zing zing." Investigating, he found a group of Negro children between the ages of 8 and 12 sitting in a circle, clapping their hands in unison to the words of the leader in a complicated ring game, a player being eliminated if he broke the fast rhythm of the hand claps. The obscure melodrama of the game revolved around a legendary character named Jacqueline. Whenever a player made a mistake or did not think fast enough, everyone shouted, "Jacqueline!" and he was out. No one knows who the unfortunate Jacqueline was, or how she demonstrated her historic slow-wittedness, but the name fits the syncopated rhythm of the game, which goes like this:

Leader: One, two, three and a zing zing zing. Number One.
No. 1 (innocently): Who, me?
Leader (fiercely): Yes, you.
No. 1 (untroubled): Couldn't be.
Leader: Then who?
No. 1: Number Two.
No. 2: Who, me?

Leader (angrier): Yes, you.
No. 2: Not me.
Leader: Then who?
No. 2: Number—
All: Jacqueline! You out! You too slow!

Schwartz made *One, Two, Three and a Zing Zing Zing* for Folkways Records four years ago, but it was picked up first by teachers and playground instructors and is used in teachers' courses at Bucknell, Teachers College at Columbia, New York University and other colleges. The reason why it has come into public attention now is that his newest effort, *The Story of New York*, was chosen to represent the U.S. in an international radio festival, calling attention to all his eavesdropping on the city. About half the material in his children's record is familiar ("I asked my mother for 50¢./To see the elephant jump the fence"), but the remainder is often electrifying: a combination of homemade Mother Goose rhymes and wild jungle rhythms, with Negro and Puerto Rican children beating on homemade drums, wooden benches and metal wastepaper baskets. The cryptic sentiments expressed in children's ball-bouncing games ("Once an apple met an apple./Said the apple to the apple"), and the curious, Emily Dickinsonlike broken rhymes of the girls' rope-skipping games ("I never went to college,/I never went to school") give them a haunting, cadenced air.

In gathering his material, Schwartz first made a few records of very elementary children's games. He took these to playgrounds and vacant lots and let the children take them home if they had phonographs. The following week he returned and recorded the games they knew, then with his enlarged collection went on to the next juvenile assembly ground. "There's a good deal of sound hunting in Europe," says Schwartz, whose interest grew out of his work for the Navy during the war. "In fact, there's an organization called the European Sound Hunters Association. But most American sound hunters are after specific sounds, like Professor Kellogg of Cornell, who records bird songs. I go after sound like a sportsman after game. It's a great sport, and anybody with a tape recorder can follow it. Just walk around the city and listen."

—ROBERT CANTWELL

151

ROUNDUP

Photographed by TONI FRISSELL

Their hoofs stir the dry ground to miniature clouds of dust, hanging in the crisp light of the early morning sun which has not yet risen enough to warm the blue Wyoming hills beyond, as a

herd of horses is driven down from their nighttime range to the dude ranch corral. The scene, freighted with the nostalgia which every city dweller feels for the Old West, is at the Valley Ranch, near Cody. Adventurous guests sometimes rise at dawn and ride out to help the hands round up the herd. And any dude can become, for a magic time, at one with Buffalo Bill.

HURTLING HYDROS

Photographed by
JOHN G. ZIMMERMAN

None of the creatures which inhabit the world of sport are quite so fearsome — and lovely—to see as America's Gold Cuppers: the unlimited hydroplanes which bellow out of hibernation on summer's hot, calm days. These enameled monsters — like Detroit's Gale V which "Wild Bill" Cantrell is hurling at you on the opposite page — are powered by Rolls or Allison aircraft engines which are supercharged to the bursting point. At top speeds (some have briefly reached 200 miles an hour) they hurtle clangorously on the verge of flight, with only sponsons and half the propellor arc in contact with the water. When they herd for combat—on Seattle's Lake Washington, or California's Lake Tahoe, or the Potomac or Detroit Rivers — they seem to assume a kind of dazzling pugnacity of their own. The men who drive them know both fear and the euphoria induced by the pure feel of speed. In the stretches they seem to ride in a howling river of sheer power; on the curves they must fight nerve-racking battles with the force of torque and often make their wild, sliding left hand turns with their rudders flung far right to counteract it.

The feel of speed and danger communicates itself to the most unknowing spectator on the banks — and the big hydros draw enormous crowds. There are few who can hear the exhausts of the Gold Cuppers rise to their deafening, brazen howl in the drive to the starting line, who can watch the high, curtain-like "roostertails" of spume rise up, up, up behind the speeding hulls, without feeling their pulses pound. In the distances of the course the boats seem to disappear — only sound is discernable and high, white fountains of water marching around the turn. And always, after a while, there is one bright hull hurtling for the finish line — delivered from peril into victory. And after that, amid an astonishing silence, the feeble, moving sound of humans applauding something brave.
—PAUL O'NEIL

154

A bright, bellowing squadron of unlimited hydroplanes chews the blue water of the Detroit Riv

feathery spume as drivers test their craft in a warm-up for climactic Gold Cup competition

GRASSY
BATTLEFIELD

Photographed by JERRY COOKE

For most days of the year the giant concrete eagles atop the stadium at the West Side Tennis Club in Forest Hills, N. Y., stare in complete boredom at the inactivity below them. The seats in the big horseshoe are empty; a community statute forbids their use for entertainment other than tennis. The green turf of the center courts, pampered like a rare orchid, is kept unruffled.

Then suddenly for a brief 10-day period in late summer — the period overlapping the dying days of August and the borning days of September — you can almost see the feathers rise on the motionless birds which form a grim guard over the arena. Deeply tanned young men and women in inevitable white move around with catlike grace. The place swarms with spectators. These are the U.S. National tennis championships — men's and women's singles and mixed doubles.

1956 marked a milestone in the American sport, steeped in the tradition of Little Bill Johnston, Big Bill Tilden, Ellsworth Vines and Donald Budge. This was the 75th birthday of national competition in a game which began with rackets like butterfly nets and balls as dead as sponges. Today the rackets are strung with violinlike tautness and the fuzzy white balls are precision-made and changed every seven games. But the scene is little changed. The same serenity and dignity of years gone by still pervades Forest Hills' tennis acres during these climactic 10 days.

For some of the young men and women who come to Forest Hills, the trip is confined to early-round matches on the outer courts (right). It is a long and difficult step from there to the massive 13,500-seat concrete stadium in the background, where tennis heroes of every year defend their positions against the always-pressing ranks of the young.

—William F. Talbert

Providing a backdrop reminiscent of England's historic Wimbledon, the clubhouse at Forest H

...enched in afternoon sunlight, surveys 12 impeccably manicured acres with more than 52 courts

THE GREAT GAME OF TENNIS

by ROBERT GORDON MENZIES
Prime Minister, The Commonwealth of Australia

LAWN TENNIS, as games go, is a new game. It was not so many years ago that it was a polite garden-party accomplishment. I can, myself, remember the jeering remarks of the "working" youth as white-flanneled players went by. Yet today, on thousands of public and municipal courts, no other than the "working" youth is hard at it. The game of the privileged few, in less than half a century, has become the game of the many. This reflects in part a marked rise in the standards of living, but it also shows the vast attraction of the game.

Not long ago I was astonished to hear Sir Norman Brookes, in a reminiscent mood, recall that when he first played as a boy the tennis ball had no cover as we know it today. We can say, therefore, that the development of today's game, and the implements used in it, spans the lifetime of one man.

I am a much younger man than Norman Brookes, having been born in 1894. Yet I can remember, as if it were yesterday, how some ruling woman champions served underarm, wearing skirts down to the ground, playing a steady baseline game, never venturing to the net. The first woman to go up to volley and to smash was regarded as a miracle or a monstrosity, according to the point of view.

In Australia the popularity of tennis is enormous. It is actively played by hundreds of thousands of people, and (such are our fortunate conditions) from one year's end to another. Australia's eminence in the game surprises many people. "How does it happen," they say, "that a country which has only just reached a population of 9,000,000 can so consistently have produced teams which, over a long period of years, have been outmatched in success only by the United States?"

The answer is simple enough. Australia, for tennis purposes, is one large California. The varying climates of the six states have this in common: They favor outdoor sport and outdoor living. Material standards of life are high; leisure is abundant. Good food and fresh air are the common lot. Most dwelling houses stand in their own grounds and gardens. For all these reasons, our inbred love of sport finds opportunity and expression. Even the most hardened theoretical socialist finds in games a satisfaction for his natural zest for private enterprise and individual initiative. I know that people have been heard to say reproachfully that Australians are too fond of sport. If this meant that we were a nation of mere onlookers at professional sporting spectacles, the criticism would be powerful. But the truth is that we are a nation of games-players who look at others only on occasions. There are, in Australia, 250,000 registered competitive players, *plus* at least 500,000 who play nonofficial tennis in a purely private way. Behind all the traditional informality and indiscipline with which we are credited, you will find the fitness, the resourcefulness and the competitive spirit which have made the Australian soldier world famous in war and which, in peace, have wrought a national development and construction which have earned the praise of so many perceptive visitors.

Thus it is that tennis has taken its place among the great popular games in Australia and has become one of the influences which form the national characteristics.

Yet one of the fascinating things to witness is how the popularity of a game can affect the game itself, and the position of its leading players. When a game becomes so popular as a spectacle for thousands or scores of thousands, the game becomes big business. To the public or private provision of thousands of tennis courts there is *added* (I emphasize *added*, because the active playing of the game continues to expand) the large-scale and costly provision of spectator accommodations, the intensive organization of competitions, the handling of interstate and international tours.

All this has meant an inevitable change in the activities and nature of the leading amateur players.

ter courts at Forest Hills are ringed with
of spectators during championship play

163

THE GREAT GAME OF TENNIS

The old amateurism has been replaced by the new, and we have seen the rise of professional play.

There were great advantages in the old amateur days. I will not dwell on them too long, for there is no more weakening emotion than yearning for the "good old days." The times change and we must change with them. But I will briefly state what I believe those advantages to have been and will then examine more closely what I believe to be the reasons why the old amateurism at the top level has passed away.

As a lad, just good enough at the game to know what it was about and how strokes *ought* to be played, I first saw Norman Brookes, Rod Heath and A. W. Dunlop; some years later there was my friend Gerald Patterson. Let me assume them to be examples of what I call the "old" amateurism.

Each was a distinct individual, with unforgettable characteristics of style and play. Heath had beautifully controlled ground strokes. Dunlop was a born doubles player, with a fine sense of position. Gerald Patterson had a villainous backhand drive, but could rely on the most violent service I have ever seen. Nowadays, when so many first-rate players seem cast in the same mold, when intense coaching has created so much standardization, I frequently find it difficult to remember other than facial differences between the playing characteristics of half a dozen of the greatest players.

Put this down to my ignorance or lack of perception if you like. But is it mere perversity on my part to say that Brookes lives in my mind's eye because of his nonconformity? He was one of the first to adopt and modify the then-new "American" service. In his use of it speed was secondary; placement was of the essence. It was as deep as the service line would allow. Its direction was such that the receiver always had to move quite a lot, to forehand or backhand, to play it. As soon as he served, Brookes moved in. Such was his control of service direction and length that he limited the scope of the return, and even appeared by some magic to control its actual direction. In spite of this, powerful opponents would seek to check him by driving to his feet as he advanced to the normally fatal midcourt half-volleying position. They soon discovered that to Brookes the half-volley was a weapon of attack, not of defense. Time after time I have seen him sweeping half-volleys first to one deep corner, then to the other, with his opponent sweating up and down in vain.

What a player! His long trousers perfectly pressed, on his head a peaked tweed or cloth cap, on his face the inscrutable expression of a pale-faced Red Indian, no sign or sweat or bother, no temperamental outbursts, no word to say except an occasional "well played." A slim and not very robust man, he combined an almost diabolical skill with a personal re-serve, a dignity (yes, dignity) and a calm maturity of mind and judgment. I have sometimes suspected that a modern coach, given control, would have hammered out of him all the astonishing elements that made him in his day (and his day lasted for many years) the greatest player in the world.

Brookes was an "old" amateur. He had means adequate to enable him to indulge his hobby. He was not overplayed. There were few Davis Cup contests. Each match could be approached with a fresh mind and spirit. But time has moved on. Big tennis has, as I have said, become big business. The cost of putting on good matches, with special stands and expensive organization and vast crowds of spectators have all involved today's player in almost continuous play, in tournament or exhibition games. Under the modern circumstances of high taxation, few people can afford such "leisure." The "old" amateur has, in Australia at any rate, practically disappeared from the top ranks. And so we have entered a period when some promising boy of 14 or 15, his education hardly begun, is picked out for coaching and development and joins the staff of some sporting-goods firm. Brookes played his first Davis Cup in 1905, at the age of 28; his last in 1920, at the age of 43 when, in the Challenge Round, he took both W. T. Tilden and W. M. Johnston to four sets—one of the most remarkable feats in lawn tennis history. Today a player is described as a "veteran" by his middle 20s.

There are those who will tell you that the "old" amateurs played when the game was "slower," and "softer," and that they could never have lived with the modern champions, with their "big" services and "fierce" overheads and "devastating" ground strokes. (You notice that I am a student of sporting journalese.) I do not decry the modern players, whose skill I admire, and who have given hundreds of thousands of us pleasure, when I say that both Tilden and Johnston, at their peak, could have beaten any 1957 amateur at his peak: and they were at their peak when Brookes played them.

But the "new" amateurism—the semiprofessionalism of the great sporting-goods firms (which, we must concede, have done much to develop the game) is here to stay, unless, indeed, it is replaced by complete professionalism or (as I think not improbably) international tennis becomes "open" to both amateur and professional, like golf or cricket. The alternative may well be that the professional promoters will come to regard the Davis Cup as a training ground for quite young amateur champions, to be recruited to the professional ranks later.

Whether we like it or not, the cost of maintaining modern international sporting teams and providing facilities for large armies of spectators to see them play inevitably tends to create a "business" atmosphere. There is another aspect of the matter. The modern proliferation of sporting journals and the expansion of the sporting pages of ordinary newspapers have led the talented, but young and mentally and emotionally immature champions into the glaring light of publicity — extravagant praise and biting criticism being more common than expert and moderate judgment. Too many are coming to regard the player as a bondslave of the public; we say that he has "obligations." If his form leaves him he is rejected and forgotten. If, at the height of his form, he abandons competitive sport in favor of a business or private career in some profession, he is not infrequently accused of "letting the public down." There are many youngish men living in some unskilled occupation today who are simply the victims of these processes. It is not to be wondered at that talented young amateurs increasingly gaze at the professional recruiter with an expectant eye.

I HOPE I will not be thought discourteous if, writing for a distinguished sporting journal, I say more about the impact of a good deal of modern sporting journalism upon the lives and minds of young and talented players.

As every man engaged in public affairs knows, it takes a great deal of strength of mind and balance and experience to ignore ignorant criticism and to select and be influenced by informed and just criticism. Boys of 20, playing some game under the eyes of the entire world, under strain, would be phenomenal if they knew how to deal with the mental problems of ignoring or evaluating criticism. If some become swollen-headed as a result of extravagant praise, and others sullen or moody under extravagant blame, it is not to be wondered at. I have sometimes advised young champions at tennis or cricket to give up reading the criticisms until their current series of matches is over. This is on the very sound principle that, though real experts always write understandingly, the pungent criticism of players by those who do not and never have studied the game cannot possess much value.

There is, for those of us who love these games, nothing more pleasant than a vivid account of some match in the press or over the air. Both the ear and the imagination are stimulated. But the occasional extravagant commentator who thinks his opinions are more important than the story of the game is a constant irritant. Nor do I, for one, want to read lurid stories (usually quite fictitious) about alleged personal quarrels among players. It may be thought to be proof of advancing years if I say also that I still prefer a lively report of a Davis Cup match I cannot attend to a series of glossy paragraphs about the love life or matrimonial intentions of the players— but I do.

What is the effect of the Davis Cup or other contests on international relations? The accepted answer is "good." It appears to be widely believed that the spectacle of two or four young athletes fighting out a Davis Cup tie, or a Wimbledon or Forest Hills final, is in its very nature a contribution to international understanding and good will.

This is, I think, substantially true; but it is not inevitably true. The truth is that it depends for the most part on the players, partly on the sporting critics, and of course partly on the spectators. A skillful but ill-tempered and uncontrolled player, glaring at umpires and spectators alike, can in an hour do his own country's reputation for sportsmanship immeasurable harm. You know how fond we all are of generalizing from single instances. An American slams his racquet into the ground and makes rude noises at a linesman. "Ah," says a non-American spectator—"These Americans! Always want to have their own way!" An Australian, at Forest Hills, puts on a childish act. "Look!" says an American spectator— "The trouble with these guys from down under is that they can't take a defeat without blaming somebody else." Both statements are nonsense. But they are made, all too frequently.

As the simple onlooker, I do not find the reasons for these occasional tantrums very difficult to understand. It might be useful to try to analyze the problem a little.

Sporting crowds are anything but fools, particularly when the game they are watching (which most of them have played) requires great skill and much subtlety of tactics and execution. There will, of course, be some fools among them; and some inscrutable law of Providence seems to have ordained that fools are frequently more vocal than wise men. But in Australia, about which I can speak with closer knowledge, a great crowd at a Davis Cup tie sees and understands a great deal of what is going on. It is quick to distinguish between the bad temper of a player whose conceit makes him blame somebody else for his own error, and the honest annoyance with *himself* of a player who is tensed up to do his best for his side and falls into a blunder. No more popular player or more creditable American ever came to Australia to play Davis Cup than Ted Schroeder. Yet frequently I have seen him going back to serve after netting an easy volley, shaking his head and talking to himself with whimsical but violent disapproval. We all loved him for it. It was a natural and human part of his keenness and his will to win.

It is my own opinion that alleged "incidents" are grossly exaggerated in the reports. If we require, as we do nowadays, that mere boys should devote their lives to the game, in spite of their immaturity in general matters, we should not hypocritically expect that their demeanor will at all times and under all circumstances resemble that of a student of mental and moral philosophy. It is not uncommon to find an elderly businessman, fresh from roaring at some underling across his desk or over the telephone, glaring reprovingly at the tennis player who has displayed a sudden spark of ordinary humanity. My own complaint about the young champions of today is not that they complain too much, but that they smile too little. Perhaps it is inheritance: someone once said that the "English take their pleasures sadly."

To sum up, I think that by and large the players in Davis Cup matches have done a first-class job for international good will and understanding. The United States, since the war, has sent to Australia many fine players. With trivial exceptions, they have been outstanding athletes, intelligent and courteous. They have helped Australians to think well of Americans as a whole. I have never listened to one of them making a speech of thanks or of congratulation without marveling at their poise, their fluency, their choice of words. They have made me an admirer of American education.

I have one very happy recollection of how a player can go wrong, and then go right so splendidly that his original error is almost affectionately remembered. Tony Trabert, a superb young champion, was defeated in a crucial match at Melbourne in 1953—defeated by a stroke or two in a match he had looked like winning. In his bitter disappointment he made publicly rude remarks about the behavior of the crowd. (The crowd had, in fact, blended patriotism with judgment very fairly!) There were adverse comments on Trabert all over Australia.

The following year, at Sydney, Trabert and Seixas took the Davis Cup from us by the most concentrated exhibition of skill, fitness and determination I had seen for a long time. Speeches were made when the Cup was handed over. Trabert's turn came. There were 25,000 in the stands, and probably a couple of million listening in. Trabert had a magnificent ovation. He smiled, looked around the stands, and said: "Thank you for that. I was wondering what you would do. A year ago I said some foolish things. But I think I can tell you that I have learned from experience!" The applause was deafening. The Stars and Stripes flew high!

I wish (if you can print such a heresy) that I could be as sure of the contribution to international good will of the sporting critics and writers. The best are, of course, superb. But to paraphrase the old nursery rhyme—

But when they're bad they're horrid.

All of the great international games are deprived of some of the good they otherwise do by the type of writer who looks for mischief—ferrets out and exaggerates personal incidents; writes about tennis as if it were a civil (and not very civil) war; and ends up by producing all the news *not* fit to print.

Still, great games and great nations can survive such blemishes. When I come toward the sunset of my own life and find myself thinking of tennis, it will not be the sensation-merchants I will recall. It will be the eager figures of Rosewell and Trabert and Seixas and, further back into what will be a misty past, the fierce power of Patterson's service and the calm, white-clad mastery of Norman Brookes. These are the figures that live.

AUTUMN

The sharp clamor of geese passing high in the dark,
not dogs barking off in barnyards, is what we heard
and imagined their strong riding.
The football punted away over the copper beech
was lost forever;
but in the sanctity of the thicket,
there we found a brood of bob-white
with piteous, round and golden eyes
under the wind.
All along the beach at night the bass fishermen stand,
joined to the running sea by their lines.
Today was green as a bottle,
the air contained in glass.
Cows lowed fearfully and the
geese came down from Canada
and walked in the pastures.

—GILBERT ROGIN

FOOTBALL AND FANFARE

IT COMES with the solid thwunk of leather on leather. The leaves are turning in the north but summer is not yet over in the southern states and only the sound of football turns the pages of the season to fall. From now until the first of January when the final arguments are settled in bowl games, the vast preoccupation of the nation will be football — its heroes, goats, triumphs, tragedies and excitement. It is a peculiarly American preoccupation — the crowds, the color, the spectacle, the blare of bands and the bright, quick ballet of cheer leaders.

It is a wonderful time of the year. No sport colors a season more than football; for all its difficulties and its commercialism, it is a symbol of romance to Americans, and they cannot sit in stadiums (or listen to a game broadcast or watch one on television) without a reaction, somewhere in their souls, to its legends; to something compounded of Stover at Yale, the prose of F. Scott Fitzgerald, the half-forgotten memories of George Gipp and Brick Muller and Jim Thorpe, of Centre College on its day of glory, and all the storied halfbacks who won the game and the girl and lived happily ever after. It is at one time the march music of autumn (*the scene at Princeton, opposite*) and the pleasantly sad song of nostaglia, and, if it brings about for a few months a mild madness among the populace, well, why not?

—TEX MAULE

UCLA team is power in rhythm as it serpentines out of huddle. Strong-side end leads

yers to the line of scrimmage, going to either the right or the left, depending on play

*The gymnastic simplicity of her bright red costume
sets off the complicated baton-twirling and acrobatics
of pretty Santa Ana (Calif.) High School cheerleader
between the halves of Los Angeles Coliseum game*

The military tradition is served grandly
at Ole Miss, where epaulets and plumed hats
are worn by the Rebel Band Majorettes,
pride of the University of Mississippi

A line of Redondo (Calif.) High girls
shakes white pompons in rhythmic display
of skill at Los Angeles Coliseum

Football's victory rites are as stylized as the bullfight: the sweaty linemen shake hands and the halfback is bussed by the pretty cheerleader (Ole Miss beat TCU to set off celebration

Army first string races into action at West Point's Michie Stadium after rest and w

wisdom from Head Coach Earl Blaik (brown fedora) as the massed Cadets prepare a cheer

The Notre Dame quarterback barks the signals, the line coils, and here is the way it begins

MARK KAUFF

I TAUGHT BUD WILKINSON
TO PLAY FOOTBALL

by PATTY BERG as told to SETH KANTOR

ONE SEPTEMBER DAY I was matched with Jackie Pung in the Ardmore, Oklahoma, Women's Open Golf Tournament. Jackie is a wonderful pro—the kind who figures to beat you every time out. She and I were the halfway leaders and, going into the traditionally critical third round, I had her by one stroke. We drew a large gallery. The afternoon was scorching. I wasn't.

Normally, I don't have long-game troubles, but she was maintaining such tough pressure on every hole, I knotted and wasn't getting anything off the tee. The cup began to look as big as Sir Gordon Richard's monocle and, worse yet, I started thinking about a football game being played 85 miles up the road at Norman.

Going out for fairway shots and in between holes, there was a guy in our gallery with a portable radio, keeping the Oklahoma-Texas Christian game muffled to his ear. I would ask him every so often what was happening and it seemed that "my" team, Oklahoma, also was having a nowhere afternoon. The Sooners were being outplayed by a highly inspired opponent. So was I. But that isn't why Oklahoma was my team. Bud Wilkinson is their coach; that's why. Bud has been a special hero of mine for 25 years—ever since he was 13 and I was 11 and we lived on the same block in south Minneapolis and played on the same football team.

Anyway, I chipped short and went down a stroke to Jackie Pung at Ardmore, just as the first half ended with the Sooners behind 0-2 at Norman. It was 7-9 after three quarters; then it got worse. Oklahoma trailed 7-16 in the fourth quarter and I was three down to Jackie. Somehow, Wilkinson and Berg just had to rally.

An almost storybook finish unfolded after all. Texas Christian slowly sank into the west and Oklahoma biffed and bammed to win 21-16. And Miss Pung finally weakened too. By weakened, I mean she probably didn't have enough strength to do 50 push-ups after coming in four under par, beating me by five strokes.

When everybody had deserted the course for the day, though, I began to think about the terrific determination that had made Bud Wilkinson a great athlete back home; the same determination he now quietly shovels into the Sooners to make them the nation's top collegiate football team. I went back out to the practice tee. I finally discovered my stance had been too wide during the afternoon and I'd been pushing the ball. I got my feet in a closer box alignment and began to get a decent coil into my backswing. The ball began to ride 25 and 50 yards more on the drive. I relaxed again.

In the next day's final round, I went under par and won the tournament, one-up over Jackie. Wilkinson and Berg had come through okay—just like winning a big one again for the old "50th-Street Tigers."

The Tigers were my team when we were kids. I played quarterback, Bud Wilkinson was right tackle, his older brother Bill was left tackle, and that's where my intelligent quarterbacking came in. Bud was the best team-player we had until he and Bill started to argue. They were the best, or maybe the worst, arguers I ever saw because every time they started in, words led to knuckles. And when Bill and Bud had a fist fight, everybody stopped everything to watch. They had nothing but classic battles. The Tigers lost a few crucial ones that way: games called on account of the Wilkinson brothers. Therefore, as quarterback, I kept Bud and Bill separated by three big boys in the line, which cut down a lot on games lost.

I TAUGHT BUD WILKINSON TO PLAY FOOTBALL

The "50th-Street Tigers" competed in everything from kick the can to bob-sledding all year long. In hockey, I was a forward, Bud was goalie. In baseball, I was an outfielder, Bud pitched (and argued with his catcher, one William Wilkinson). In football, I called the plays, and that's where Bud really learned the game. The huddle conversation would sound something like this:

Berg—"Roger and Stanley go out for a long pass. John, you take out that big guy with the green sweater. Okay, now, Boots, you hike the ball back to Marty when I say '22.' Marty fakes a long pass, see, and heaves me a lateral instead and I'll go through right tackle. We need the yards. Remember, you guys. '22.'"

Wilkinson—"Are you coming through me again?"

Berg—"That's what I said."

Wilkinson—"What's the big idea? You been carrying the ball off right tackle all afternoon. Aren't you bright enough to go someplace else for once?"

Berg—"Now look, Bud. You just shove your man out of the way and lemme through."

Wilkinson—(nothing for Berg but a nasty look).

But time after time, he would open those wide holes. He blocked hard and consistently gave me the safest running room on the field. I ran where it was padded the softest and that was always the path behind Bud. A couple of years ago, I visited him at Norman and he drove me out to watch the Sooners practice at Owen Field. He gathered them around and said:

"This is the kind old lady who taught me how to play football. She did it merely by running right-tackle slants so often I had to learn to block opponents to keep her from trampling me."

Most of the Tigers, 14 of us, lived on one block of Colfax Avenue South, between 50th and 51st streets, in Minneapolis. I was the only girl and I knocked the stuffings out of any kid who said I couldn't play. (I was the one who lived at the corner of 50th, which is why we weren't called the "Colfax Tigers.") This must sound as though we were being raised in the midst of an unshaven, slouch-cap, slum area. Colfax South actually was pretty fashionable.

We all came from a well-to-do environment and a heavy majority of the Tigers now are prosperous business and professional men. Bud never had to worry. There was a substantial real-estate business, his just for the growing up and inheriting, no matter how he played. But, I don't know, every once in a while there seems to be a neighborhood street somewhere which houses a fiercely eager bunch of youngsters, much more highly competitive than youngsters on other streets around them—because of a lot of sociological reasons, I guess. Our one block was like that. The Tigers grew up together, well-mannered and smart, extremely robust and full of rivalry. And Bud Wilkinson was always right in the midst of it. He was fast,

strong, an excellent student and almost passionately determined to win at anything.

"Try, try, try," he would say, when another team was giving us a tremendous struggle. It was the kind of determination you would write off as pure Horatio Armstrong Merriwellism if you didn't know Bud. And he used to say it time and again to keep us going. "Try, try, try." Slow, deliberate words. His face would be so serious. I won't ever forget that about him.

Charles P. Wilkinson, a widower during those years, did a fine job of raising his two boys in the spirit of our fierce eagerness, but there was one time I clearly remember him wondering just how far all that spirit could possibly go. It was a Saturday in 1930. I was 12. Bud was 14. I had grabbed a baseball bat and walked from my house at 5001 Colfax to the Wilkinson house at 5015 Colfax and had knocked there. Mr. Wilkinson answered.

"Can Billy and Bud come out and play?" I asked.

"Play?" Mr. Wilkinson stammered. He has always had a lot of charm and poise. This seemed to shock him. "Young lady, don't you know what time it is?"

"Yes sir," I said. "A little after nine."

"At night!" he said.

"Yes sir."

"It's pitch-black dark outside."

"Yes sir."

"Aren't you aware of the fact that you have been playing baseball with my sons for some ten hours already today and now it is night?"

"Yes, sir."

"Go away."

Mr. Wilkinson still kids me about that. I guess the good old "50th-Street Tigers" never did know when to quit.

A number of the boys became big high school football stars and Bud went off to Shattuck Military Academy where he set scholastic and athletic records that have stood for 20 years. Then he went to the University of Minnesota, majoring in English, playing goalie on the hockey team, captaining the golf team and lettering three years in football. He would run by the long, lonely hour in those days, building his endurance in dashes and wind sprints to improve himself in everything. For instance, he learned to push himself hardest when he was fatigued—for the sheer sake of determination—a major thing he has trained his football teams to do in recent years.

Not many people ever knew the most important story of Bud Wilkinson at Minnesota. He was 20 when he was graduated, but he already had unceremoniously given up more reward than most of us can achieve in any similar period of time.

He was a cinch to be an All-America guard in 1936, his last year of football. Both he and Ed Widseth, the big tough tackle, had been most outstanding on Bernie Bierman's all-time greatest line for two years. But

Coach Bierman had a backfield problem in 1936 and was in desperate need of a fast, strong, clever combination man, a signal-calling blocking back. So Bud didn't even consider his personal glory for a minute. He volunteered to come out of the forward wall, giving up his only chance of becoming All-America, to take over a new position for the sake of the team. He called the plays that year, and Minnesota drove with power sweeps and short-side reverses to a National Football Championship. Still, his backfield work was so polished he went on to quarterback the College All-Stars to their upset victory over Green Bay in 1937.

Furthermore, Widseth and Wilkinson had been elected co-captains for 1936, which was something Bud really deserved. But he gave that up, too. He learned that one of the other players was being dropped from the squad because of study troubles. Bud thought it all out, decided what was most important to him and quietly went to Coach Bierman—to suggest that the other boy be named co-captain with Widseth. He hoped it would be an exceptional incentive for the troubled player to settle down scholastically and hang on with the squad. That's just what happened. The other boy took Bud's place of honor and wound up as a great backfield star. Bud never talked about what he did.

Wilkinson the coach is like Wilkinson the player, except the fire he had as a Tiger chokes off somewhere around his collar button now and slips out quietly. He never shouts at his players. He never berates anybody for a dumb play. But the fire gets all pent up in his insides. I know there are nights when he slips off by himself to the gymnasium to work out as hard as he possibly can, to exhaust himself so he can sleep.

In football, Bud is a positive thinker all the time. He never puts undue pressure on his players by telling them they're great. But he never lets them think they aren't better than the other guy. His main interest at the university is education, though, and he can't stand the idea of a boy coming to Oklahoma just to play football. His teams haven't lost a conference game since he took over as head coach in 1947 and his teams have won 10 for every one they've lost against all comers, which makes the alumni simply delighted. He has a contract running through 1962 on account of that. But Bud is doing things in his own way—insisting that his athletes maintain good marks and seeing that over 90 percent of them are graduated into fields primarily non-athletic. No other coach before him had that kind of success at Oklahoma. The alumni are happy with his educational ideas, too. He *is* a winning coach.

And I'm very happy I used to run through right tackle all the time. It would have been a shame if Bud Wilkinson had wound up as just another businessman.

OFF AND PACING

Photographed by MARK KAUFFMAN

Spread-eagled on their precarious perches inches from flying hoofs, drivers urge their smooth-striding charges onward in the pacing classic of the year for harness racing fans—the Little Brown

Jug, held in early fall at picturesque Delaware, Ohio. For generations the premier attraction at county fairs, sulky racing today is also a thrilling nighttime spectacle in many of our largest cities. The rhythmic grace of the Standardbred horse, straining for speed within the hobbled restraint of his gait, makes a portrait reminiscent of many a Currier and Ives print.

FAIRWAYS OF OCTOBER

Photographed by JERRY COOKE

ONE of the last things that needs a press agent to extol its charms is autumn. Perhaps, in the days before color photography reached its present state of fidelity, there was some slight justification for a man's turning to his neighbor and rhapsodizing: "Quaff the wine in the air, Llewellyn, and, while you're at it, drink in the Joseph's coat of colors that garbs yon slope where, thanks to the sour acidity of the soil, the deciduous trees are even now sweetly transilient, like a traffic light gone amok, all colors flashing. Of the white-limbed birch, the swirling leaves underfoot and the cloudless azure of the deft empyrean, I will not sing, for my soul is full enow of beauty." This last is a wise decision. Fellows of this cut may have made good conductors of the Poet's Corner in the local weekly, but they made bad neighbors, for if there's anything that's hard to take in grandiose doses it is someone's letting you in on the obvious as if he were endowed with gifts of perception and appreciation denied his grosser fellow men.

In introducing the portfolio of lovely photographs which begins on the opposite page, let us stick to unadorned fact. The pictures were taken at the Meadow Brook club's relatively new course in Jericho, N. Y.— a handsome test of golf in any season. Each member of the foursome shown at right limited his remarks to the general area of its being a beautiful day for golf. Of course, any day that is not an irretrievably bad one is a good day for golf. And a fine spring or a fine autumn day — well, Llewellyn, the cup runneth over.

—HERBERT WARREN WIND

The offbeat beauty of late autumn is a wonderful setting for golf—the air is invigorating,

ass *indecently green. Framed in flaming trees, the fairway is gently dappled with shadow*

A lone golfer prepares to drive down the long, quiet fairway of the 8th hole at Meadow Brook and (below) a brisk twosome, casting fall's long shadows, moves off the leaf-speckled 13th green

THE INCOMPLEAT GOLFER

IN ADDITION to the backswing cougher, the silent caddy and the terrible-tempered partner who has bet too much on the match, there is one other fairway menace whose presence insures you will *never* learn the blasted game. This is the helpful partner, the man whose business it is to keep you cheerful through the most harrowing disasters which can befall a man with a golf club in his hand. His techniques are transparent, his motives clouded, but the net result is you never learn anything, least of all how bad your game really is.

For instance, your drive is a piddling roller which never gets in the air and looks more like a double-play ball than a tee shot. "That'll run all day," chirps our menace.

Your next shot is a horror which goes chattering into the woods on the right and out of sight. "You just quit on it a little," soothes friend partner, mentally congratulating himself for stepping out of the way before you quit. Your approach shot is a smother hook which runs erratically diagonally away from the green and into the deep rough. "If you'd kept your eye on it, that would have been a perfect shot," marvels our undisturbed pal.

On the putting green, you get a last-minute seizure and the ball squirts away at right angles to the hole but, because it's so far off line, manages to stop hole high on the other side of the green. "Your distance was perfect," enthuses your tormentor. "Burke says distance is more important than accuracy in putting."

Your next putt is a spasm-ridden stab which roars past the hole on the left side, missing by inches, but going so fast it would have hopped the hole like a freight going over a trestle anyway. It comes to rest back out on the fairway. "Perfect line!" shouts your friend. "You just pulled it a little."

Then there's the sand-trap shot where you plaster the ball, as well as the sand, and it arcs out in a shower of silica over the green and into the trap on the other side. "Atta boy," counsels the optimist. "The idea is to get out of a sand trap in one. That's all the pros try to do." He knows all the time it's going to take you four to get out of the trap you're in now.

Then there is the goofed shot which zooms into the air directly overhead like a pop foul behind home plate. "You just teed it a little high, sport," muses your helper. "Try teeing it a little lower."

Finally, there is the complete miss, the fan-out where the club head swooshes several inches over the ball, leaving you tied up in a 30-handicap knot, feeling as though you'd just broken your back. "An absolutely perfect practice swing!" shouts your partner. "Now, do that when you swing at the ball and it'll be 295 yards straight down the middle."

If you really don't care whether your game improves or not, it's O.K. to play golf with this fellow. A word of advice, though: Don't get in a gin rummy game with him.

—JAMES MURRAY

OVERTURE TO A CLAM BAKE

Photographed by ROBERT J. SMITH

Their reflections glistening in the wet sand, clam diggers of all ages take advantage of a low tide and a lovely November day to hunt the succulent, jumbo-sized bivalves which inhabit Pismo Beach, Calif. A family sport that requires no equipment beyond a digging fork, the hunt is nearly always successful. And anyone who has dabbled his toes in the cool wet of a tide-washed beach knows how much fun it is.

BIRDS, DOGS AND GUNS

THE MINNESOTA HUNTER at the right is every hunter wherever ring-necked pheasant can be found. He walks in a riot of autumn color and tastes the clean tang of autumn air. With pride he has watched his dog range field and pry into dense cover until the cock was found. The bird flared briefly. The hunter felt a primitive surge of emotion as it fell to his gun and the dog bounded away to fetch. Other hunters may range damp alder bottoms for the fleeting woodcock or walk cool woods in search of grouse. They may roam southern pineland for quail and wild turkey or gladly shiver in a north country blind as approaching winter scatters ducks before it. But all these hunters, regardless of what or where they hunt, feel a need in common — the need to refresh an over-civilized spirit with purposeful solitude on Nature's terms.

The clean line of a bird lifting against the blue of an October sky is an evanescent thing, gone in the whirring beat of frantic wings, but no one who has ever watched it can see autumn come again without looking for the sight once more. Ages ago man hunted to live. Who can say that he doesn't still?

—THOMAS H. LINEAWEAVER

The inner reward of good teamwork is written on the faces of this Minnesota
hunter and his dog after they have collaborated to bring down a cock pheasant

The tensest moment in pheasant hunting: the cock is going all out against the autumn sky,

g breaks point, the hunters must hold their fire briefly or risk ruining the bird for table JOE COUDERT

On the rolling sandhills and open prairies of the Armstrong Ranch in south Texas, quail

hunters trundle bumpily along behind a busy bird dog. The hunting caravan of specially

built safari cars is equipped with everything from bourbon and tamales to needles and thread,

with saddlebags, chuck boxes, fitted-in leather gun satchels, hors d'oeuvres and can opener

His decoys artfully positioned, the duck hunter stands ready behind his cover of reeds, hopefully expectant, as dawn breaks over a lake in Texas to light a vivid and treasured moment of the great outdoors

DMITRI KESSEL

MY LIFE AS A SPORTS WIDOW

by CORNELIA OTIS SKINNER

At THE TIME of our marriage 25 years ago, my husband's sporting interests centered solely and passionately about horses: riding them, employing them for the pursuit of hounds, observing them at race meets, judging them at horse shows, even paying formal calls on them in their stalls. I tried, as a blushing bride, to go in for the fancy. But it was my husband who did the blushing—when I donned the lovely habit I'd bought when I was at Bryn Mawr: tweed knickers, sleeveless jacket and stout army puttees.

My husband agreed that indeed the outfit must be just the thing for Colorado but not exactly right for the New York or Long Island riding set. Furthermore, as I'd be riding sidesaddle (an announcement that turned me pale), we'd better see about getting some proper equipment—from London. An Oxford Street tailor, one of those "By Appointment" fellows, made me a sidesaddle habit so extremely heavy I could barely carry it about on foot, let alone lift it onto a horse. My boots, from Peal, were worthy of a guardsman. The historic Lock & Co. "built" or more accurately *cooked* me my bowler hat. At the fitting they brought it forth from some hat bakery, steaming like a pudding, and clamped it on my astonished head.

I vastly admired my appearance in this highly authentic and more highly expensive ensemble. The admiration, however, was not shared by any horses, and my riding career (mercifully for both horse and rider) was short-lived. Abandoning for all time the idea of seeing my picture in *The Spur*, I divorced myself from any active sports participation and resigned myself—well, more or less—to becoming a sports widow.

My sports widowhood might be divided into three periods: the horse, the duck and the retriever. My husband's obsession during the first half of the horse period was fox hunting. Having abandoned any hope that his wife might in time become what I believe is called "a fine woman to hounds," my spouse found some solace in the fact that I could go along with him for a few weekends to upper New York State, where there was a hunt of which he was a member, and enjoy the privilege of observing the goings-on. These took place in a stretch of hill and valley I in my ignorance called lovely cow pastures but which, I was told, was "good galloping country," the very sight of which would cause sportsmen to dilate their nostrils and start dropping their final g's.

During my first stern initiation I learned one hard and fast rule of the world of outdoor sports. In order to qualify as first class, a sport must involve acute physical discomfort. All worthwhile sporting events start at break of day—which means that all participants must get up and dress a good two hours ahead of the break, long before the heat has been turned up in private home, country inn or motel.

Never having been one of those exhibitionists who

go swimming on New Year's at Atlantic City, I found it a matter of acute pain to shiver into my clothes in a glacial room. The pain turned to fury when I found out that I might have remained in bed much longer than my husband. For it takes a hunting gentleman more time to get into the proper attire than it takes a debutante to dress for a ball.

Why people who are about to be doused in all manner of horse sweat, flying mud, slimy ditchwater or even their own life's blood, should dress with the dainty care of a foreign minister about to attend a court levee, I don't know. But I do grant that there is something of the grand manner about it, like the Bourbon aristocrat taking a pinch of snuff while mounting the steps of the guillotine. And I must admit that my husband, resplendent in white breeches, gleaming boots, impeccable stock and red—I said *pink!*—coat, mustard vest and a reinforced silk topper, was pretty as a Christmas card. And I felt that I really "belonged," as we drove to where "hounds were meeting." Horses were also meeting, and also human beings, but they are never mentioned.

For the nonparticipant, there are several methods of following a fox hunt. One may tag along at a distance on a horse. One may dash on foot via frantic short cuts to various points which it is hoped will be viewing ones. Or one may, like me, pursue a zigzag course, equally speculative, through side roads and lanes in a car. Our car was a convertible, and my concession to sport was to keep the top open, even when it was raining.

Lest anyone assume that this nonsportswoman lacks all feeling for beauty, let me record right here that the sudden weird sound of that melancholy little horn has turned my hair to electric wires and that the sight of horses with their bright-coated riders streaking across a slope, or of hounds streaming in a yelping torrent out of an autumn copse, has caused me to bawl like a baby.

Repetition, however, can make for satiety. I gave myself an honorable discharge from the mechanized hunt-followers corps after a certain near disaster that occurred one weekend when I had brought my father along to give him a taste of the bracing life into which his daughter had wed. With the show-off authority of the half-smart explaining a subject to an ignoramus I gave him a running commentary offensively peppered with terms like "giving tongue," "breaking cover" and other John Peelisms.

I had, meanwhile, taken a small side road, my reason being, I said, that I thought the fox would go "down wind." Sheer bravado on my part. I had no more idea of which way the wind was blowing than what down it meant. Father made the politely attentive face that showed he wasn't listening. Then suddenly he went tense and cried "Watch out! You're going to hit a dog!" A lean furry animal darted past

the front wheels and only a violent jamming on of brakes prevented our squashing it. As it scuttled into an adjacent field, we paused in wild surmise, caught breath and gasped in unison "Good God! It's the fox!" We watched it lope easily away to safety. Then, both of us being underground members of the Animal Resistance, we shook hands and never told a soul. What would have happened had I run over the creature is a supposition too frightful to dwell upon. I should certainly have had to leave the community, the state and, in all likelihood, my husband.

And while we're on horses—which, thank heaven we are not—I'll mention other equine activities which over the years have forced me into sports widowhood. I don't count horse racing, which I happen vastly to enjoy. But I *do* count horse *showing*, which I happen vastly not to.

I tried. I really tried. My husband, who did a lot of judging in those days, suggested that perhaps if I were to go along with him and watch him judge, I'd acquire a taste for the thing. Watching a horse judge at work is like watching a chess champion at play. There are long, long periods when absolutely nothing happens. The horse-show judge stands in the center of the ring, most of the time quite motionless. Occasionally he tells someone who tells the riders who in turn tell the horses when to vary their routine. Occasionally he makes mysterious notations on a pad. Occasionally he carries on a whispered conversation with a co-judge. At last the horses are lined up, their saddles removed and, as they stand there nude, he walks appraisingly around each one, signs something which proves to be his final decision, watches the ring master attach the ribbons, then retires with the co-judge for what I presume to be a drink. And there you have the thrill of watching someone officially judge a horse. I made a friendly pact with my husband to the effect that every time he insisted I go with him to a horse show, I'd insist he go with me to the Museum of Modern Art. It works out very well. I go to Madison Square Garden for the ice carnival, and his shadow has yet to fall beneath the Calder mobile.

A COASTING ACCIDENT, which resulted cruelly enough in my husband's losing a leg, ended his riding career. But not my sports widowhood. For after the horse, the wild duck raised its pretty beak.

Again I made a brave attempt and again there was brought home to me that basic sportsman's rule of self-torture. Duck hunters get up even earlier than fox ones. In fact, it isn't early at all. It's just terribly late the night before. This entails the gulping down, either in your own icy kitchen or in an overheated dog wagon crowded with truck drivers, of a nocturnal breakfast—traditionally mammoth, despite the fact that only a few hours previously you have stuffed yourself with dinner and drinks. On possibly four occasions I tasted the primitive joy of deep-freezing from dawn to dusk in a duckblind and never seeing a bird. For, not being a "gun," I was always told to cower silently out of sight (fingers well stuffed into ears) while the marksmen let fly their volleys and, sometimes, felled their prey. Then I abandoned any ideas of being either a spectator sportswoman or an apathetic decoy. Now when my marital Nimrod and our mallard-minded house guests arise at 3 a.m., I lie in bed. But I don't sleep. As soon as duck enthusiasts put on their shooting togs, they go fearfully virile. Their voices deepen to a roar—a subdued roar, so as "not to wake Cornelia"—and, because their boots and breeches must weigh half a ton, the effect when heard through a closed door is that of a number of romping dinosaurs.

And, speaking of that attire, until I found out that other duck fanciers were the same way about their shooting clothes, I kept secret the horrendous state of my husband's. Ordinarily, he is a gentleman of meticulous cleanliness, and so, as far as I can in all propriety make out, are his duck-shooting companions, but why, I ask myself, must their garments remain undesecrated by dry-cleaning as though they were Coptic textiles? Well-seasoned shooting clothes are doubtless delicious to the dog in the duckblind, but in the evening when the hunter comes home from the hill and starts warming up over a fire—!!

During the season, my husband goes out about three days a week, and being a good shot, always gets his limit. Personally I am all for amending the game laws and limiting the limit. For although he manages to distribute a fair amount of the trophies among his duck-eating acquaintances, the overflow remains in our iceboxes, whence all superfluous delicacies are removed to make way for the spoils of the chase—and sometimes I do mean *spoils*. If the weather is "right" (meaning I wouldn't quite know what), a few "brace" may be "put out to hang." In everyday parlance, a few pairs dangle like rag mops outside the back door until they are "properly hung," which is just a day or so before the buzzards start coming up from southern New Jersey. For a duck should be approaching a state of fine Stilton in order to suit the sportsman's palate. And, as everyone knows, the correct way to cook it comprises very little more than holding it near the oven.

Shocking as it may be to admit, I don't really care for wild duck even if it has remained for some time *in* the oven. And I don't think that biting into Number Four shot is an adventure in good eating. Thank God, I say, for the game laws that confine the duck season to two or three scant months!

But there are, alas, other months and other games. The latest aspect of my sports widowhood is the retriever trial. We live in Long Island, where the retriever trial has taken over like the tent caterpillar.

For those half-wits such as myself who never knew what a retriever trial was, let me briefly explain that it is an all-day and several-day performance at which retrievers and retriever fanciers gather together to go one by one through a series of tests involving intelligence, obedience, perception and physical prowess, on the part of the dog, that is. Some take place on land, others on (and in) water. Birds are either shot in flight or their extinct bodies are concealed in grass and the retrievers one by one go forth, find the creatures and bring them back in tail-waving triumph. Sometimes the dog is allowed to watch which way the bird falls. The concealed ones he must ferret out in a sort of canine treasure hunt, directed in this by the handler, who from afar blows piercing blasts on a shrill little whistle and goes through an arm-waving set of semaphore signals which are retriever code for orders like "Turn right!" "Get back!" "Come forward" and "Drop dead, you dope!"

Here, I was assured, was one sport I could follow with zest. Everyone loves a field trial! The people love it, the dogs love it, even, it would seem, the birds love it—although they don't always capture the spirit of things.

I TRIED once or twice to capture it. There's no denying that the dogs are lovely to watch for a time. But the time can start seeming interminable, and the waits between the acts are more drawn out than intermissions at the ballet. At first I made shy little attempts to relieve the monotony by wandering in a friendly fashion among the other spectators. But, while a retriever is working out a problem, chit-chat among the humans is bad form. I once made the mistake of going over and scraping acquaintance with certain of the dogs lined up for the next series—a gross breach for which I was severely reprimanded. A retriever about to go on line is like a tenor about to go onto the stage of the Met. You mustn't pat or distract him.

Once again I granted myself a sports divorce, this time on the grounds of field trials. But they are not the only kind, I soon learned. There are lesser occasions known as *sanction trials*, meaning that when a dog wins, the owner gets congratulations instead of a silver ashtray, while the dog receives an encouraging pat instead of a Ph.D. Our place, it seems, is just right for a sanction trial because, as I was told by one of the judges with kindly approval, "the land is so nice and uncared for."

The opening series starts in a field directly in front of our house. Cars and dog-laden station wagons assemble on a rise a bare 60 yards beyond my bedroom windows. Need I remark that the field trial, like all clean, God-fearing sports, starts at break of day?

As lady of the manor, I thought at first it behooved me to get up and out and greet the arrivals as they came. To my intense relief I found that people concentrating on handling dogs don't want to be bothered by a hostess hospitably burbling, "Do step into our poison ivy!" The fanciers can't even be bothered with coffee. As one lady enthusiast explained, she just didn't dare pause because she was "running in the open."

But I do my running indoors. Someone has to stay there anyway to comfort our house dogs, two Norwich terriers and a small mutt, all of whom start quaking at the first crack of a shotgun and continue in an all-day state of terror. The mutt keeps jumping up into my lap for sanctuary, while the elder and supposedly more intrepid terrier cowers behind the water closet. They all three periodically throw up.

The solution, I find, is to betake myself and house dogs off to a cabin a few miles away overlooking the Sound and spend a serene, ungunshattered day. For me there are books to browse through and never quite read, for the dogs there are rabbits to chase after and never quite catch, and for us all there is the delight of picnic lunch followed by swinish sleep. In the late afternoon we return home to find the field trial over and the house crowded with happy sportsmen shedding wet clothes, getting into dry ones, trying to locate lost car keys, phoning to tell children Mummy and Daddy may be a little late and to go on with dinner—everyone drinking and talking at once and nobody listening to a word anyone else is saying. I grab a glass and join in the hearty fun. Best of all, in this as in other sports, no one has ever noticed my absence and everything works out merry as a marriage bell.

RUN, RABBIT, RUN!

Photographed by HY PESKIN

In hot pursuit of a mechanical rabbit that stays 20 feet ahead, long-striding greyhounds skim over the 5/16 mile oval at Phoenix, Arizona, achieving speeds of close to 40 miles per hour and cov-

ering as much as 15 feet with each bound. Each has been trained not to crowd, try to bite, or otherwise foul other dogs during a race. Despite their appearance of frailty, greyhounds are tough and tireless on a race course or when engaged in their ancient task of pursuing game. And, as the photograph proves, few greyhounds are grey —color having nothing to do with purity of breed.

THE ELITE AT LAUREL

Photographed by RICHARD MEEK

As INCONGRUOUS as it may seem for a sport which has been growing annually since the end of the second World War, Thoroughbred racing in America has, until as recently as 1952, lacked much of the dignified respectability that one instinctively associates with racing in so many other countries.

One U.S. track is today leading the way in erasing the misconception that racing over here can never match the dignity of Longchamp and Ascot. The Washington, D.C., International — usually referred to now as simply the Laurel International, after the Maryland track at which it is run — represents the closest thing to open world competition that has ever been seen in this country. For one thing, it is a turf race from a walk-up start — conditions found highly acceptable to foreign horsemen, who come, by invitation only, to compete for $100,000. All foreign entrants receive full shipping and housing expenses. Consequently, for this mile-and-a-half classic, the management of Laurel in recent years has brought to the track silks from many different countries, including those of such distinguished owners as Her Majesty Queen Elizabeth, the President of Ireland and Sir Winston Churchill.

A traditional feature of the Laurel International, and a major event on the Washington social calendar, is the annual pre-race ball. Here in the grand ballroom of Washington's Sheraton Park Hotel, brilliantly decorated with the silks of all the world's great racing stables, the elite of the capital, including Supreme Court Justices and Cabinet members, gather to discuss turf matters and bring new dignity to the U.S racing atmosphere.

Guests shown arriving at the International Ball on the opposite page include British Ambassador Sir Roger and Lady Makins (*top center and top right*), Justice and Mrs. Tom Clark (*left foreground*), and Justice and Mrs. Stanley Reed (*lower left*).

—WHITNEY TOWER

Guests at International Ball walk between banners to a ballroom decorated with suspended horse fig
and tablecloths made up like racing silks. Present are ambassadors, Cabinet members and socia

THUNDER IN THE LINE

Photographed by HY PESKIN

FROM HIGH UP on the 50-yard line, you can see the plays traced out on the field in precise patterns of red and white, meticulously and well, as the San Francisco 49ers attack toward the Cleveland Browns' goal-line. The blocks boom and crackle and you can hear the clear popping noise of the armor of football in hard, quick contact. The backs move with the elegant grace of all great athletes, and the thunder in the line is a physical thing as the big men strain and clash and the holes open briefly and close. Once in a while, a ball-carrier breaks suddenly into the clear, running with a certain strong economy of motion, the legs churning swiftly, the player shifting direction and speed with a wonderful prescience, the tacklers coming up and fading away, and all of it stirring a warm, deep emotional response in the spectator. Perhaps nowhere else in the wide world of sport is there a single sequence of action which has in it so much of drama and excitement. This is professional football — big, agile, expert men doing with immense authority the thing they know how to do superbly well.

In the pictures on the following pages, you can feel some of the tremendous physical impact and the great team effort that puts the professional game, to the knowing fan, in a class completely apart from college football. Here, as in every other sport, the player who devotes a good part of his life to the mastery of a particular skill is the best. These are the dedicated ones, the mighty pros.

—TEX MAULE

Leaning ponderously against the thrust of San Francisco blockers, the heart of the mighty Clevelan

own line blunts the impact of a 49er thrust in the tough trench warfare of professional football

THE LOVELY, LEAPING LIPIZZANERS

Photographed by JERRY COOKE

THE ALABASTER STEEDS pictured opposite and on the following pages amid the pillared opulence of Vienna's ancient Spanish Court Riding School are Lipizzaners — the greatest equine performers in the world and a national treasure beyond price. Having survived a long, perilous exile during and after World War II, they are shown here restored to prewar glory in their ancestral home.

In the ritual accompanying their performance, in the trappings of the horses and the uniforms of the riders, little has changed since the Holy Roman Emperor Charles VI built the school for the breed 222 years ago. The cavalcade enters single file and high-steps across the sawdust-strewn quadrangle to the loge of honor. Then to old dance music the lordly beasts respond to their riders' almost imperceptible commands by pirouetting and doing the Spanish walk in which they raise diagonally opposite pairs of hoofs and hold them aloft in a semblance of floating. These exercises, reminiscent of the horses' early stage of training, are followed by courbettes (*pictured at right*), the stallion advancing in leaps on his hind legs, forefeet never touching the ground; ballotades, leaping high and wide with legs retracted like folded wings; levades, raising and folding the forelegs while the haunches support the full weight of the body. The finale is the traditional Great School Quadrille, a sequence of intricate steps brilliantly performed in absolute unison. It is a performance of statuesque high school dressage that has no peer anywhere else in the world.

text continued on page 219

Learning levade, stallion is schooled by Colonel Podhajsky. Horse should hold pose several seconds with or without rider

Starting courbette, a dramatic procession from the levade, horse is first taught balance on short rein from ground

Flying through the air like a wingless Pegasus, Lipizzan stallion performs a ballotade

The Spanish Court Riding School derives its name from the origin of the first Lipizzaner mares, not from its equestrian style. The breed, which contained Arab blood, was imported from Spain in 1565 by Emperor Maximilian II. The term Lipizzaner refers to the village of Lipizza, near Trieste, where Maximilian's brother, the Archduke Charles, established a stud in 1580.

In their long history the Lipizzaners have had many great masters, but perhaps none more important than the present head of the school, Colonel Alois Podhajsky, undoubtedly one of the finest horsemen and trainers of horses in history. It was Colonel Podhajsky, a lean, hard, ramrod-straight man of 59, who saved the Lipizzaners from extinction during the war. It was in 1944, as the front moved close to Vienna and bombs plastered the city, that he took alarm for his horses, then numbering 70. He applied to the German command in Vienna for permission to evacuate them. "Bad for civilian morale," he was told. "If the Lipizzaners go, people will say the war is lost."

Secretly casting about for an Austrian haven, he found, in northern St. Martin, an abandoned stable once used by Empress Maria Theresa as a pony relay. Rail transportation was insufficient even for troop movements, but Podhajsky recognized the accent of the officer handling northbound traffic as that of a native Viennese. "You wouldn't want the Lipizzaners to die, would you?" he asked him. Few Viennese could resist such an appeal, and shortly the colonel was able to begin evacuating his cherished steeds, together with their equipment, grooms and riders, in freight cars, two or three at a time. As the first Russian troops entered Austria, the last of the Lipizzaners were headed north.

A month later a fresh danger threatened when the 20th U.S. Corps rolled into the area of St. Martin. Podhajsky's grooms, without whom maintenance of the stables would have been impossible, were soldiers in uniform and therefore subject to imprisonment on sight. But luckily there happened to be on the U.S. headquarters staff a horse-fancying major who explained to the corps commander what the Lipizzaners stood for. Podhajsky was invited to stage an exhibition for General George Patton, a passionate equestrian and, in his youth, an Olympic contestant.

Patton sat enthralled through two hours of the Lipizzaners' most dazzling stunts, then rode one of them himself in a few exercises. (This horse was Favori Africa, whom Hitler had been about to appropriate as a gift to Hirohito, when war with Russia made delivery via Eurasia somewhat awkward.)

After the Great School Quadrille, Podhajsky rode up to Patton and, hat in hand, craved the protection of the U.S. Army. Patton guaranteed it. He also promised to move the stud farm, which the Germans had shifted to Hostau, Czechoslovakia, now lying in the path of the advancing Russians, back to its original location in Piber. Podhajsky flew to Hostau to supervise the operation. The herd crossed the Czechoslovak border, mares and foals in trucks, stallions afoot, under an escort of five U.S. tanks. Russian officers attached to the Alien Property Commission tried to halt them. The tank commander threatened to open fire. The horses went through.

Displacement from Vienna during the years of military occupation following the war did not curtail the Lipizzaners' ring appearances. They toured Middle Europe, France, England. After an exhibition in London, Queen Elizabeth rode Pluto Theodorasta, who excels in on-the-ground exercises, at Buckingham Palace. In 1950 the Lipizzaners, 14 of them, crossed the Atlantic for the first time and played Madison Square Garden during the National Horse Show.

Since their earliest triumphs the Lipizzaners, which, with rare exceptions, are born black, brown or grey, but become pure white by middle age, have been a frequent theme of art and literature. No textbook, however, exists on their dressage. Of the several score Lipizzaners foaled each year, only a small number are judged likely to succeed as performers and are selected for training. The techniques, as complex as those of painting or music, have been handed down chiefly by word of mouth. The training of the riders, who must be crack horsemen to begin with, takes, on the average, a year; of the stallions, starting when they are 4, three to five years. Once fully trained, the Lipizzaners can look forward to a long professional career. They are seldom retired before 25 and may live five to ten years after that.

Of the classical school movements, some are copies from nature, like the play and fighting of horses in the pasture; others are adaptations of maneuvers formerly used in combat. Untrained Lipizzaners often leap up on their hind legs simply out of high spirits, a natural courbette. The pirouette originated in medieval combat, when the rider feinted an attack (half pirouette) and wheeled to return it (full pirouette).

A mare or rejected stallion will be sold by the Austrian government if Podhajsky recommends it, but this he refuses to do unless the horse exemplifies the characteristics of the breed and the purchasing stable is a recognized one. The waiting list is long. The colonel approves less than half a dozen sales a year, with the price ranging between $600 and $800.

There are several families of Lipizzaners in America, and one or two of the horses have been exhibited with success. If the scarcity of first-rate trainers on this side of the Atlantic can be overcome, soon a number of the famed whites may be thrilling U. S. audiences with their matchless grace in the show ring.   —JOHN KOBLER

STRIPER MAN

Photographed by GARRY WINOGRAND

Some men will fish for years and never catch a striped bass. There is a fascination to the pursuit of this elusive warrior who ranges off certain U.S. shores that enters the very bone and fiber of a striper man; hour after hour, in predawn darkness, in midday heat, or in the wild, wet world of night he will cast out his line, reel it in, and cast it out again into the turmoil of the heaving sea. Here such a man has finally tasted triumph: in the foaming surf off Montauk Point, Long Island, a striper has struck his lure, fought with legendary stubbornness, and now weary, comes to gaff.

IT'S A GAUDY SHOW

Photographed by MARK KAUFFMAN

ALL PROFESSIONAL WRESTLING (which has been described as all gall) is divided into two parts: heroism and villainy. This is not an accident. It was discovered long ago that a contest between two clean-cut young athletes generates less emotion in the spectator than a struggle between one clean-cut athlete and one dirty-cut athlete. Of the approximately 3,800 wrestlers who populate the 335 arenas in the U. S., one-half are clean-cut and the other half are dirty-cut.

Although there are almost as many heroes as heels in wrestling, on the opposite page it's villains 3 to 1. Perhaps embarrassed at being in such bad company, Hero Bobo Brazil (upper right) has turned his ornate back. Villain John Tollas (upper left) holds a bouquet presented by admirers. At lower left is the insufferable, unconscionable, monocled "Lord" Blears; and at lower right, Kubla Khan, a man who has plumbed the depths of fancy dress and perfidy.

Prior to World War I wrestling was a pretty prosaic business, and a contemporary account of a title match between champion Frank Gotch and George Hackenschmidt in 1908 notes that "one hour after the start nothing approaching a hold had been gained by either man." No modern wrestling fan would wait a solid hour for Hold No. 1, and neither would any TV director.

Many of the wrestling holds which so delight televiewers today — the airplane spin, the surfboard and the drop kick, to name three — can only be applied with the skilled complicity of one's opponent. One, the Indian death lock, is so complex that the assistance of the referee is sometimes required.

There is some argument as to how Frank Gotch would make out with the modern crop of TV wrestlers. A few experts believe he could beat them all in one night; others think it would take two. Actually, the argument is beside the point. Professional wrestling, circa 1958, owes only a slight debt to Gotch and Hackenschmidt and not much more to the amateurs. Its true forebear is the morality play, and its true concern is not with athletics but with good, evil and gate receipts. The curtain is about to go up. Turn the page and watch the plot unfold.

P. S. You may hiss the villain.

—RICHARD W. JOHNSTON

222

THE AGONY
OF COMMUNICATION

Stoicism does not count for much with wrestling fans, who would feel defrauded if not allowed to share the exquisite tortures of their heroes. On the opposite page Hero Wilbur Snyder grimaces as long-haired Villain John Tollas howls as he prepares to flip Snyder to the mat. At right Bobo Brazil registers alarm, though it is he who has the hold (a scissors) on Gene Kiniski. At lower right Warren Bockwinkle's face contorts in agony as Villain Bulldog Pleeches (*red trunks*) bears down on a wristlock, and directly below, Matt Murphy (*green trunks*) and Mike DeBiasie suffer the dual devastation of a double arm stretch. Actually, the pain projected from these twisted countenances was slight compared to that happily received and endured by the spectators who witnessed the matches on a recent evening at the Ocean Park Arena in Santa Monica, Calif.

A VILLAIN
PUT TO FLIGHT

As every good American knows, sportsmanship and courage are inevitab[ly]
allied; so, conversely, are brutality and cowardice. One nice thing abou[t]
wrestling is that it wholeheartedly affirms these fundamental beliefs. He[re,]
for example, we have the hateful Kubla Khan, snarling sadistically as [he]
applies first a double wristlock and then a knee drop (*below, left and righ[t]*)
to the admirable but overpowered Mike DeBiasie. What happens, thoug[h,]
when Mike retaliates (*bottom*)? Kubla flees (*opposite*), shrieking in terr[or.]

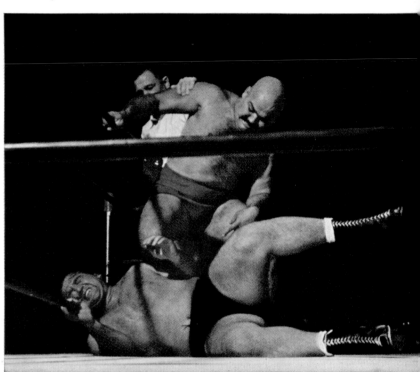

A MODERN MORALITY PLAY

The plot is simplicity itself. Evil seems sure to triumph over good. The evil man uses every sinful device at his command and it appears that the long-suffering good man will never be stirred to retaliate in kind. Meanwhile, the referee appears to be blind; he makes only the feeblest of protests at the vil-lain's outrageous conduct. The pictu[re] above is a sample. Man Mountain Dea[n] Jr. has Sandor Szabo backed into th[e] corner and is butting him with his b[ig] belly while Sandor emits loud cries [of] "Hah! Hah!" On page opposite, uppe[r] left, Dean holds Szabo with a perfect[ly] legitimate headlock, but pulls Szabo['s]

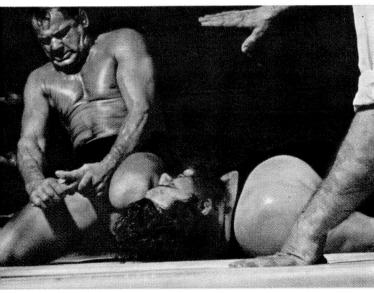

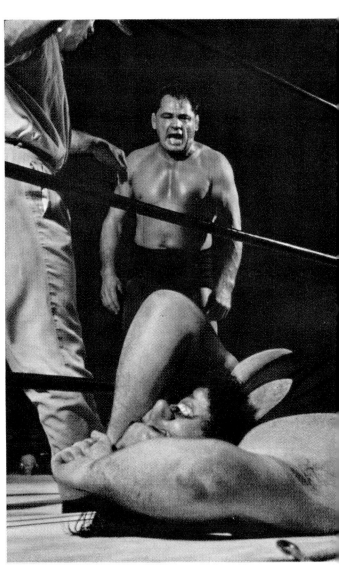

air while the referee is unable to see that he is doing. Lower left, the heroic Szabo has at last rebelled; he holds Dean's shoulder down with his knee while bending back the fingers of one hand. And at right, Szabo stands triumphantly, for the moment, over Man Mountain, having thrown him with a "suplex." Events up to this point have moved women at the ringside (*left to right below*) to clench a fist, threaten with the back of the hand, assault Dean with a shoe, and suffer exquisitely for Szabo. In reply to the question, "What do women see in wrestling?", amateur psychiatrists ask, "What do men see in burlesque shows?" For what both men and women saw at the conclusion of the Dean-Szabo match, main-event feature of the thrice-weekly card at Hollywood Legion Stadium, see page following—bearing in mind, before turning, that in wrestling, as in life, the wicked sometimes seem to prosper.

VICE IS ITS OWN REWARD

The morality play comes to a happy conclusion as men and women spectators rise to their feet to give the raspberry to the fallen Man Mountain and cheer the noble Szabo. The lesson is plain enough to the true aficionado. Any wrestler who persists in using dirty tactics, who habitually violates every precept of fair play, such a scoundrel—is sure to be on next week's card.

THE WRESTLING CROWD

AWAITING the entrance of the wrestlers for the next feature match, the crowd is strangely silent. The men chew their cigars; the women, most of them middle-aged, sit thoughtfully. A reverend in a clerical collar walks down the aisle and takes a seat in what would be the press section if the press attended wrestling matches.

The hawkers yell out their wares confidently, addressing the spectators as equals, not deferentially as at the tennis matches or the horse show. There are soldiers and sailors here and there in the crowd. It is an adult crowd; the law of this state says that boys and girls under 16 may not attend professional boxing or wrestling matches.

In one of the $5 seats sits an astonishingly thin man with a face like the edge of a knife and a wisp of a mustache that he keeps trying to brush away. He listens to a question and shakes his head.

"I will not give you my name," he says, "but I will give you my philosophy. I have paid $5 to attend a program of professional wrestling because I consider the wrestling arena to be the natural refuge of the thinking man. Outside is the great absurd world in which traffic signs flash 'Don't Walk' in all directions at once and television commercials show men lathering half their faces with a recommended shaving cream and half with Brand X."

He shudders and draws the back of his hand rapidly back and forth across his knifelike face as if honing himself.

"When I left home this evening," he continues, "my brother-in-law lay fast asleep on the hide-a-bed sofa in the living room reeking of after-shave lotion. If I were a man instead of a mouse, I would throw him out, but my wife is a strong woman and would break me in two.

"Here a man can speak his mind, take his stand, applaud virtue and denounce evil."

Suddenly, there is a great roar from the wrestling crowd and the thin man jumps to his feet with the others, brandishing his fist and screaming unintelligibly. Down the aisle, lifting his feet high as if he were stepping in something unpleasant, comes a wrestler wearing a cap and gown, as for a college commencement exercise. He is attended by a lackey who wears long hair tied in the back with a small ribbon, a style reminiscent of George Washington as a young man. The wrestler is clearly Professor Shire, described in a program note as a graduate of Northwestern University and thus, in wrestling values, entitled to professorial rank. As the Professor enters the ring, he doffs his mortar board, revealing his bleached blond hair, and the booing mounts in volume. An unescorted young woman, wearing her hair in a ponytail, cups her hands to her mouth and yells, "G'wan home, ya bum, ya." A fat woman in a white hat and green sweater races to ringside as if to attack the Professor, but instead she holds out an autograph book, which he signs with an evil smile. Another fat lady, wearing a flowered black dress, scurries down the aisle and stops to aim a Brownie Hawkeye flash camera at the Professor, who is now mincing around the ring, lifting his feet high in the manner that infuriates the crowd.

The crowd boos are shut off as if someone had turned a switch. Then, almost at once, the crowd erupts again, but this time into applause and cheers. Down the aisle comes one of the heroes of the evening, Cowboy Carlson, a tall, gangling man wearing green calico chaps and a broad-brimmed hat. He, too, has bleached blond hair, but the crowd does not find it offensive. He walks with a rolling gait like a man who has just swung down from a horse. The thin man is on his feet applauding, and the autograph seeker and the Brownie camerawoman rush to their ringside stations. A distinguished-looking man in gray keeps jumping up from his seat and his wife keeps pulling him down by the coattail. As the referee enters the ring, the boos mix with the cheers and the girl in the ponytail hairdo cries out with splendid impartiality: "G'wan home, ya bum, ya!"

The pattern is repeated all evening. The villains enrage the crowd with an assortment of remarkable dramatic skills. Lord Carlton of England looks at the crowd as if it were dirt. Fritz Wallick of Germany, with his monocle and Prussian haircut, compounds his hatefulness by facing the crowd and giving it a Fascist salute. The crowd becomes a lynch mob shooting blanks.

Everything is orderly, logical and proceeds according to plan. By the time the big match of the evening is announced, the thin man looks relaxed and happy, the girl in the ponytail is composed and quietly smiling. But a man leaving early passes the wrestlers' dressing room and catches a glimpse of Professor Shire sitting on a bench, cap and gown lying at his feet. He holds his bleached head in his hands. He does not look like a man who has suffered physical injury in the ring. What he looks like is a man who has been happy in the evening's charade and now dreads to face the great, absurd world outside.

—GERALD HOLLAND

RHINO!

Photographed by WELDON KING

The rhinoceros is an irascible beast, not particularly happy to have its picture taken. You can either stand a long way off with a telephoto lens, or depend on fleetness afoot and come up close. Joe Marsicano, with the 12th Gatti African Expedition, tried the second method one fine day in Zululand. Walking cautiously, with one eye on his jeep, Marsicano angles toward a suspicious black rhino. A moment later (right) it charges — and the photographer dashes for his car.

*At full gallop an infuriated cow rhino, followed by her calf, hurtles upon
fleeing jeep. Seconds later the animal caught the car and overturned it.
As the rhino worried the jeep, its riders escaped to another nearby*

THE GENTLE ART
OF SWORDPLAY

by PAUL GALLICO

SINCE fencing is the most exciting participant game in which two persons may indulge, it would seem to me that a small fortune might await someone who could devise a method of teaching it that would be less tedious than the existing curriculum and would take a year or two off the time it takes to learn how to skewer your opponent properly while yourself remaining unharmed.

For the art has everything to recommend it to the passionate competitor or the tired businessman in need of exercise and relaxation. It is cheap; it is convenient in that it may be conducted in any fair-sized room or hallway, on a terrace, lawn or in a cellar. *Salles* devoted to it are conveniently located in big cities. It is not time consuming; an hour and a half between five-thirty in the afternoon and seven is sufficient, including shower and changing. Three times a week is enough to keep a man fit, entertained and happy.

And it is enthrallingly exciting and absorbing. In the entire field of sport there is no more dramatic way in which a man may master another—if you exclude boxing, which is, of course, only a game for hopeless adolescents willing to have their brains addled and features warped to prove not very much.

Unfortunately, it takes time to learn fencing's unnatural posture and simplest maneuvers, to train the legs, the eyes and, above all, the hand. It takes even more time to become sufficiently experienced in combat to enjoy to the full the delights of making a monkey out of a fellow citizen—or citizeness, since one of the three weapons, the foil, may be practiced in mixed company.

The fencer never stops taking lessons to the end of his days. And those days are long for, unlike other sportsmen, the fencer may continue to compete and enjoy himself through the sixties and into the seventies. One of the toughest old boys in the Épée Club of London, who still fights and places regularly in club fixtures, is 74.

Unfortunately, the American is all-out impatient for play. It won't work with fencing. It takes the beginner six months before he gets his legs sorted out and another month before his hand responds automatically to stimuli. After two years he can begin to fight in earnest. But all the time he is learning he is getting exercise employing limb and wind, doing hard, sweat-producing work, disciplining himself and acquiring the rudiments of a fascinating skill which will never leave him.

To begin with a few definitions, there are three standard international weapons available: the foil, the épée and the saber. They are different in size, shape and weight and each has its own set of rules.

The foil is a light, whippy, four-sided blade with a button on the end. Its target is the torso only.

The épée is a stiff, three-sided dueling sword, an adaptation of the rapier, with a large bell, or guard. Its target encompasses the entire body from mask to shoe tip, including hands and arms; its pseudo intent is simple and direct: to disable or kill swiftly. In many tournaments one touch settles the issue, for it is assumed that if one were hit anywhere by this weapon, one would be unable to continue. It is symbolically deadly and hence most interesting.

The saber is both a cutting and a thrusting weapon; the whole upper part of the body is vulnerable, including head and arms, and the rules of attack, parry and riposte are such that experienced *sabreurs* communicate with one another in phrases in the manner of people engaged in performing a duet on instruments.

THE GENTLE ART OF SWORDPLAY

Indeed, the French word "phrase" is a part of saber language and denotes a series of questions and replies via the blades, so that their clashing sings a recognizable song. The cutting and slashing movements appeal to—well, cutters and slashers.

I started fencing when I was 36. Today, 20 years later, I can hold my own in good company; I compete on club teams in New York, London and Paris, have fought as a member of a team in both the U.S. and British Nationals, take lessons regularly, keep my weight down and never travel without jacket, shoes and glove. Mask and weapons I can borrow wherever I happen to be, for fencing is a brotherhood as well as a sport.

Thus I have fenced in Istanbul, Athens, Paris, Tel Aviv, Marseilles, Rome, Florence, Milan and Venice, London and The Hague. I fence crossing the Atlantic on the *Queen Elizabeth*, the *Queen Mary* and the *Ile de France*. Upon arriving in a strange city at home or abroad, I commission the hotel porter or concierge to ferret out a fencing club or fencing master. A couple of hours later I am on the strip, with the local boys queuing up to take a crack at the visiting fireman.

My specialty is the épée, or dueling sword. My second weapon is the foil. Today, at 56, I have begun taking saber lessons—left-handed. Five years from now I will be a fair saber fencer. In 10 years I'll tackle anyone. Sure enough, the legs have gone and the reactions have slowed down, but the guile increases. I can't catch the youngsters any more, but if a kid wants to hit me he's got to come close enough to touch. That's all I ask. Youth is served, but fencing really is a game for the middle-aged and the mature. Captain Charles De Beaumont recently won back the British épée championship at the age of 52. It is great for the ego when, aging but knowledgeable, you flummox some flaming and impetuous youth and coax him to impale himself on your point.

In boxing you feint with foot, head or hand. You do the same in fencing. In a fight you take the initiative, moving in with leads, or back-pedal and wait for a chance to counter. The same holds for a sword fight. With gloves you try to block an opponent's lead or jab. With a weapon this is called a parry. And in the ring, having nullified your opponent's lead with a block, you try to knock his head off with a timed counterpunch. Fencers call the same thing a riposte. And the purpose of both games is to hit without being hit in return.

But whereas boxing is brutal, inflicting pain and eventually serious injury to brain or optic nerve, the fencer is protected by canvas jacket, wire mask and glove. Injury is the result of accident rather than design. The fencer's aim is to establish an intellectual as well as a physical superiority over an opponent. To do so, he uses an adaptation of the same weapon with which men once disputed in terms of life and death.

One of the chief charms of fencing is that it is never quite possible to divorce the sport in one's own mind from its romantic and lethal background. And in spite of precautions, accidents do happen from time to time. In épée fighting the three-pronged, needle-sharp *pointes d'arrêt* fastened to the tip of the weapon to aid in registering hits by catching in the cloth of glove or garment sometimes find a weak spot in material or seam and slit open a segment of epidermis, which bleeds most satisfactorily. Sabers can leave a handsome welt. A broken foil can become instantaneously dangerous and deadly.

STEEL is a man's weapon. It has always been the great equalizer. Little men have brought big men crashing like storm-stricken oaks by sliding six inches of it gently into their bodies. Speed and guile offset brawn and size; trickery can take the measure of knowledge. The men who fought with the sword risked everything, for to carry death to an opponent they had perforce to expose themselves. In this age, defeat is the penalty instead of death. But when you go into a bout, the old ghosts seem to rise up beside you and whisper, "Careful—don't let him come too close—he may be going to try the Italian trick*—keep your point menacing his eyes—a man is afraid for his eyes—don't believe that opening where his sword arm has dropped —it is a lie—he is deceiving you—I believed that once and look—I am dead!"

One of the most fascinating sides to fencing is its revelation of a man's character. By his point ye shall know him. His style and comportment give him away. A few minutes with a man on the strip and you will know whether he is timid, aggressive, honest, dishonest, trusting, deceitful, tricky, guileless, decisive or indecisive, stubborn or easily swayed, impetuous or craftily patient. You read him like a book and you yourself are not able to conceal from him for long what kind of human being you are.

Personally, I find the stiff, triangular-bladed dueling rapier known as the épée the most satisfying of the three weapons, possibly because of the three sharp points affixed to the tip which achieve an actual penetration into some part of the opponent's clothing, for penetration is the swordsman's aim and satisfaction even if, in fencing's civilized adaptation, it is no more than a sixteenth of an inch. The points do catch and hang and sometimes even draw a small quantity of blood. I do not particularly enjoy bashing a man on the nose with my fist and seeing him drip gore, but to

---

* In the 15th century, an Italian master, Achilles Gazaio, came to Paris and grew wealthy teaching the bravos one trick— passing the blade of the sword through the legs of the opponent, then drawing it back quickly and cutting the tendon back of the knee. Once brought to earth, the victim could be finished off at leisure.

236

prick an opponent with my steel and see his jacket stain a little pink at wrist or elbow is, for me, a thrill.

Oddly, it is just as enjoyable to suffer a slight wound in this game and later sport the cicatrice. I once had some five inches of forearm ploughed open when the épée prongs entered a defective seam in the leather-and-canvas glove. My opponent made profuse apologies and did his best to look concerned, but found it difficult to conceal his delight, particularly when examination revealed that the cut, though long, was superficial. About this time I began to feel noble and gallant myself, the wounded warrior. Épée points always leave scars; mine proclaims that I am a sword fighter and I will exhibit it at very slight provocation.

Épée matches are the only kind which may be scored electrically, and all competitive bouts are now conducted with electrified swords whose points depress a small spring that makes a connection to ring a bell and light a light when a hit is scored. The fighting of this weapon affords the deepest psychological satisfaction, for it eliminates all human error as well as human vanity. The reluctant-to-admit-a-touch fencer is at the mercy of this loaded sword that rings out its own victory and illuminates the victim. Menaced with it, you fence as carefully and tensely as though your life depended on it, straining to avoid its viper bite and the public humiliation resulting when your opponent slips beneath your guard or otherwise diddles you to light your light and ring your bell.

The rules and punctilio of fencing—the salute with the weapon, the repetition of this gesture and the handshake at the end of the match, the gentlemanly restraint, the immediate and unswerving acknowledgment of a hit when there are no arbiters present—are modern and artificial adjuncts to a game which, when conducted for business or political purposes a half a millenium ago, was completely dirty and savage, and in its technique and play bore little or no resemblance to modern bouts with foil, épée or saber.

As a matter of fact, no two ancient weapons were alike, as each bravo purchased his sword or had it made to suit his own measurements or heft—long, short, whippy, stiff-bladed, hilt- or point-heavy—and the only rule when steel was unsheathed was kill and kill quickly, if necessary by foul means, such as throwing a handful of dirt into your opponent's eyes.

The origin of the development of "seconds" in duels had a most practical basis and came about when the challenged party to a duel in the *bois*, foolish enough to arrive alone for the encounter, found himself set upon by friends of the challenger who held him while the challenger ran him through and then went off to take bows. Eventually the news leaked out and the boys took to showing up with friends of their own, which often led to a free-for-all on the spot and later to the punctilio of seconds, as well as the principals,

crossing swords, and later still to the purely representative function of the second.

You might believe that fencing calls for a certain kind of excitable foreign temperament, and one tends to think of the sport mostly in connection with fiery Europeans with moustaches. But the fact is that fencing has a temperament, a life and behavior all its own, which it grafts onto Anglo-Saxons, Americans, Swedes, Englishmen, Danes or what not, for they all shout and yell on the strip and carry on like maniacs. I have seen some very cold British fish in action, including doctors, Q.C.'s, businessmen and a Sea Lord, and it moves them all alike. Only the week before writing this I was in a competition at the Lansdowne Club in London; there were ten of us, nine Englishmen and one American, and there we were shouting, hollering and running at one another, stamping our feet and bellowing "Ho!" and "Ha!" and "He *la!*," cursing misses, howling with anguish over errors and behaving most un-British. Temperament was all over the place.

You bellow or shout at your opponent for two reasons. One is to panic, frighten or at least disconcert him, a perfectly legitimate and permissible maneuver in what is otherwise a gentleman's game. The other reason is that, during a long mental duel which frequently precedes the physical clash—a period of lightninglike feints, probes, shiftings of feet, head, hands, changes of distance, maneuvers for range and balance —the tension becomes so unbearable that release brings explosion. Once the die is cast and the attack is launched, bringing on the fury of crashing blades, cries are torn from the contestants that they are unable to control.

Fencing, more than any other sport I know, is a game of will power and spirit. There is no quicker way to get licked than to take the strip timidly, in awe of an opponent. On the other hand, there are few games where a confident and capable performer can take such command at the outset and impose his will upon the other long before swords or bodies have clashed. I once met, fenced and beat an Olympic champion before I knew who he was. I missed the name. To me he was just another Joe with an épée in his hand, and I set out to take him. Later, when I found out who he was and we fenced again, he murdered me.

I N FENCING, there are periods where two opponents are in contact with another through the medium of two thin shafts of steel. These are very like antennae down whose length messages of strength, weakness, anticipation, nerves, tensions, plan and counterplan are broadcast. Each pressure on the blade, each beat, each probing for the weak and strong of the weapon has its separate meaning to both fencers. It is as though, while the intellect is occupied moving feet and bodies for advantageous positions, the swords were holding an independent conversation, most of which is wool-over-the-eyes, shameless deceit, a blind and a tissue of lies. For the only time a fencer does the expected is when he has managed to make it wholly unexpected to do so. The element of surprise is vital, and a crafty fighter will spend minutes building up premises of false security in his opponent's mind, deluding, seducing and lulling him.

Again, a wary opponent will suddenly realize that his nervous and quivering blade is telling too much and not only giving him away but affording his opponent the opportunity to take command of it. Then he will disengage himself and his steel from all contact. With communication broken, the men become like two wary fighting cocks, for now it has become a pure guessing game, but one which can instantaneously explode into violent action as each attempts to lead the other into mistakes.

It is a creative game, since one is constantly improvising. Yet there is little in fencing for the spectator and in particular the layman, for this is an affair of *feeling* as well as participating or seeing. It is a highly emotional sport, but the emotion is shared only by the contestants, leaving the observers usually high and dry, with only an occasional visibly pretty hit to applaud.

And now, should you find yourself interested in joining our company of the romantically bemused, here is a quick rundown on what is needed. Since all fencing begins with lessons in the classic fleuret or foil, acquire a pair of these, costing four or five dollars apiece, a mask, glove and jacket. Slacks and ordinary sneakers will do for the beginner. The whole outfit won't cost more than fifty dollars and will last for years.

You can find a fencing master and take private lessons but it is better to join a fencing club and become steeped in the curious and appealing atmosphere of fencers and fencing. The club professional will give you lessons, and the older members and club hot-shots will give you tips and fence with you occasionally and keep you from forming bad habits before your good ones are set. The first year or so it is also a good idea to put up a target in your room at home and lunge at it every day. This makes for accuracy and teaches you to aim and keep your point in line. It is a good idea to start kids when they are 14 or 15, but you can begin at any age and become a good performer if you are not in too much of a hurry.

One thing I can promise you: you'll thank me someday if I have managed to get you started. You can take the word of one who has had a crack at most games played by two or more people. For sheer fun and excitement, fencing beats them all.

WINTER

The dwindling bear within the earth's skin
fishes the liberal river of his dream
and knows no season.
The fish in the high interiors of the sea
glides tranquil miles below the storm;
the wreck comes down, absurd.
That roaring metropolitan dark
where a prizefighter falls
is a private season
ruled by the timekeeper's reckoning,
the soft machinery of the heart.
Elsewhere and outside
snow burns slowly its white fire.
A skier in his splendid freedom
regards the deep way of his descent.
A skater, hands folded behind,
bends through circles
as through sleep.

—GILBERT ROGIN

ICE-SKATING TIME

THE FLAT SHEEN of smooth ice is a wonderfully inviting thing to see. Long before men climbed into the air with the help of a clattering engine and an awkward imitation of a bird's wings, the sensation of flight was easily come by on any cold winter day if a frozen pond and a pair of skates were at hand. Of all man's inventions, none has given him a better illusion of airborne lightness or equipped him more admirably with the tools for grace than the basically simple device he calls the skate.

Not that skating is easy. The palette of an unmarked ice rink demands a delicate blend of strength and coordination before it yields a picture as cleanly drawn and charming as the one on the opposite page. Figure skating has been described as "a disciplined passion, an absorbing art." When the artist is a world champion, like Tenley Albright at right, the execution has the lightness and grace of ballet. But no one needs the artistry of Tenley Albright to find the magic in a frozen pond or a skating rink. It is there for the youngster trying his balance for the first time, and it is there as well for the grey-flanneled businessman who seeks his youth again on the rink at Rockefeller Center.

On a country pond in Maine the ice is unswept and there are no rink-side cafes, but there is a bonfire and a sunset, and even the dogs can share in after-school fun; in New York the lights of the city sparkle above the bright swirl of the Wollman Memorial rink in Central Park

The skating rink at Rockefeller Center in New York shortly after dusk on a winter's evening le

this from the 51st floor of the RCA Building. Fifth Avenue runs across the top of the picture

THE GRACEFUL VIOLENCE

OF THE

BULL RING

Photographed by MARK KAUFFMAN

HE is the enemy. He is a bull — big, perhaps 1,000 pounds of lightning speed and smashing power. The whole top of his neck is a tossing muscle capable of flinging a horse into the air. The muscle flexes and humps tight when he is angry. He comes trotting out of his dark box into the bright sunlight of the ring, head up, looking nervously about. He charges and the sand sings under his feet.

In midwinter the high season for killing this bull is at hand in some 200 cities and towns of Mexico. Many Americans make the short trip across the California border from San Diego to visit the bull ring at Tijuana, where photographer Mark Kauffman took the brilliant series of pictures on the following pages. Some who watch for the first time are revolted; others are enthralled. These photographs show what a bullfight is: blood and fury against grace and courage, a spectacle of violence, a supreme test for animal and man.

Mexican bullfighting comes to a grand climax each season in Mexico City, in the big, 50,000-seat Plaza Mexico, the largest bull ring in the world. Here many of the best of the world's officially-invested Killers of Bulls are assembled. The impresario will pay these stars from $4,000 to $6,000 per appearance, and since theirs is a year-round business, carried on in countries in which income taxes are matters for gentle laughter, they take home very large sums indeed — the great Manolete netted $250,000 yearly for his Mexico City appearances alone — larger than those of any other professional athlete in the world. The bullfighter who survives at or near the top for eight or 10 years can expect to buy his own castle in Spain or Mexico's elegant Jalisco and settle in very comfortably.

—JOHN STANTON

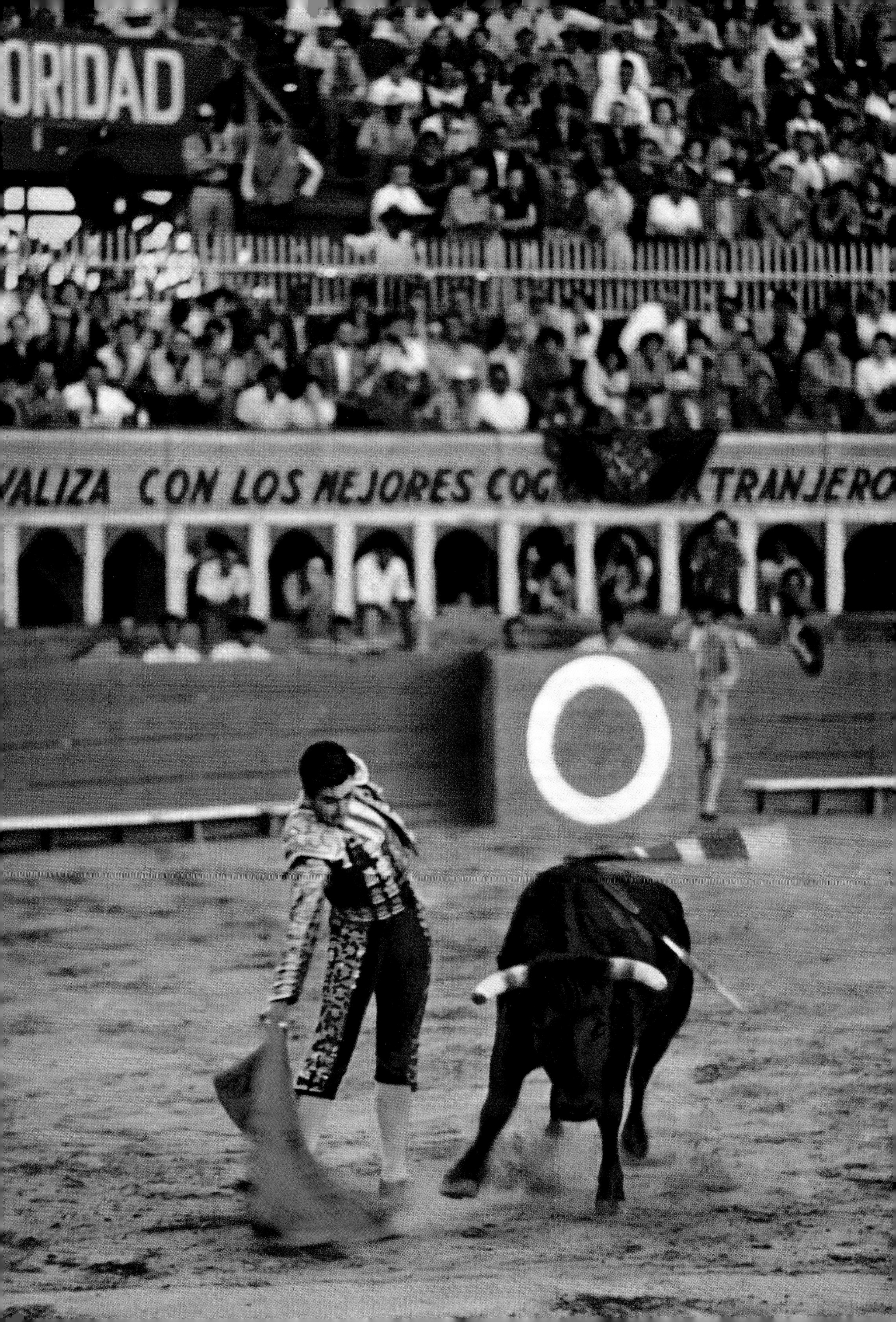

ORIDAD
VALIZA CON LOS MEJORES COG
TRANJERO

THE PICADOR

The bullfight proper starts with the appearance of everybody's enemy, the *picador*. To the novice fan he is evil itself —a brawny-armed bravo who rides a well-padded, blindfolded but pathetic old horse and lures the bull into charging it. Then, while the bull is snorting and straining, he

BANDERILLERO

After the picing and rival demonstrations of cape work by the *matadors*, *banderillas* (barbed sticks) are sunk into the bull to help wear down its strength. Here Carlos (Little Canes) Vera, a better *banderillero* than he is a *matador*, places a pair in the manner called "force to force." At left

cks an inch and a half of steel at the end of a nine-foot
le into its back, producing the afternoon's first shocking
ht of blood. To veteran fans the *picador* is even more sin-
er. His job is to "pic" the lifting (or goring) muscle atop
e neck, slowing the bull without ruining its will to attack.

But most pic farther back, making the bull less belligerent
—and drawing boos from the *aficionados*. Bullfighters afoot
are in the ring to take the bull away from the horse after
the picing. But the one in picture at left is risking a fine
by being out of his appointed place at the left of the horse.

calls the bull. As it charges (second picture from left),
era runs toward it, lifting his arms with the *banderillas*
gh, and leaves the ground. Bull and man come together
hird picture) and Vera sinks the sticks where they belong:
gh on the shoulders, close together and well back of the

neck. The shock stops the bull for a split second; his head
comes down seeking something to strike, and Vera, using the
banderillas as levers, twists away from the horns, throwing
his arms up (fourth picture) in the traditional signal that
he, for one, thinks (correctly) that the job was well done.

THE FAENA

THE FINAL ACT before the death of
the bull is the *faena*, a series of
linked passes by the *matador*. He
comes to the bull alone, armed only
with his courage, his sword and the
muleta, a small red cloth draped over
a stick. There, to the limits of his
skill and spirit, he tries to mold sudden violence into slow grace; to bring
the charging bull's horns closer and
closer, slower and slower, until the
spectators catch fire and the plaza
shakes with short, breathless growls
of *"Olé"* that stop in the air as the
bull whirls to charge again. It isn't
easy; it doesn't always come off; desperately reaching for it, *matadors* often mix such ornamental frivolities
as the *Lacernista*, a pass named for
the Spanish bullfighter who invented
it and which the Mexican Carlos Vera
is doing at right, with more fundamental passes. These bring the bull
in, head low, horns outreaching, close
on the right or, more dangerous, closer
on the left of the bullfighter. But
even in the heat of the *faena*, the
matador must study his bull—which
horn it hooks with and how fast its
eyes move—for in a few moments his
life will depend on this knowledge.

THE APPROACH OF DEATH

The *matador* is in most danger just as he kills his bull. Some of history's greatest—Antonio Montes, Manolete, and others—suffered their own death wounds in this moment. Here Rafael Rodriguez, best of the current crop of Mexican bullfighters, prepares to kill in the classic 18th-

century style called *volapié*, flight afoot. Having made
certain that the bull's eyes are following the *muleta* in
his left hand rather than the sword in his right, that
its front feet are planted close together, thus opening
wider the gap between its shoulder bones on top where the
swood must go in to strike the vital organs, Rafael is
ready. Sighting down the slim steel blade, which curves
downward at the tip, he begins his charge from a position in profile to the bull. For the wearied and bleeding
animal, death within the next few moments is inevitable.

THE MOMENT OF TRUTH

Lunging toward the bull, the *matador* moves out the *muleta* (*above, left*), to draw the horns down and to his right. As the sword goes in (*above, right*), in what bull-fight fans call "the moment of truth," he is directly over the horns. The bull, wounded unto death, has but to lift its head to drive a horn into Rodriguez's groin or stomach. But Rafael pivots away, and the bull, vomiting blood, falls down and dies.

MANOLETE THE MAGNIFICENT

HE was slim, unsmiling, with a tragic air about him. Perhaps it was partly drilled into him by a shrewd manager, for bullfighting is a cynical business at best, and perhaps it was partly born in his own spirit, for Manolete could see the end coming.

He would stand in front of the bull, the thousands around him dead silent, sword in his right hand, and offer the *muleta* with his left, low, inches to the left of his thigh and groin. The bull would charge and there would be one agonized grunt of *"Olé"* from 50,000 throats and then silence again as he turned to face the bull. The tension would build, bit by bit, tighter and tighter, until he killed the bull, and then people would explode. Crying men would throw their hats and coats into the ring. Shivering women would throw their undergarments to him as he walked in sad triumph around the ring. He would pick them up and, with a gesture half salute, half as if about to drink a toast, throw them back to their owners. But there would be no smile; just the same somber look with which, at Linares, Spain, on Aug. 28, 1947, he killed a Miura bull in the same instant that the bull mortally wounded him.

It is, perhaps, hard to understand. Most of the Americans who see some part of the bullfighting proceedings in Mexico or in Spain each year will turn away from the blood and pain, utterly revolted—an attitude, it should be hastily explained, that is perfectly normal; in fact it is shared by many Spaniards and Mexicans. Others will recognize in the elaborate formalism of the bull ring the need for a special knowledge, somewhat like the special knowledge one must take to the ballet or to a baseball game; their interest will drift off. Some, following recent literary trends, will swallow their squeamishness and declare themselves delighted. A few, having had the good luck of running up against a good bullfight first crack out of the box, will fall enraptured and become *aficionados*. Unfortunately this is usually the first step toward becoming a *villamelon*, a boastful fellow who loftily pretends a highly dubious expertese in the ancient arts of tauromachy. In fact the new *aficionado* will soon discover that he has joined a cult whose members spend their time, while the bulls snort in the background, disdainfully sniffing at one another.

This horrible snobbism reaches its height in the *porra* and *contra-porra*, the shirt-sleeved gentry of bullfighting's left-field bleachers who occupy the sun-drenched seats on either side of the judges. They express their opinions brutally. They make shocking references to intimate parts of the human body. But always and inevitably, their attention, their emotion, the compelling force of those demanding and bestowing instincts which center in the guts, will finally focus on the bull.

He is implacable, magnificent. He may spot a piece of paper floating down from the crowd. He will spear it on one horn and rip it to shreds with two angry shakes of his head. Seeing the proffered cape of one of the bullfighter's assistants he charges, head down and horn hooking. From behind a fence the bullfighter nervously studies him: does he charge straight? Which horn does he favor?

He is death; and therein lies his final fascination. The crowd, shrill and excited, looks at him and shivers. And then, to conquer death, to bring him to his knees with grace and beauty, the matador steps swiftly into the ring.

In Plaza Mexico the *porra* and *contra-porra* remember the day they jeered Manolete for refusing to place *banderillas*, and assigning the job to one of his assistants. He took the bull directly before his critics. There he executed one of the most beautiful and dangerous passes in bullfighting—the *natural*. It is dangerous because the cloth is in the bullfighter's left hand and the sword, which must remain always in his right, cannot be used to spread the cloth wider. The bull comes very close. Manolete did this with slow, certain grace; but it differed from many others he did during his career in this way. Not once as the bull roared past him did he look at it.

He was staring with cold contempt up into the seats at the people who had jeered him. They gasped. Still with his head back, staring up at the people, he turned and brought the bull by again. That wrenched the first *"Olé"* from the crowd. Nine times he passed that bull and not once did he look at it. Then, fixing it in one spot, he turned for one last stare. He touched his body where, according to Spanish mythology, human courage resides. Then he turned and killed the bull.

—JOHN STANTON

255

PATTERNS

ON

HARDWOOD

Photographed by HY PESKIN

THE SWIRL of players on the opposite page, against a background of the Boston Garden's parquet floor, illustrates both the nature of professional basketball today and the chief reason for its accelerating popularity. The game is played by patterns rather than predetermined movements, and the variety of patterns is unlimited. Thus, as play follows play in speedy sequence, the knowing spectator has the fun of trying to anticipate what each participant will do to further or impede the progress of the ball upcourt to its ultimate destination — a metal ring 18 inches in diameter suspended 10 feet above the hardwood floor. And his guess, often, is as good as that of any man on the court.

For example, at the top of the page, New York's Carl Braun (4) has attempted to run Minneapolis Defender Vern Mikkelsen (19) into Braun's teammate, Richie Guerin (9). As a consequence, at least four different pattern plays may emerge:

1) If Braun's maneuver succeeds, Defender Bob Leonard (21) will switch from guarding Guerin to picking up Braun. At this instant, it appears that Braun is already half a step ahead of Mikkelsen so that the switch in assignments may take place even if Mikkelsen is not stopped completely.

2) If the switch takes place and Mikkelsen cannot recover in time to pursue Guerin closely, Braun may pass the ball to Richie for a close-in shot or layup.

3) If Mikkelsen does recover quickly but Leonard comes out slowly, Braun may stop suddenly and try his favorite overhead jump shot at the edge of the key.

4) Finally, Ray Felix (19) is obviously taking advantage of the fact that his defenseman, Clyde Lovellette (34), is watching the progress of Braun's maneuver. He is slipping away from Lovellette, and if he succeeds in getting clear under the basket, Braun may pass high to him for an easy tap-in.

There are, of course, a dozen possibilities. As soon as one is played out, a new pattern and its options will unfold. This is basketball at its best — demonstrated over a 4½-month season by 80 of the best players in the world.

—JEREMIAH TAX

256

At the end of a typical Boston fast break led by Bob Cousy, all five Celtics have arrived upcourt against only three Rochester Royal defenders; Cousy, relatively unhampered, lifts for one-handed jump shot at basket

A Rochester free throw misses the basket, and now another classic pattern unfolds: the battle for the rebound

BASKETBALL'S CREATIVE GENIUS

IT is always a little misleading to talk about the astonishing things Bob Cousy can do with a basketball because it tends to distort a true appreciation of his genius for the game. Though you are apt to forget it some nights when a poorly played contest seems to consist almost entirely of tall men shooting from outside and taller men battling lugubriously under the basket, basketball, good basketball, is a game of movement. As in hockey, Rugby, soccer, polo, lacrosse, and other kindred games where two opposing teams try to gain possession of the ball and advance it toward the enemy's goal for a scoring shot, the really gifted players are not necessarily the high-scoring specialists but the men with an instinctive sense of how to build a play—the man without the ball who knows how to cut free from the opponent covering him, and, even more important, the man with the ball who can "feel" how an offensive maneuver can develop, who can instantly spot a man who breaks free, and who can zip the ball over to him at the right split second. Without this latter breed—the play-makers—basketball, or any other goal-to-goal game, can degenerate into a rather ragged race up and down the playing field.

Cousy's greatness lies in the fact that he is fundamentally a play-maker and that his legerdemain, far from being empty show-boating, is functional, solid basketball. Equipped with a fine sense of pattern, superb reflexes, he also has peripheral vision which enables him to see not only the men in front of him but a full 180° angle of the action. Thus, like nobody else in the game—unless it be Dick McGuire of the Knicks on one of his outlandish hot nights—Cousy can open up a seemingly clogged court by appearing to focus in one direction, simultaneously spotting a seemingly unreachable teammate in another area, and quickly turning him into a scoring threat with a whiplash pass. There is implicit deception in Cousy's straight basketball, which is the secret of any great player's success, and it is only in those exceptional circumstances when extra measures pay off soundly that he resorts to his really fancy stuff.

Well aware that his feats of manipulation draw the crowds and help to keep the league healthy, Cousy will flash a few of his special effects near the end of a game in which the outcome is already surely decided, if he previously has not had a chance to use them. Aside from this, he is all function. There has been only one occasion, for example, when he has deliberately trotted out a little of the old razzle-dazzle to show up an opposing player.

This occurred a few years back in one of those high-pitched battles between the Celtics and the Knicks. Sweetwater Clifton of the Knicks, who can handle the ball with his enormous hands as if it were the size of a grapefruit, had been, as Cousy saw it, indulging himself far too prodigally in exhibiting his artistry and appeared much more concerned with making the Celtics look foolish than in playing basketball. This aroused Cousy's French. The next time he got the ball, he dribbled straight up to Clifton. Looking Sweets right in the eye, he wound up as if he were going to boom a big overhand pass directly at him. As he brought the ball over his shoulder, however, Cousy let it roll down his back, where he caught it with his left hand, and, completing that big windmill thrust with his empty right hand, stuck it out towards Sweets in the gesture of "shake hands." It brought down the house.

"It was an old Globetrotter trick I'd seen them use and had practiced for my own benefit a couple of times," Cousy explained not long ago. "I shouldn't have done it but I was awfully sore at the time. Naturally the newspapers played it up that there was a feud between me and Clifton. The next time we played New York I looked Clifton up and told him I was sorry about the incident, for I was. Clifton isn't a wise guy. He's a helluva nice guy. I should have taken that into account at the time."

—HERBERT WARREN WIND

ROSE PRINCESSES

Photographed by MARK KAUFFMAN

The young ladies perched prettily on their rose-covered float owe their position to a flower-throwing picnic which took place in Pasadena, Calif. a long time ago. Dr. Charles F. Holder returned

from Europe in 1888 and told friends: "I saw a lovely thing in Rome. They called it a Battle of the Flowers. Why couldn't we . . . ?" The people of Pasadena could and did. Now the Tournament of Roses parade before the Rose Bowl football game moves 8 million flowers from one end of Pasadena to the other before some 45 million TV spectators. The girls move with the flowers.

WONDERFUL WORLD OF SNOW

Photographed by

JOERN GERDTS and RICHARD MEEK

IN November and December the first snows sweep into the mountains, and now the special world of the skier springs into being. It is a world of sun and excitement; of exhilarating runs checked by rhythmic turns; of flashing speed heading down and down past towering evergreens, with the glistening snow wheeling in beneath your skis, rocking them and twisting them in challenge. It is a world of the senses: there is the good smell of melted wax just brushed on the skis and the coolness of new snow sifting down across your face; there is the surging blood called up by a fast run and the pungency of hot chocolate in the warming hut; there is the low hiss of ski tips cutting through unbroken powder snow on a silent mountain.

Skiing is also a world of challenge. Every hour on skis is a chance to run a bit better and to reach for those moments of perfection in speed and balance that are like flying. Such moments come often to expert skiers like Ronnie Youngberg, who is shown at right spinning flawlessly through the difficult, knee-deep powder snow on Mt. Millicent, Utah.

Such are the rewards. To the enthusiast, nothing quite matches the fine elation of skiing, or the evenings spent afterwards in front of a lodge fire. And whether the skier chooses to carve a single track down the lovely snow fields of the western mountains, or to run through twisting alleys of pines on the eastern slopes, he will have plenty of company. Four million Americans now ski. And over two hundred major lifts built in the last twenty years to keep them skiing now climb snow faces of U.S. mountains from the Appalachians to the Sierra Nevada.

The photographs on the following pages — of the Utah mountains by Joern Gerdts, and of a New England carnival by Richard Meek — attest to what every skier knows: a large part of the fun of skiing lies in meeting and mingling with other skiers. One and all are joined by a feeling of comradeship in escaping together from the ordinary in life out into the wonderful winter world of snow.

—MORT LUND

...ing is a sport of high speed and stamina
...some and for others a way of taking the sun,
...in any case skiing is a sport of sociability.
...re in the Alta-Brighton area near Salt Lake
...y friends gather to exchange small talk
...ong the forest of stacked skis and poles at
...bottom of a beginner's slope; snow bunnies
...p one another with waxing skis and putting on
...dings; and a father gives his young daughter
...boost on the rope tow at Little Mountain

Across from Mt. Baldy's ski-marked slopes, a lone skier stirs up a cloud of fresh powder as s

...s beneath a cornice of snow in Cardiff Pass on her run down toward the main parking lot

Jostling through small traffic jam, a ski carnival crowd at Vermont's Middlebury College he

ck for campus past a lovely grove of Norway spruce after the day's competitions are over

i carnival spirit draws on the exuberance of college students like these at Middlebury
o will stand in a blizzard half a day to watch the racers dart through the flags on a
lom course and then stay up half the night for a jazz party in a fraternity house

FOOTPRINTS
ON THE FAIRWAY

Photographed by

MARK KAUFFMAN

As THE TOURNAMENT golf trail winds, it is 5,000 miles — and 1,000 holes of pressure golf — from California in January to the Masters at Augusta in April. Just about all of the country's outstanding playing professionals make this long, sun-swept haul, variously known as the grapefruit circuit, the winter swing, or simply "the tour". The annual motorized migration begins in Los Angeles in the first week of January, proceeds across the dry, golfable Southwest and South at the pace of a tournament a week (save for one week open for rest and recuperation), and winds up some three months later with the climactic Masters.

At right is the opening scene of the winter show. The air is chilly and dew sparkles on the fairways as a sparse but eager gallery tramps through the morning haze after one of the Los Angeles Open's early-starting threesomes. Later in the day the January sun will burn hot from a cloudless sky, and thousands of gaily dressed southern Californians will swarm the course to watch and applaud the always astonishing skill of the name stars: Middlecoff, Mangrum, Littler, Burke, et al. But that is later, and the early-morning fans content themselves by watching the lesser-knowns, on the theory that one of them may someday develop into another Ben Hogan or Sam Snead.

—HERBERT WARREN WIND

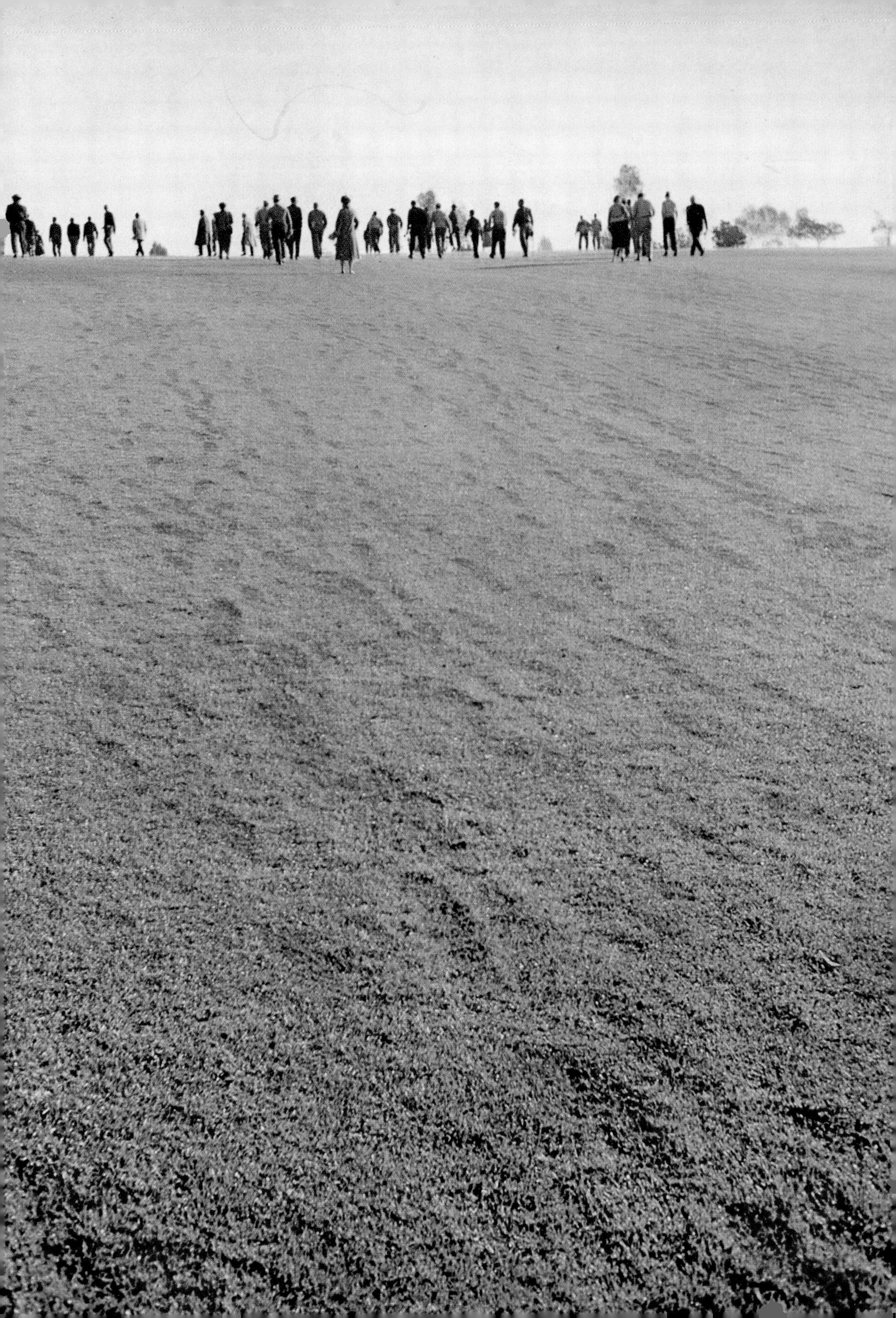

Jim Turnesa, an early starter in the L.A. Open, propels two putts across the dew-heavy practice green

WHAT RUGBY MEANS
TO ENGLAND

by ALEC WAUGH

I AM NOW in my middle 50s. A short while ago I was playing golf with a near contemporary who had gone to Princeton. After the game we fell to talking about the '20s, which he had spent mainly in New York while I had been in London. We compared our separate experiences during that hectic period. Suddenly an idea struck me. "I believe," I said, "that this is the chief minor difference between us—I as a Londoner every Saturday afternoon between mid-September and mid-April was playing Rugby football while you as a New Yorker were shooting squash in the Racquet Club."

He looked surprised and his eyes ran me over. I am short and stocky, 5 foot 6, and my weight since my late teens has vacillated between 150 and 160. "You played Rugby till you were nearly 30?" He is quite a bit bigger than I, but he had played no football after he had left high school. He hadn't been heavy enough to make the team, he felt, and there were other games. "Weren't you exceptional?" he asked.

I shook my head. "I was a very average player. One of many thousands. Rugby is played in the majority of our public schools. Most of us who are any good go on playing afterwards."

"Rugby every Saturday between mid-September and mid-April. That's quite a thing!" he ruminated. "It must fill a very special place in English life."

Now, in retrospect, I can see it does. But at the time, to play Rugby every Saturday through the winter was the most natural thing for me to do, for the very simple reason that it was the thing I wanted to do most.

I have joined in many arguments as to which is the best game to watch. Much is to be said for many. But I have little doubt that the best winter game for a young man to play is Rugby football. It has everything to recommend it. It is fast and hard; it is rough but it is not dangerous. You get bruised and shaken but bones are rarely broken; no special padding is

prescribed; you wear shorts and a jersey. Dexterity and speed are as important as weight and strength. It is essentially a team game, but it is highly individualistic. The majority of points are scored not as the outcome of a concerted movement but through an opportunist taking advantage of an opponent's slip. Each player develops his own style.

It is, moreover, a very simple game. You learn it by playing it. No long apprenticeship is served. My own experience is that of many thousand others. At my preparatory school, from 9 years to 13, I played soccer. On my first afternoon at Sherborne, my public school, I was instructed with 20 other new boys in the rudiments of Rugby. It bears resemblance to American football. It would be surprising if it didn't; after all, both games stem from the same source. *Tom Brown's Schooldays*, in its account of a school-house match at Rugby School in the 1830's, describes that source. Both fields look alike, with a similar type of goal post, and the object of each game is the same, to get the ball over the opponent's line, after which you are allowed a free kick at the goal. But whereas the game that was introduced into America via Canada in the 1870s developed rapidly into its present form, Rugby stayed the way it was. My younger son is playing today at Sherborne virtually the same game that his grandfather played there 75 years ago.

In Rugby there are few complications. The ball cannot be passed forward; it is fatter and less pointed than the American ball, and you cannot fling long one-handed passes with it. There is as much dribbling with the feet and the gaining of ground by long kicks into touch as there is running with the ball under the arm. Body blocking is not allowed. There are no substitutes, no huddles, no interruptions except for serious injuries. The rules consist of a few straightforward DON'TS.

There are 15 players on each side, and I was told on that first afternoon how they are disposed—eight forwards, six backs and as a last line of defense a single fullback. I was then shown how the eight forwards form themselves into a three-row phalanx—it is called a scrum—and, with bent backs and arms around each other, join issue with the opposing pack. The ball is then slid by one of the backs under their feet, and the two packs shove and struggle in an attempt to heel it to the backs, who are spread out behind them in the open, waiting to initiate an attack.

My first lesson lasted for half an hour. I was then ordered to watch a practice game on the upper ground. It was the first Rugby match that I had watched. I was fascinated by its speed and its variety. In all athletics I doubt if there is a finer sight than a fast backfield movement, the ball heeled quickly from the scrum, each back running straight, making all the ground he can, drawing his opponent before he passes laterally till finally the ball reaches the wing man, who makes for the corner flag in a desperate attempt to outswerve and outpace the fullback. I longed for the day when I should be big enough to play in such a game.

That half hour of explanation and the watching of that "upper" was all the preliminary instruction I received. The next day I was posted to a house game. I cannot say that I enjoyed it. I was playing with boys bigger than myself. I felt very lost. I was terrified of making myself conspicuous by doing the wrong thing. I was equally terrified of doing nothing. The game was watched by a prefect who urged us to keener efforts. Abuse was mingled with his exhortations. "Go low. Drop on the ball, run straight, don't funk," he shouted. I was afraid that my ignorance would be mistaken for cowardice, and at half time I surreptitiously rubbed mud into my knees to give the impression that I had plunged adventurously under the feet of the attacking forwards. I was infinitely relieved when the final whistle went. But within a week I had found my feet.

The simplicity of Rugby is one of its great merits. It is easy for a novice to pick it up, and it is possible for the ex-public school boy to continue playing it after he has come down when he is working in an office, with no time available for midweek practice, which is impossible, I fancy, in American football, with its profusion of "plays," its elaborate deception schemes, its mathematical positionings.

The proof of Rugby's excellence lies in the fact that so many men play it after they leave college. Games are compulsory at English schools, and it is natural for a schoolboy to be anxious to succeed at them. Prestige and popularity depend upon his prowess on the field. The reputation and standing of a school is in large part determined by the skill of its footballers and cricketers, and it stands a man in good stead in later life to be able to say he was in his school XV. "A ribboned coat" is the opening to many appointments. But it is quite another matter to go on playing Rugby after you have left school, when you are under no compunction, with no rewards attached, obscurely before an uncrowded touch line, simply out of a love of the game. And that is what thousands of men do.

My own case is typical. When I was posted to the army reserve after World War I at the age of 21, I joined Rosslyn Park, a London club. For seven years I turned out every Saturday between mid-September and mid-April. I had been in the first XV at Sherborne, but as a forward weighing 150 pounds. I was too small to earn a regular place in the first Rosslyn Park side. For the most part I played for the second or "A" XV against public schools, second-class clubs and the "A" XVs of other first-class clubs.

Each Monday evening the selection committee met, and on the Tuesday morning I would receive a card. "You are selected to play vs. Bishop's Stortford. Train 1:15 Liverpool Street. Meet at barrier. Tickets taken." I observed no training rules, but I kept fit. I confined wild parties to the first half of the week. On Friday I dined at my parents' house and was in bed by 10.

SOMETIMES when I woke on the Saturday, I would wonder why I still went on playing football. It was cold and wet. Liverpool Street station at 12:30 on a Saturday is a shambles. I should lunch in a crowded buffet off a soggy sandwich. The train would be packed and I should have to stand. The ground would be a quarter of an hour's walk from the station. The pavilion would be a drafty converted army hut. There would be small wash tubs, tepid water and no electric light. Why on earth was I still playing Rugby?

Now and again I felt like that on a wet Saturday morning, but the moment I reached the barrier and saw the familiar faces that mood left me. From week to week the side changed little, and the nucleus was carried on from one year to the next. We had a fund of jokes to share. Though I had to stand in the train, the journey passed so quickly that I was surprised to find we had arrived. It was still spattering with rain, but that made it, I reminded myself, perfect football weather for a forward. The pavilion was indeed drafty, but I did not notice it. I was impatient, like a horse at the starting point. I was young, fit, tingling with a sense of battle. It would be a game in which nothing was at stake; no caps or cups were to be won; afterwards there would be no elation in victory, no deep despondency in defeat. I can remember in detail every house and school match in which I played at Sherborne, but of my seven years with Rosslyn Park I can only recall occasional incidents and the look of certain grounds. Yet, though there was no drama in that later football, I enjoyed the actual playing of it more than I had at school.

And after the game, despite the tepid water in the shallow tub, I was suffused with the agreeable languor that follows violent exercise. Next day I should be stiff and slow in movement, but at the moment my bruises were still soft. I felt pleasantly exhausted, no more than that. After the game there would be a heavy tea with fruit cake and thick fish-paste sandwiches. We would be too tired for much talking; that could wait till afterwards. For always after the game seven or eight of us, on our return to London, would raid Dehem's oyster bar off Shaftesbury Avenue and drink many pints of lukewarm beer, eat a steak and kidney pudding and argue about this and that till closing time. So it went on every Saturday from mid-September to mid-April for seven years.

Rugby football made the pattern of winter life for me, as it does in Britain year after year for many thousands of ex-public school boys. I was lucky to have that pattern. The seven years between 21 and 28 are crucial in a young man's life. He is establishing himself in his career, he is falling in and out of love, he is discovering himself. Myself, I had at that time a half-time job as an editor in a publishing house. On the other days I was writing articles, short stories, novels. I had many problems, emotional and professional. It was an immense relief to me to be taken every week out of the circle of those problems into the wholesome atmosphere of football. It was a relief to all of us.

It is a curious two-dimensional friendship that links the members of a Rugby side. In one sense we all knew each other very well. We knew who was reckless and who was cautious, who was a fair-weather player and who was at his best in an uphill fight. We all liked each other, for that is the great merit of team games, that you only play with congenial people; however brilliant as an individualist a player may be, if he is boastful and a bully, he soon ceases to receive that Tuesday morning postcard. In one sense I knew inside out the men with whom I played regularly with Rosslyn Park. In another sense I scarcely knew them. I knew little of their backgrounds. I knew to which school each had been, and the kind of job he worked at. But I had no idea who his parents were or from what kind of home he came. For the most part we were bachelors, but more than once I was surprised to find that someone I had known for three seasons was married and a father. When we parted outside Dehem's at closing time, we passed out of each other's lives until we met at the station barrier on the following Saturday.

There is a quality of anonymity about football friendships, and sometimes on Saturday evenings when I caught the tube back to my flat in Kensington, I found myself thinking ruefully of the inevitable day when I should give up Rugby. Very few men play it after 30: you lose your speed, your wind gets short and your bones brittle, you are shaken badly when you are brought down heavily. I had seen many friends drop out of the game, usually in the same way. They caught a chill, or a minor injury prevented their playing for three weeks. When they played again, they were out of training; they excused themselves on the following Saturday; they vowed to get back into training and never did. If the rhythm is once broken, it is not resumed when you are nearing 30.

One day that would happen to me, and as my tube rattled westward I vowed to myself that when my turn came to stop playing, I would not drop out of the game altogether; I would become a referee or a touch judge so that a winter Saturday would still mean football for me. It didn't though. When my time came, I was like all the others. I let golf and matrimony impose their own new pattern.

That is the one sad thing about Rugby football. When you give up playing it, you drop out of the game altogether. I am a life member of Rosslyn Park, but I never go to the old Deer Park to see them play. I have lost touch with every former member of the side. As a retired cricketer, I go to Lord's on a summer evening, certain of meeting half a dozen old friends in the pavilion, but a Rugby international in the vast arena at Twickenham provides no common meeting ground.

When you walk off a Rugby field for the last time, you walk out of the world of Rugby. Maybe that foreknowledge adds a keener savor to one's enjoyment of the game during the years when one can play it. Certainly the savor I got from it lingers still upon the palate. For me, in retrospect, the early 1920s do not mean wild parties and the fast dollar half as much as they mean Rugby football.

FLURRY OF FLAMINGOS

Photographed by MARK KAUFFMAN

Traditional symbols of racing at Hialeah are the track's flamingos, which are herded across the infield by Seminole Indian children on the day of the rich Flamingo Stakes. Winter racing interest is divided between events at major tracks in Florida and California *(next page)*.

Flanked by the swift-moving shadows they cast upon Santa Anita's hard, fast dirt track, horses and riders maneuver for position in a stakes race during the California park's mid-winter season

THE LADY HORSEPLAYER

THE MANAGEMENT of Laurel race track in Maryland recently undertook a brave campaign designed to put order and logic into the mental processes of women—not all their mental processes, to be sure, but at least those functioning when they bet on horses.

Feeling that women rely much too heavily on intuition in selecting the horses they bet on, Laurel arranged a series of four educational lectures. The first was given before 60 more or less attentive ladies in the clubhouse lounge by Raleigh S. Burroughs, the dignified, spectacled editor of *Turf and Sport Digest*.

"I say study the horses and know their records," Mr. Burroughs began, "and then you won't make any foolish bets. The average person isn't emotionally adjusted to be a horseplayer. The thrill of the race is too much for him or her; the thrill of the long shot is too much. People make a lot of foolish bets without providing themselves with adequate information."

Some of the ladies nodded and some wrote in their notebooks; some kept reading the racing literature they had brought along.

"Don't try to bet every race," Mr. Burroughs went on. "The handicapper has to make a selection, but you don't. When you bet, think of the reasons why a horse is a favorite. Don't think you have to make a lot of money on every race. If you bet a favorite $5 to show and he pays $2.80 for $2, then you've made $2. If you do the same in the next race, you've made a total of $4."

Mr. Burroughs went on in that vein and then answered a few questions from the audience.

All in all, it seemed like a most satisfactory session, and as Laurel officials congratulated Mr. Burroughs and each other, the lady bettors gathered in little groups and compared notes.

"I was at Bowie the other day," said a middle-aged lady from Washington, "and it was a beautiful sunny day. I sat in the sun and read my program, and there it was: a horse named Noble Sun was running. Naturally I bet on him. He paid $19."

Another woman nodded. "The other day at Bowie," she said, "I decided to bet on horses with white forefeet. I had five winners. Today I'm going to bet on My Boots." She looked around and then explained: "One time I had a dog named Boots."

Suddenly there was a whole chorus of voices:

"I bet black horses. They always look so strong."

"I go down in the paddock and look at the owner. Then, somehow, I always feel I can tell whether his horse has been doing well or not."

"I bet horses with nautical names because my son is in the Navy."

"But what," someone asked, "would you do if there were two horses with nautical names in the same race?"

"Oh, then," said the nautical bettor promptly, "I'd flip a coin."

The second lecturer in Laurel's lecture series was Walter Haight, racing writer for *The Washington Post*. Wearing baggy pants and a sports jacket, he peered over his horn-rimmed glasses and saw what he was up against. After speaking briefly on the subject of scientific betting, he dropped all pretense when one of the ladies asked him his choice in the daily double.

"I always play six and three," said Mr. Haight promptly, "because when my son was 8 years old he had a football uniform with the number 63 on the back."

The ladies hurried out to the betting windows and a little later those who had followed Mr. Haight's hunch collected $97 for $2 after Extra Easy, No. 6, had won the first race and Knockabout, who was No. 3, had taken the second.

Which, if it is not scientific, is likewise not hay.

—GERALD HOLLAND

TRACK NIGHT AT THE GARDEN

Photographed by HY PESKIN

THE SKI-JUMPER may revel in his dizzy glide down the mountain and soaring leap into space—but he would think twice before attempting it without any snow. The blades which flash on the winter pond gather rust in the dark of a closet when the pond is not covered with ice. Yet the sport of track and field (the very words conjuring up visions of lazy spring days with the sun beating down upon white-laned clay and cinder tracks) begins, for many, indoors, when those familiar tracks are layered over with February slush. It is this that makes indoor track an anachronism in the world of sport — but, fortunately, a magnificent anachronism even so.

Indoor track would have a *raison d'être* if it served only as a preliminary conditioner for the big season outdoors, a chance to warm up and stretch winter-laxed muscles. But since the New York Athletic Club introduced the idea some 89 winters ago, indoor track has gained a very special—and very spectacular—niche all its own. Here, in great arenas like New York's Madison Square Garden, shown on the following pages, banked yellow boards replace the black and red cinders, the brilliance of artificial light apes the brilliance of the sun, and formally-jacketed spectators sit in place of the shirt-sleeved and casually-shod crowd which will gather, outside, later on. If there is, perhaps, too much smoke and too much noise and the track seems much too small, there is something else, too: the sense of closeness and intimate contact with the young men in bright sweatsuits and running shirts who jog around elbow to elbow, and the appreciation of tactical problems one finds only when runners must compete not only against other runners but against the confining space and sharp, dizzying curves which are a part of the whole. Occasionally, as in the vault by Olympic champion Bob Richards on the opposite page, one also finds perfection — no wind, a smooth runway, and, for a moment, the hush which falls over 18,000 people captured by the drama of a man's struggle and final attainment of a lofty goal.

—ROY TERRELL

A faint puff of smoke from the starter's gun and five figures driving in unison toward t

rst of many turns signal the start of indoor track's most featured race—the magical mile

LONG JOURNEY INTO HEIGHT

VILLANOVA UNIVERSITY's big, black-haired and exceedingly competent pole vaulter, Don Bragg, experienced a certain understandable regret when he made his last appearance of the winter season at Madison Square Garden. Bragg cleared 15 feet for the 19th time at the Knights of Columbus Games and heard the last of many bursts of wild applause. At the same time he could not avoid a vast sense of relief. In four years of traveling between Villanova and New York for winter meets, Bragg has endured logistical complications which would have daunted even a bull fiddle player or the mother of quadruplets, for a pole vaulter cannot hit the road with empty hands.

Bragg's particular pole—a Giltal Vaultmaster—has many things to recommend it. It is made of light alloy steel, is stiff enough, as most poles are not, to support his 195 pounds and can be tastefully wrapped in a blue canvas case—the gift of his father—which bears the legend: "Don 'Tarzan' Bragg—15 feet 9 inches or Bust." It is, however, 16 feet 3 inches long—longer, one might say, than a giraffe's neck.

Every Thursday, if he is to vault at the Garden on Saturday, Bragg must telephone the stationmaster at the Pennsylvania Railroad's Villanova station and say, in effect: "I'm coming. Get ready." On Friday he must carry the pole up 20 steps from the basement of the athletic field house and walk it a quarter mile to the station and get it aboard the Paoli local for Philadelphia. This is a relatively simple operation—by walking to the back of the train he can push it through the door in the end of the last car and lay it in the aisle, although he must watch it henceforth like a hawk to keep other commuters from stepping on it.

At Philadelphia's 30th Street station, however, things get more complicated. Early in his career Bragg tried to angle a pole through the vestibule of a Pullman car in Philadelphia; one end tilted up, came in contact with the pantograph of the electric locomotive and caused an alarming, lightninglike flash. Bragg escaped being fried on the spot, apparently because of the canvas case, but the high voltage current melted one end of the pole like wax. The railroad instantly set up a loading procedure calculated to keep the vaulter intact.

Bragg's appearance, with pole, at Philadelphia now causes a wondrous turmoil. The locomotive of the train he is to ride is uncoupled and moved down the track out of harm's way, and current in the overhead wires is shut off before he is allowed to get his gear aboard; the same rigmarole goes on at Pennsylvania Station in New York before he can get off. After that, he faces the problem of getting the pole 13 long blocks uptown to the Paramount Hotel. During his first three years, by pleading and cajoling, he was usually able to find a cab driver who would glumly consent to let him lean out the window and clutch the pole to the side of the taxi. Now, however, cab drivers will have no part of him. The pole must be carried on to its destination through thousands of goggling pedestrians.

This chore Bragg has finally managed to place upon other shoulders. For four years he has had to endure the hard fact that sprinters, hurdlers, weight men and broad jumpers have no sympathy at all for a man with a pole. But Villanova now has a promising freshman vaulter named Ron Brady, a fellow who not only understands Bragg's problems but appreciates his instruction and example; Bragg has grandly turned the pole carrying over to him. Even so, Bragg worries as he rides uptown in New York. He is certain that Brady will not stop in a bar, or leave the pole in a hock shop, or tie a red flag on the end of it and slip it into a passing truck. But even a fellow vaulter might fall prey to amnesia, or get mugged by scamps in the employ of a scrap-metal combine. With the KC meet ended, Bragg still looked a little remote and preoccupied; he had to get back to Villanova one more time.

—PAUL O'NEIL

The world's best shotputter, heavy-muscled Parry O'Brien, explodes the leather-covered iron ball peculiar to indoor meets out past 60 feet

MUDLARK

Photographed by PHIL BATH

Mud has always held a fascination for small chil
dren, barefoot boys and pigs. Add to that lis
California sports car people, who have discovered
the old English pastime of sluicing through the
best available mire in light machines. Very likely

bored with highways, the Britishers some years ago took to the woods, sought out the ruggedest terrain they could find for speed runs and hill climbs and other tests of automotive stamina, and thereby invented the "mudlark." Here a couple of bespattered mud cats are barreling through the slop in the MG Club of America's English Trials. The locale is the Mecca Valley, the season for true believers is from January to May, and everyone has an extraordinarily muddy good time.

THE LOOK OF FEBRUARY

Photographed by HY PESKIN

THE WINTRY VISAGES of the deeply concerned men weren't easily come by. Very likely they had their origins in Canada, where almost all of the good hockey players come from. From November to April, whenever the ice formed and for as long as the hard cold was in the air, the young boys tied their skates to their sticks, hoisted them across scrawny shoulders and followed long blue shadows to the pond. After school and on Saturdays it was always the same — the loud thwack of wood on wood, the shouts, the brawling, the laughing and cheers, and in the gloom of dusk, going home, crisp steps under tired, aching bodies. They grew stronger and better. The town began to notice. "That Claude Planton can move, can't he?" "Tommy Ashton might make it. He doesn't scare."

The eyes were quicker. They saw patterns in the confusion, and the performance began to catch up with the wish. Passes led the receiver fleeing down the ice. A feint, a flick of the hip and he dribbled around, back and forth with the puck, out to the side, cradle it when it comes back, soft so that it stays. Not only big men play. Little men, with eyes for the puck, snake their bodies around straining defenders, and when it is their turn to be hit, dance a jig on sharp skates against the boards, as hard to pin as a weasel in a corner. There is the winnowing of league play, the kids' leagues and the more serious school teams. The hardy survive, the agile, the unflinching ones, the competitors.

The crowds grow. There are the raucous red and blue rinks, the cut of blade on the refreshing blue-white ice, the solid heft of good padding, and in the uniforms color and pride. Men who have gone that far — Red Kelly and Gordie Howe and the other Detroit Red Wings (right) — care for what they do. It is a game for boys, but it is their life. Other men see them play and they scream, or they gasp for breath. But the players watch intently. They will rest and in a minute or more clump over the barrier to battle. Shakespeare described the look. He called them February faces.

—ANDREW CRICHTON

THE FIGHTING CANADIENS

One of the roughest of contact sports, hockey almost by definition is a fight for survival. But to the Montreal Canadiens the word "fight" has connotations all its own. With a strong injection of Latin temperament (more than half the squad is of local Quebec stock), aggressiveness is a tradition revered by Montreal fans and players alike. This means fight for every goal and, if necessary, *fight:* for individual and team honor against enemy skaters. It means, too, hot tempers on the other side, as shown here in a game between Montreal and the New York Rangers at Madison Square Garden. But most of all it means great and exciting hockey.

Fiery-tempered Maurice Richard flashes past goal

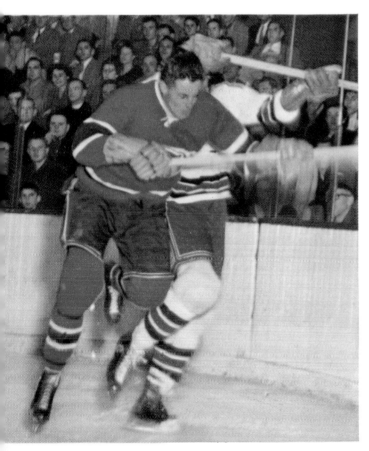

Clever-skating Jean Beliveau board-checks Rangers' Lou Fontinato, who, to delight of crowd (right), is embroiled in melee with Richard and his brother Henri

iving solo try as New York Rangers' Gump Worsley drops to block shot

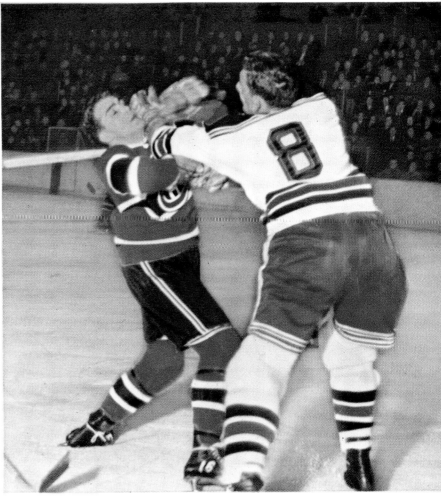

Scrappy Fontinato and game Henri Richard duel heatedly with fists

THE HOCKEY CROWD

IT HAS its finest flowering at Montreal, home of Les Canadiens of the National Hockey League. There is no crowd exactly like it anywhere. At times every member of it appears to react at the same split second so that the crowd seems to speak or roar or moan with a single voice.

It is always a capacity crowd. On the afternoon of the crucial games, thousands fill the streets outside the Montreal Forum, hoping to buy standing room. There is a waiting list of thousands for season tickets, but there is rarely one to be had. Ticket holders provide in their wills for the disposition of their precious reservations.

It is a tidy crowd. It is not permitted to smoke and so it chews gum and sucks lozenges. No vendors roam the aisles. Between periods almost everyone (except for standees who do not wish to lose their places) files out for refreshments and cigarets below the stands. No beer is sold, but there is coffee and hot chocolate and soda and hot dogs.

It is a bilingual crowd. Announcements over the loudspeaker are made first in French, then in English. In the heart of the crowd, English predominates, but the cries from high in the gallery are exclusively French. During a lull in the action, a gallery voice rings out: *"Grouille-toi!"*, which is to say, "Move!" or, translating freely, "Get the lead out!" Another voice calls, *"Patine! Patine!"* to a slow-moving player, urging him to "Skate! Skate!" Still another cries, *"Surveille ton homme!"* or "Cover your man!" Among the standees in the lower stands there is a knot of French-speaking fans, and caught and held fast by them is a red-faced little man who is the image of Jiggs of the comic strips. Unable to move, the little man is stuck for the evening with comrades he is unable to understand, and every now and then he wails: "What happened?" and "Where is everybody?" It is obvious that he has not had a drop of hot chocolate this night which happens to be New Year's Eve.

Despite the fact that it is New Year's Eve, the crowd is on its best behavior. Except for Jiggs and a few others, there is no evidence of pregame celebrating. Hockey is too serious a matter in Montreal to be blurred by too many cocktails.

Because it is New Year's Eve, there are more children than usual among the 13,000 patrons. This has been the day when French children receive their gifts and the luckiest ones have been given this extra special treat. For many, it is obviously the first hockey game they have seen. As the crowd suddenly roars, a little girl in a fur-trimmed hat, no more than 5 years old, turns to a proper-looking man in a Homburg and fur-collared great coat to ask: "What is it, Papa?" "The Rocket has the puck!" replies Papa, jumping to his feet an instant later to scream, *"Le coude, le coude!"* ("The elbow!") as he considers a Chicago Blackhawk to be giving the jab to the idol of all Montreal, Maurice (The Rocket) Richard. When the referee does not react, Papa joins a chorus of *"Choo! Choo!"*, the Gallic booing form, and then cries out as an after-thought, *"Achète-toi des longue-vues!"* This last advises the referee to invest in a pair of binoculars.

When Chicago opens the scoring in the 10th minute of the first period, a resentful murmur sweeps over the arena. Then the crowd pouts in silence. But three minutes later, Henri (The Pocket Rocket) Richard, younger brother of the

In rare, panoramic view of packed Montreal Forum, Boston Bruin player, free for an instant, steadies for shot at goalie Plante

incomparable Maurice, passes to the Rocket himself in front of the goal and the score is tied. The explosion lacks only a mushroom cloud. Seconds later, Kenny Mosdell scores again for Les Canadiens and in a box high in the rafters, a fur-coated woman spectator leans precariously over the edge to pound her fist against an advertisement in sheer joy. In the stands below, men embrace each other and pretty girls laugh and let themselves be kissed. The little man who looks like Jiggs implores the French-speaking fans who have hemmed him in: "What happened, what happened?" Nobody tells him.

Now the Pocket Rocket is slammed into the fence by Allan Stanley of the Chicagoans and is carried off with a sprained ankle, and for the first time the crowd bares its fangs. "*Choo, choo!*" yells Papa as his little girl looks up at him anxiously, "get Stanley, get Stanley!" The gallery roars, "*Assomme-le!*" which is to say, "Slug him!" Maurice the Rocket does not fail them. He nails the villainous Stanley with a bodycheck that sends him sprawling and the crowd goes off, happily avenged, to the concession stands below the stands.

Watching the crowd at the counters where the hot chocolate is sold, a stranger finds it difficult to believe that some part of the same kind of crowd participated in the recent riots at the Forum. It is better not to mention the affair in Montreal now, for the city still feels the shame.

This does not mean that the crowd has become afraid to let its righteous anger boil up a little when events on the ice call for it. Thus, in the final period, when Les Canadiens break a 3-3 tie and stage a stick-whacking, body-slamming rally, the crowd lets itself go. And when this Chicago person, this Monsieur Tiny Tony Leswick, dares to make himself objectionable to Jean Beliveau and the Rocket himself and when the idiot of a referee fails to see things as clearly as the crowd can, what is there to do but roll up newspapers and programs and hurl them down on the ice and (this is a real sacrifice for it is snowing heavily outside) pull off one's overshoes and aim them as well at the dull-witted officials? Could a man who calls himself a citizen of Montreal do less?

But depend upon the Rocket, Maurice Richard, to right matters. Setting up two of the three Montreal goals in the third period (he scored the 500th goal of his career only two nights before) the Rocket sparks the 7-3 victory, and the laughing crowd streams out of the arena with backs being slapped and pretty girls being kissed. Now is the time for the other affairs of the holiday eve and surely there has been enough of hot chocolate for this night. Except, perhaps, that the man who looks like Jiggs could do with a little. The French-speaking fans who held him prisoner all evening have started out now and he finds himself suddenly free. It is too late to learn exactly what has happened, but Jiggs does the least that any friendly fellow can do on a night like this. Throwing out his arms, he raises his misty eyes to the rafters and declaims with bilingual fervor: "Happy New Year to all from Paddy O'Brien! Hinky dinky parley voo!"

—GERALD HOLLAND

Substances amidst shadows, three figures twist graceful
in simple but telling vignette: a fine shot, a near mi

SUGAR RAY COMES BACK

by BUDD SCHULBERG

I F THE FIGHT GAME is show business with blood, Sugar Ray Robinson is its Booth, its Barrymore, its Brando. The manly art may have its seamy side, but it will survive its scandals because it is still the closest thing to Russian roulette we have in sports. A ball team plays for keeps every day, a golfer plays his heart out, but it is only in the prize ring that fame and fortune, disgrace and despair, hang on a single night, a single round or five inspired seconds that turn champions into bums and seemingly used-up contenders into legends.

That Friday night in Chicago, as Sugar Ray Robinson danced in his corner waiting for the opening bell, while Champion Bobo Olson performed a jerky stationary jog in the opposite corner, tension silenced the crowd and touched even the veteran sportswriters who expected to see the ruin of the greatest boxer of the '40s and '50s. He had been our Dixon, our Gans, our Leonard, an unbeatable welterweight and middleweight who could make the moves that reminded the old-timers of the masters. To see him feint with his shoulders, move in, slide away and counter, to see him put combination punches together faster than any ringsider could count them, to see him hook off the jab and then throw the straight right hand, was to see what the whole complex sport of boxing is all about.

But the years were supposed to have stolen the matchless grace from Sugar Ray. In this same Chicago ring 11 months earlier he had looked flat-footed and ordinary with Tiger Jones. Then Castellani had knocked him down and the satin-black man with the once-marvelous legs had had to call on a champion's memory to game it out to the final bell.

So the smart money said the twice-champion of the middleweights could never make it back. Hell, they *never* come back, remember? In the half-century of glove fighting it had never happened, and Sugar Ray with all his pride and cuteness had shown nothing in his comeback campaign to suggest that he could succeed where Corbett and Fitzsimmons failed.

So the money boys set the price on Olson at 17-5 and, despite the nostalgic interest in Ray's adventure, it became very nearly an out fight. Not a single sportswriter or manager, as I wandered around at the weigh-in ceremonies, could see it any other way but Olson. Sugar Ray might outspeed him for five, six rounds, give him a little boxing lesson maybe, but then Olson would plod on and Ray's 35-year-old legs would stiffen and the dazzler of the '40s would burn down and out.

Just the same, the slender, almost delicate body of Sugar Ray looked nicely conditioned. The years were riding him with light rein tonight. Same tense, lean, handsome face. Same light-footed rhythm as he stared across at dull-faced Bobo Olson and waited for the bell to send him out for the desperate hour.

As they joined combat, I couldn't help thinking of something another former champion and great technician had said to me about this big try. It was Willie Pep: "Don't forget Robinson took him *two* out of *two*. That's batting a thousand. You got a big edge on a guy when you know you set him down twice. I give Ray a helluva chance."

Ray Robinson, fighting for his third middleweight championship, gave himself a helluva chance. From the moment they touched technicolor-red gloves in a meaningless token of courtesy, Ray took charge. He jabbed, he moved back out of danger, he countered with a quickness of hand, he suckered Olson into right-hand leads.

And then when he had finished the series he had planned for the occasion, he paced himself by grabbing the out-thought Bobo around the waist. It was beautiful to watch, an old pro at his best; score and rest, score and rest again. Robinson had won the first round by a 10-9 margin. His eyes were sharper than Olson's, his hands so quick that the defending champion seemed ponderous. Ray's style of fighting seemed to say, "I'm smart and you're dumb. This is a battle of will and intellect. I master you."

In round two, Bobo shuffled in with reckless right hands that wheezed over Robinson's shoulder. Sugar Ray was working him like his old gifted self. Even when Olson nailed him, Ray shook it off and *boxed*, sliding under Olson's chops and firing his shots with the precision of a quick-elbowed fencer. "Maybe his legs won't hold out," an expert observed, "but it sure is lovely while it lasts."

A few seconds later a boxing precedent was flattened, along with the methodical champion. Sugar Ray crossed his right hand over Bobo's left. Olson settled from the punch like a foundering ship. The next punches were as fast as you could say bing-bing-bing-bing. A left, a classic right uppercut, another left. Down went the surly champion of the middleweights. Olson writhed and floundered. When the count reached ten, Sugar Ray was once again the middleweight champion, the only man in ring history to win

it back twice. Now the tension in him burst like a dam. He sobbed uncontrollably. He was so happy. His five managers held him aloft. He wept unashamedly, as the fallen Bobo wept the night he stopped Turpin to win the title.

In the dressing room Sugar Ray, half legend, half vaudevillian, was composed and articulate. After his poor showing against Tiger Jones, it had taken his last ounce of will power to keep going, he said. At times, with so many people ridiculing his comeback it had seemed like a nightmare. "But I came to Chicago knowing I had did everything it was possible for a man to do," he orated. He thanked the few sportswriters who had not sold him short. He thanked God. He thanked his loyal wife Edna Mae. He thanked Lou Radzienda, the Illinois Boxing Commissioner, "for whom it's a pleasure to box." He thanked Jim Norris. He thanked Joe Glaser, "my agent, who has offices all over the world and is now negotiating for the sale of my life story."

To these skeptical ears, the Ray Robinson third inaugural speech was Chautauqua oratory, Professor Archie Moore style. In the old days a fighter was a man of many blows and few words. Nowadays they may have to take out cards in Actors Equity. But during the five or six precedent-shattering minutes he was in the ring, Sugar Ray, like Basilio a week before, proved that a boxing champion is a symbol of what the human will can do under terrible duress.

ORDEAL OF A CHAMPION

Photographed by GARRY WINOGRAND

A COMMON OPINION about prizefighters and boxing in general is that boxers are essentially brutal and that the sport depends for survival on a residual atavism in man — his family relationship to the lower animals. These photographs might easily lend themselves to a fortification of that opinion.

It is a good thing, therefore, to think for a moment about some differences between men and brutes. No brute, for one thing, fights for fun. A boxing kitten sheathes its claws. A dog will growl and bark in mimicry of desperate doings at play, but will expend itself seriously only in defense of serious enterprises — like the sanctity of the home, which must be preserved at all times against letter carriers.

Men do fight for fun and are distinguished thereby from brutes. The vast majority of prizefighters make very little at the game. And amateur boxers, who sometimes fight with extraordinary fury, have no hope at all of making money. They fight for glory, a word that neither dog nor cat nor Derby-winning horse would understand.

Carmen Basilio, who is here shown losing his welterweight championship to Johnny Saxton in a grueling 15-round bout, likes to say that he fights for money. This is a proud cliché of the professional, as exaggerated in its way as another bromide that comes up from time to time when boxing men look deep into an emptying cup and say, with profound sentimentality: "I never knew a fighter what wasn't a gentleman." Boxers are, in truth and with few exceptions, amazingly gentle outside the ring. Neither Saxton nor Basilio ever has said a nasty word about the other. Prizefighters differ in this respect from bridge players. In the end Basilio won his title back, without words.

The subtleties of boxing, the brilliance of thrust and parry, are often obscured by blood. But, except by accident or mismanagement, the rules protect a fighter from permanent harm. At the same time the sport keeps alive an ideal of manly courage, useful in our time. Perhaps the greatest value of boxing lies in preserving the notion that rational man can survive any ordeal, once he braces himself for it.

—MARTIN KANE

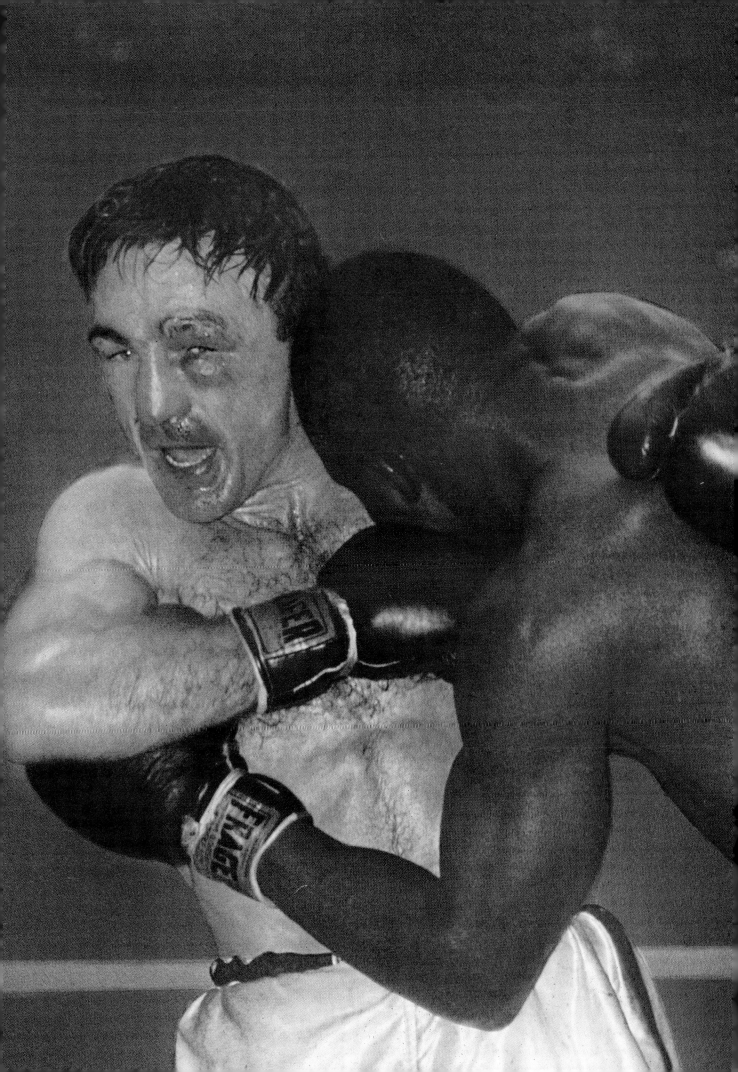

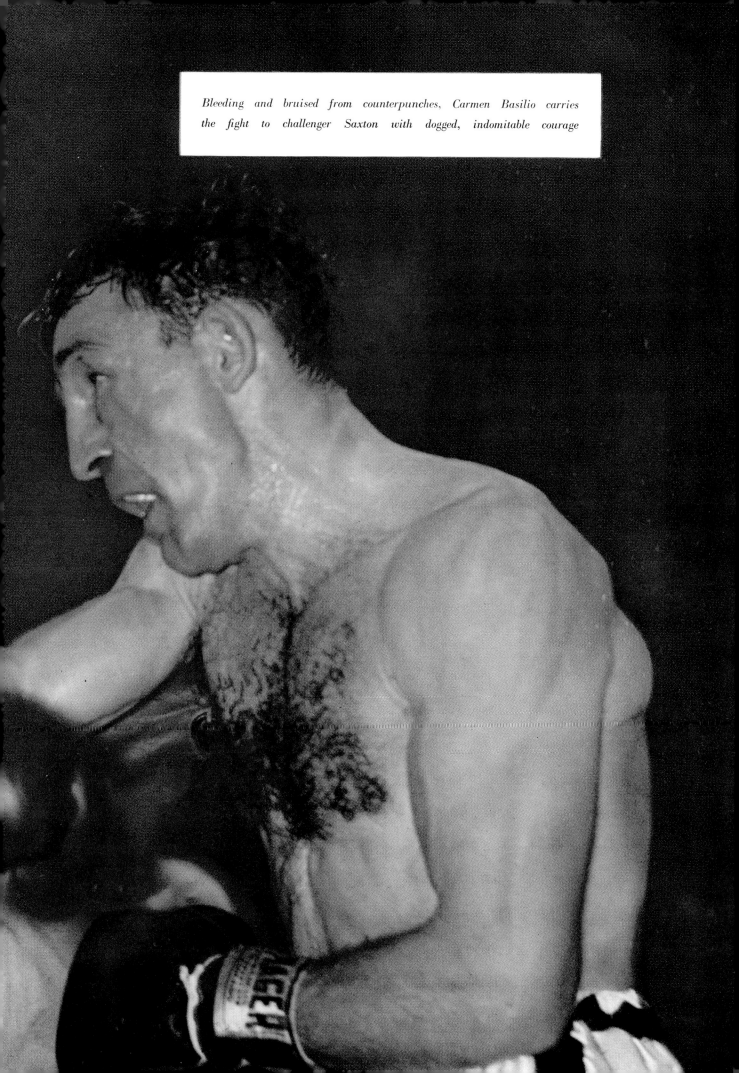

Bleeding and bruised from counterpunches, Carmen Basilio carries the fight to challenger Saxton with dogged, indomitable courage

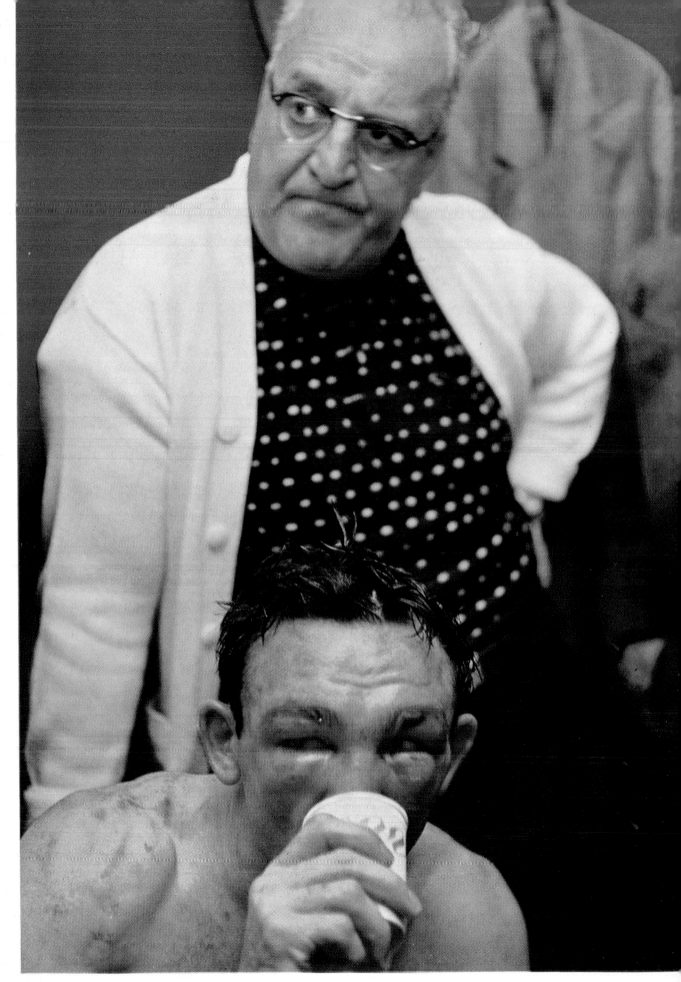

Eyes puffed and cut, defeated Basilio sips tea as manager surveys Chicago dressing room with sour distaste

THE UNIVERSITY
OF EIGHTH AVENUE

by A. J. LIEBLING

IN EVERY GREAT CITY certain quarters take on the color of an industry. Fifty-second Street between Sixth and Fifth Avenues in New York, for example, is given over to strip-tease palaces. In addition to electric signs and posters advertising the Boppa La Zoppas and Ocelot Women inside, it can be identified in the evening by the thin line of nonholding males along the curb who stand on tiptoes or bend double and twist their necks into periscopes in what must surely be an unrewarding effort to see through the chinks in the draperies. This is known as the old college try, since it is practiced largely by undergraduates.

Forty-seventh Street between Sixth and Fifth, for another example, is devoted to polishing and trading diamonds. It is lined with jewelers' exchanges, like North African *souks* with fluorescent lighting, inside which hordes of narrow men rent jumping-up-and-sitting-down space with a linear foot of showcase immediately in front of it. The traders who don't want to sink their funds in overhead stand out on the sidewalk. There is a social distinction even among them: between two-handkerchief men, who use one exclusively for diamond storage, and one-handkerchief men, who knot their diamonds in a corner of their all purpose *mouchoirs*.

The block on the west side of Eighth Avenue between 54th and 55th street is given over to the polishing of prize fighters. It has a quiet academic charm, like West 116th Street when you leave the supermarkets and neighborhood movie houses of upper Broadway and find yourself on the Columbia campus with its ivy-hallowed memories of Sid Luckman and Dwight D. Eisenhower. It is a sleepy block whose modest shops are given over to the needs of the student body —a couple of hock shops, a pet store and a drugstore which sells bandages and gauze for taping fighters' hands. A careful etiquette reigns in this student quarter, as it is impossible to know if you can lick even the smallest man looking into the pet shop next door

to No. 919 Eighth Avenue, which is the Old Dartmouth, or Nassau Hall, of the University of Eighth Avenue.

Old Stillman, as this building is named in honor of the founder, is three stories high, covered with soot instead of ivy and probably older than most midwestern campuses at that. It is a fine example of a postcolonial structure of indefinable original purpose and looks as if it had been knocked down in the Draft Riots of 1863 and left for dead. It hides its academic light behind a sign which says "Stillman's Gym," against a background resembling an oilcloth tablecloth from some historic speakeasy specializing in the indelible red wine of the age of F. Scott Fitzgerald and Warren Gamaliel Harding. Maybe that is where the artist got the canvas; it is an economical neighborhood. The sign also says "Training Here Daily," and in smaller letters "Boxing Instruction—See Jack Curley." This is the university's nearest approach to a printed catalogue. Doctor Lou Stillman, the president, knew when he put out his sign in 1921 that an elaborate plant does not make a great educational institution. In the great schools of the Middle Ages, scholars came to sharpen their wits by mutual disputation. Prize fighters do likewise.

The narrow window of the pet shop is divided by a partition, and the show is always the same. Monkeys on top — which is Stillmanese for "in the feature attraction"—and a tolerant cat playing with puppies underneath, which is Stillmanese for the subordinate portion of the entertainment, as for example a semifinal. Dangling all over the window are parakeets and dog collars. The window draws very good, to stay with the scholastic jargon, before noon when the fighters are waiting for Old Stillman to open and around 3, when the seminars are breaking up. A boy wins a four-rounder, he buys a parakeet and dreams of the day he will fight on top and own a monkey. There was a time when a boxer's status was reflected by the flash on his finger; now it is by his pet. Floyd Patterson, for example, owns a cinnamon ringtail.

Whitey Bimstein, the famous trainer, had one of the pet-shop monkeys hooking off a jab pretty good for awhile. Whitey, a small bald man with sidehair the color of an Easter chick, would stand in front of the window darting his left straight toward the monk's face and then throwing it in toward the body, and the monk would imitate him—"better than some of them kids they send me from out of town," Whitey says. Then one day he noticed a cop walking up and down the other side of the street and regarding him in a peculiar manner. "I figure he thinks I'm going nuts," Whitey says. "So I drop the monk's education."

"You probably couldn't of got him a license anyway," Izzy Blank, another educator, said consolingly.

The modest entrance to Old Stillman is the kind of hallway you would duck into if you wanted to buy marijuana in a strange neighborhood. There are posters for the coming week's metropolitan fight shows —rarely more than one or two nowadays since television has knocked out the nontelevised neighborhood clubs. There is a wide wooden staircase leading up to the gym. Although Dr. Stillman locks a steel grille across the doorway promptly at 3, keeps it locked until 5:30, when working scholars come in for the poor man's session, and then locks it again religiously at 7, the joint always smells wrong. Dr. Stillman, like so many college presidents nowadays, is not himself a teacher but rather an administrator, and the smell in the hall makes him feel there are limits to academic freedom. He is a gaunt man with a beak that describes an arc like an overhand right, bushy eyebrows, a ruff of hair like a frowsy cockatoo and a decisive, heavily impish manner. He has the reputation of never having taken any lip off anybody, which is plausible, because he seldom gives the other fellow a chance to say anything. In earlier stages of his academic career he used to speak exclusively in shouts, but now that he is in his latter 60s, his voice has mellowed to a confident rasp. The great educator has never, so far as is known, himself put on the gloves; it might prove a psychological mistake. Stillman excels in insulting matriculants so casually that they don't know whether to get sore or not. By the sixth time Stillman has insulted a prize fighter the fighter feels it would be inconsistent to take offense at such a late stage in their personal interrelationship. When that happens, Stillman has acquired the edge.

Dr. Stillman has not been so styled since birth. His original surname was Ingber, but he got into the gymnasium business by working for a philanthropist named Alpheus Geer who ran a kind of Alcoholics Anonymous for burglars trying to go straight. Geer called his crusade the Marshall Stillman movement, and he thought the best kind of occupational therapy was boxing, so he opened a gym, which young Ingber managed. The burglars got to calling Lou Ingber, Lou Stillman, and after they stole all the boxing gloves

and Mr. Geer quit in disgust, Ingber opened a gymnasium of his own, farther uptown than this Old Stillman, and legally adopted his present name.

Occasionally Dr. Stillman has a problem student who does not know when he is being insulted, and then he has to think up some more subtle psychological stratagem. Tommy (Hurricane) Jackson, a heavyweight who has to be driven out of the gymnasium at the end of every session because he wants to punch the bag some more, has been a recent disciplinary challenge. Jackson, who is 6 feet 2 inches tall and of inverse intellectual stature, would occupy a boxing ring all the time if Stillman let him. He would like to box 15 or 30 rounds a day, but this would be of no value to his fellow students, even those who worked with him, because Jackson is a purely imitative boxer. He waits to see what the other fellow will do and then does it right back at him until the guy drops from exhaustion. Against a jabber he will jab and against a mauler he will maul; it is the exact opposite of Sam Langford's counsel: "Whatever that other man want to do, don't let him do it. Box a fighter and fight a boxer." Jackson will box a boxer, after a fashion, and fight a fighter, in a way, but he can never decide for himself. Knowing this, most boxers who work with him step in with a right to the jaw, planning to knock him out before he can begin his systematic plagiarism. But he has a hard jaw. Whitey and Freddie Brown, his trainers, who are partners, attribute his lack of originality to an emotional conflict, but it has not yielded to any kind of permissive therapy like buying him a .22 rifle to shoot rats, or letting him drink soda pop on fight nights. "He is not too smart of a fellow," Freddie Brown has concluded.

Jackson, when not exercising, likes to walk around Stillman's with a shiny harmonica at his mouth, pretending to blow in it. A small, white camp follower trails in his wake, completely concealed from anybody in front of Jackson, and plays a real tune on another harmonica. It is Jackson's pose, when detected, that this is an elaborate joke because he could play a tune too, if he wanted to. Dr. Stillman once invited him to play a tune into the microphone with which the president of the University of Eighth Avenue announces the names of students defending theses in the rings. "Give us all a chance to hear you," he snarled invitingly. Tommy backed off, and Stillman grabbed a moral ascendancy. Whenever Jackson is obstreperous now, the good Doctor points to the microphone, and the Hurricane effaces himself.

To gain access to the hall of academe you must pass a turnstile guarded by Professor Jack Curley, the assistant to the president who the sign says is the fellow to see about boxing instructions. The only person who ever did was a follower of Father Divine named Saint Thomas. Curley signed him up as a heavyweight contender before letting him through the gate where the managers could see him. Saint Thomas was a hell of a natural fighter if you believe Curley, but they split on theological grounds such as he wanted Father Divine, *in absentia,* to okay his opponents by emanation. Later he backslid and stabbed a guy, and is now in a place where he has very little opportunity for roadwork. The sign is as sensible as one would be on the door of Yale saying "Instruction in reading and writing, see Professor Doakes." Old Stillman is no elementary school.

There are two ways of getting by Professor Curley. The more popular is to invoke the name of some manager or trainer you know is inside, claiming an urgent business mission. Professor Curley will deny he is there, but if you ask some ingoing fighter to relay the message, the fellow will come out and okay you. Curley will then assume the expression of a baffled witch in a London Christmas pantomime, but he will let you in without payment. The second method is to give him 50¢, the official price of admission, which he doesn't expect from anybody who looks familiar. Through decades of practice he has trained his facial muscles not to express recognition, but he is violently disconcerted when the other fellow does not demand to be recognized. After you give him the 50¢ he has another problem—whether to say hello. This would be a confession he had known you all along. He compromises by giving you what is known on campus as "a cheap hello," looking over his shoulder as if he might be talking to somebody else.

On the main floor of Old Stillman there are two boxing rings set close together. The space in front of the rings is for spectators, and the relatively narrow strip behind them for boxers and trainers. To get from one zone to the other, the latter must pass directly in front of Dr. Stillman, who stands behind an iron rail leaving a passageway perhaps two feet wide. This is a big help in the collection department, because a boxer who is in arrears can't get into the ring to spar unless the president, who doubles as bursar, gives him an extension. When granted, this is usually on the grounds that the delinquent has a fight coming up.

Boxers pay $6 a month for a locker and $11 a month for a dressing room, which means a stall just wide enough for a rubbing table. The de luxe dressing rooms have hooks on the plywood partitions. Stillman has a microphone in back of his stand and in the back of his head a rough list of the order in which fighters will go into the rings. Some fighters he knows by sight; trainers have to prompt him with the names of others. Most of the present crop, the Doctor says, he would like to forget as rapidly as possible. When he says the names into the mike they come out equally unintelligible, so it doesn't matter. Most of the spectators know who the guys are anyway, despite the increasingly elaborate headgears which make them look like Tlingit witch doctors.

In the days when 375 boxers trained at Stillman's and the majority actually had bouts in sight, there was

considerable acrimony about the scheduling. Trainers were afraid that some of their boys who needed sparring would be crowded out. Now that fewer fellows use the place and are in less of a hurry, everybody gets a chance. The enrollment at Old Stillman is less than a hundred, which is not bad when you reflect that there are only 241 licensed professional boxers in the whole of New York State and this number includes out-of-state fighters who have had to take out a license for a New York appearance.

The main operating theater at Stillman's is two stories high. There is a gallery which, in the halcyon days before television, used to accommodate spectators, but which now serves as a supplementary gym. The light and heavy bags are up there, and so is most of the space for skipping rope. In pre-television times Stillman's had an extensive bargain clientele of fans who couldn't afford the price of admission to regular boxing shows, but now these nonholders see their fights free.

Only knowing coves come to Stillman's these days —fellows who have more than a casual interest in boxing or are out to make a buck, like the diamond traders. Few managers today have offices of their own —there are only a half-dozen such grandees—and the rest transact their business walking around Stillman's or leaning against the radiators. There are seats for ordinary spectators, but managers consider it unprofessional to sit down. Even managers who have offices use them chiefly to play klabiash or run up telephone bills; they think better on their feet, in the mingled aura of rubbing alcohol, sweat and hot pastrami-on-the-lunch-counter which distinguishes Old Stillman from a gym run by Helena Rubinstein or Elizabeth Arden.

The prevailing topic of conversation at Stillman's nowadays is the vanishing buck. Boxers are in the same predicament as the hand-loom weavers of Britain when Dr. Edmund Cartwright introduced the power loom. Two boxers on a national hookup with 50 major-city outlets can fill the place of 100 boxers on top 10 years ago, and for every two eliminated from on top, at least 10 lose their work underneath. The boxer who gets the television assignment, though, is in the same spot as the hand-loom weaver who found work driving a power loom—he gets even less money than before. This is because while wads of the sponsors' tease go to networks for time and camera fees, to advertising agencies in commissions based on the purchased time, to producers for creating the drivel between rounds and even to the promoters who provide the boxers, the boxers themselves get no more than they would have drawn in an off night in Scranton in 1929. Naturally, this is a discouraging technological circumstance, but the desire to punch other boys in the nose will survive in our culture. The spirit of self-preservation will induce some boys to excel. Those who find they excel will try to turn a modest buck by it. It is an art of the people, like making love, and is likely to survive any electronic gadget that peddles razor blades.

Meanwhile the contraction of the field has led to a concentration of talent at Old Stillman. These days good feature-bout fighters, who were sure of $10,000 a year not long ago, are glad to sell their tutorial services as sparring partners for $5 or $10 a session. This is particularly true of the colored boys who are not quite champions. Trainers who in the flush times accepted only stars or near-stars as students will now take on any kid with a solvent sponsor. The top trainers, whose charges appear frequently on televised shows, still make out pretty well.

Trainers, like the teachers in medieval universities, are paid by their pupils or their pupils' sponsors. A couple of trainers working as partners may have 15 fighters, all pretty good, if they are good trainers. If they cannot teach, they get no pupils and go emeritus without salary. There are two televised boxing cards originating in New York clubs every week—the St. Nick's on Monday evening and the International Boxing Club show from the Garden on Friday. When the Garden is occupied by other events, the IBC runs its show from out of town, which is a blank margin around New York City, extending for several thousand miles in every direction but east. A team of trainers like Whitey Bimstein and Freddie Brown, or Nick and Dan Florio, or Chickie Ferrera and Johnny Sullo, figures to have at least one man in one of the three features every week, and a couple underneath. The trainer customarily gets 10% of his fighter's end of the purse. Because of their skill as seconds they are also sure to get calls to work in the corners of men they don't train. Noted Old Stillman trainers are called out of town for consultations almost as often as before television, because while there are many less fights, the out-of-town trainer as a species has for that very reason nearly vanished. In most places it is a part-time avocation.

Their reputation is international—one year, for example, Whitey Bimstein was retained to cram a Canadian giant named James J. Parker for a bout for the Canadian heavyweight championship at Toronto. Parker is not considered much of a fighter here—a good banger, but slow of intellection. In Canada, however, he is big stuff—he weighs over 210 pounds. The Canadian champion (now retired), whom Parker was to oppose, was Earl Walls, also a pretty good banger but a slow study.

Whitey took Parker up to Greenwood Lake, N.Y., where his troubles started when the Canadian insisted on doing his roadwork on the frozen surface of the lake. "He might fall through and roon the advance sale," Whitey said. Not wishing to increase the weight on the ice, Whitey declined to accompany him. He would watch him from a window of the inn where they were staying, prepared to cut loose with a shotgun if Parker slowed to a walk. Trainers blanch when they tell of the terrible things fighters will do to get out

of roadwork. Nick Masuras, one of Whitey's friends, once had a fighter up at the Hotel Peter Stuyvesant, across the street from Central Park at 86th, and every morning he would send him out to run a couple of times around the Central Park reservoir, which is right there practically. Masuras would then go back to sleep. By and by the fellow would come in panting and soaking wet, and it wasn't until three days before the fight that Nick learned he had just been sitting on park benches talking to nursemaids, after which he would come in and stand under a warm shower with his clothes on. After that Nick moved to a room on the eighth floor, with a park view. But it was too late. The guy's legs went back on him and he lost the fight. "He done it to himself, no one else," Nick says, mournfully, as he polishes beer glasses in his saloon, the Neutral Corner, which is the Deux Magots or Mermaid Tavern of the fighters' quarter. Instead of training fighters, Nick has taken to feeding them.

For most fighters, pickings are lean between infrequent television appearances—so lean that they are beginning to recall the stories old-timers tell about the minuscular purses in the '90s. One of the best lightweights in the world, for example, went up to Holyoke, Mass., from the campus on Eighth Avenue not too long ago and fought on top of the gate against a tough local boy whom he knocked out in five rounds. He had signed for a percentage of the gate which turned out to be $115. After he had deducted railroad fare, the price of a Massachusetts boxer's license and a few dollars for a local helper in his corner, he wound up with $74. Freddie Brown, the trainer, wouldn't accept a fee, and the fighter's manager wouldn't cut the fighter because the guy was broke and he would have had to lend him the money back anyway. He had been out for several months with a broken rib sustained in another fight.

The CLUB in Holyoke, one of the few stubborn survivors, functions Tuesday nights because of television boxing Monday, Wednesday and Friday.

All the great minds of the university have gone a few rounds with this problem, but none has come up with a thesis that his colleagues at the lunch counter couldn't flatten in the course of a couple of cups of tea. One school of savants holds that if the television companies are going to monopolize boxing they should set up a system of farm clubs to develop new talent. Another believes the situation will cure itself, but painfully. "Without the little clubs, nobody new will come up," a leader of this group argues. "The television fans will get tired of the same bums, the Hooper will drop, the sponsors will drop boxing, and then we can start all over again." Meanwhile a lot of fighters have had to go to work, a situation the horror of which was impressed upon me long ago by the great Sam Langford, in describing a period of his young manhood when he had licked everybody who would fight him. "I was *so* broke," he said, "that I didn't have *no* money. I had to go to work with my hands." Manual labor didn't break his spirit. He got a fight with Joe Gans, the great lightweight champion of the world, and whipped him in 15 rounds in 1903, when Sam says he was 17 years old. The record books make him 23. (They were both over the weight, though, so he didn't get the title.) After the fight he was lying on the rubbing table in his dressing room feeling proud, and a busted-down colored middleweight named George Byers walked in. "How did I look?" Langford asked him. "You strong," Byers said, "but you don't know nothing."

Langford wasn't offended. He had the humility of the great artist. He said, "How much you charge to teach me?" Byers said, "$10." Langford gave him $10. It was a sizable share of the purse he had earned for beating Gans.

"And then what happened?" I asked Sam. He said, "He taught me. He was right. I didn't know nothing. I used to just chase and punch, hurt my hands on hard heads. After George taught me I made them come to me. I made them lead."

"How?" I asked.

"If they didn't lead I'd run them out of the ring. When they led I'd hit them in the body. Then on the point of the chin. Not the jaw, the point of the chin. That's why I got such pretty hands today." Sam by that time was nearly blind, he weighed 230 pounds and he couldn't always be sure that when he spat tobacco juice at the empty chitterling can in his hall room he would hit.

But he looked affectionately at his knees, where he knew those big hands rested. There wasn't a lump on a knuckle. "I'd belt them oat," he said. "Oh, I'd belt them oat."

When I told this story to Whitey, he sucked in his breath reverently, like a lama informed of one of the transactions of Buddha.

"What a difference from the kids today," the schoolman said. "I have a kid in a bout last night and he can't even count. Every time he hook the guy is open for a right, and I tell him: 'Go twicet, go twicet!' But he would go oncet and lose the guy. I don't know what they teach them in school."

After Sam tutored with Professor Byers, he grew as well as improved, but he improved a lot faster than he grew. He beat Gans, at approximately even weights, but when he fought Jack Johnson, one of the best heavyweights who ever lived, he spotted him 27 pounds. Langford weighed 158, Johnson 185. Sam was 26, according to Nat Fleischer, or 25, according to Sam, and Johnson 28. Sam knocked Johnson down for an eight count, Johnson never rocked Sam, and there has been argument ever since over the decision for Johnson at the end of the 15 rounds. Sam's effort was a *succès d'estime* for the scholastic approach to boxing, but Johnson, an anti-intellectual, would never give him another fight.

Johnson, by then older and slower, did fight another middleweight in 1909—Stanley Ketchel, the Michigan Assassin. Ketchel's biographers, for the most part exponents of the raw-nature, or blinded-with-blood-he-swung-again school of fight writing, turn literary handsprings when they tell how Ketchel, too, knocked Johnson down. But Johnson got up and took him with one punch. There was a direct line of comparison between Langford and Ketchel as middleweights. They boxed a six-round no-decision bout in Philadelphia which was followed by a newspaper scandal; the critics accused Langford of carrying Ketchel. Nobody accused Ketchel of carrying Langford. I asked Sam once if he *had* carried Ketchel, and he said, "He was a good man. I couldn't knock him out in six rounds."

Their artistic statures have been transposed in retrospect. The late, blessed Philadelphia Jack O'Brien fought both of them. He considered Ketchel "a bum distinguished only by the tumultuous but ill-directed ferocity of his assault." (That is the way Jack liked to talk.) Ketchel did knock Mr. O'Brien *non compos* his remarkable *mentis* in the last nine seconds of a 10-round bout (there was no decision, and O'Brien always contended he won on points). Jack attributed his belated mishap to negligence induced by contempt. He said Langford, though, had a "mystic quality."

"When he appeared upon the scene of combat you knew you were cooked," Jack said.

Mr. O'Brien was, in five.

ALOFT ON A WAVE

Photographed by VICTOR BALDWIN

THE PILOTS soaring in sailplanes on the edge of the Pacific at Torrey Pines, Calif., shown on the following pages, are applying about the same skills they would in small power planes, with one substantial difference. In a sailplane the pilot is forever seeking his power, by picking his way from cloud to cloud, borrowing lift from thermals or searching for updrafts along a ridge such as that which rises 350 feet from the ocean at Torrey Pines.

In some ways, the soaring pilot still serves an apprenticeship to a more experienced traveler of the air lanes — the bird. Even the best pilot of today soars only statically; that is, he gains altitude by riding updrafts that are rising faster than the sailplane sinks. At times a pilot may spot a cadence in gusty air and get some altitude from the intermittent lulls and gusts, but in this sort of dynamic soaring, the birds are still ahead and well worth watching.

In some respects, on the other hand, the sailplanes have left the birds behind. Ridges and thermals still afford good sailing, but the experts are going into bigger lifts, the standing waves which exist on the lee side of large mountain ranges. In the lee of the Sierras around Bishop, Calif., the pilots are now soaring up to eight and a half miles. The turbulence around roll clouds encountered near such waves has at times torn sailplanes apart. Before he tries the big waves, a man should serve a good long apprenticeship on a ridge like Torrey Pines.

—COLES PHINIZY

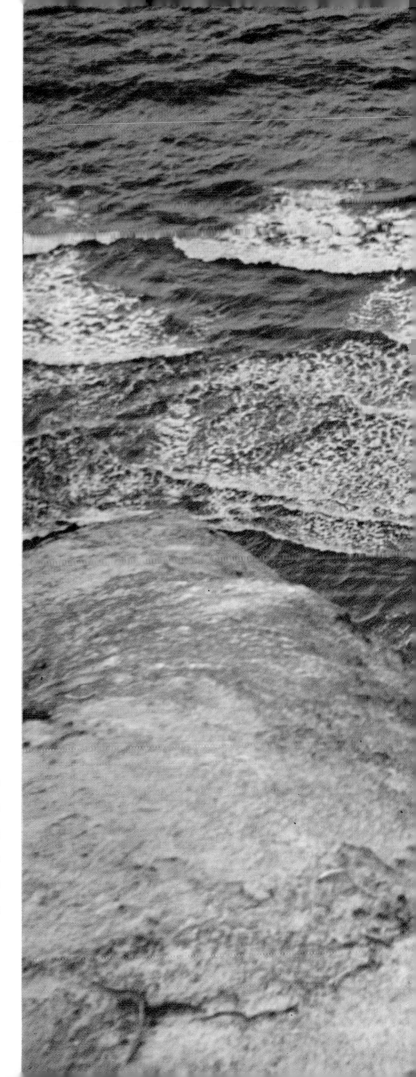

A modified flat-top sailplane skims the Pacific near San Diego after taking off from cliff in foreground. Plane is ridge soaring 20 feet above water, staying aloft by means of air currents forced upward under the wings as air strikes the cliffs, starts to rise

A California pilot banks dizzily over the Torrey Pines area (runway is at right) as his sailplane drops its towline to begin free flight. At the towline release point, planes are 300 feet off ground, flying at 50 mph

"SO THERE I WAS..."

AN AIRPLANE PILOT'S first solo is supposed to combine the thrill of a ski jump, the satisfaction of crossing a new frontier and the exhilaration of a bird. It's an unforgettable experience, the old-timers will tell you; and they are so right. I'll never forget mine, anyway. It was on a Friday the 13th.

I was taxiing past the hangar for my fourth take-off of the afternoon, thinking I should have taken up boating, when my mentor unexpectedly opened the cabin door. He just wants fresh air, I thought, and kept moving.

"How can I get out if you don't stop the fool thing?" he growled.

I put on the brakes.

"You said a half hour today. We've still got 15 minutes."

"Well, you might as well use it up. You're paying for it," he said, stepping out.

Once, in my aggressive teens, I had courted a girl for several weeks, with steadily waning hopes, and all of a sudden had found her cooperative. Then, like now, I was surprised to the point of utter confusion.

"The hell with this," I said. "I'm not ready."

"If you want to sit here talking about it for 15 minutes, it's all right with me," the instructor said. "Idling engines save us gas." He walked away.

"But I've been overshooting all my landings lately!" I hollered after him. "You said so yourself."

"If you're not landed by dark we'll bring you down with a 12-gauge shotgun," he promised over his shoulder.

So this is how they do it, I thought bitterly. No warning. Even a cold-blooded chicken hawk inches a fledgling out of the nest. He doesn't just boot it out with no choice but a good landing or a broken neck.

Well, I don't have to stand for it, I told myself, and so help me, I took off from the ground in that airplane with no thought but to get up in the air

where I could think things over. If I decided it was no good, I would simply come back and solo another day. The human mind can be shockingly stupid sometimes—and all of a sudden the ground was 50 feet below.

There was no birdlike feeling about this. All I remember is an incredible loneliness. No terrestrial predicament puts you so completely and awfully in your own hands as a solo flight in a little airplane. The doting relative, the generous friend, even the kindly stranger, have been pushed hopelessly beyond your reach.

"My gosh," I thought, "this is nothing but a form of temporary suicide."

The spasm of loneliness became so monumental that I began to feel almost ennobled by it and regretted its passing as I found myself automatically performing the little cockpit chores preparatory to landing. By the time I was on the ground I was really disappointed at how routine it had been.

"Congratulations," the instructor said, coming up with a grin and sticking his hand out.

Oddly, my hand wouldn't come loose from the stick. I pried it free, finger by finger.

"Thanks," I said, only the word didn't come out. I reached to shake with him, lost my balance on the door sill and grabbed for the strut. My hand slipped off and I nearly went flat on my face in the dirt.

Now, as we walked to the office and my knees slowly turned from rubber to bone, I began to feel a sensation somewhat akin to exhilaration for the first time, and with it came a talking jag.

". . . and the funny thing," I concluded at the end of a half hour's recital of the four-minute flight, to which the instructor listened patiently, this being part of his job, "the funny thing is that it was the best landing I ever made."

"It always is," he said. "I've never seen or heard of anybody making a bad one on the first solo."

—BILL MAULDIN

THE BIG JUMP

Photographed by DAVID MOORE

Leaning into the smooth white danger of Oslo's Holmen-kollen jump, this skier has reached a supreme moment in Nordic sport. Gathered like ants about a pile of sugar, 100,000 spectators ring his target in the distance below.

Printed by
PUBLISHERS PRINTING-ROGERS KELLOGG CORPORATION
NEW YORK CITY